"WHAT JUST HAPPENED?"

Suddenly, she was aware of the silence between them, and after the embarrassing misunderstanding of the tie incident, she decided that she had better stand up before she made another stupid mistake. She started to get to her feet, but before she could, she felt his fingers reach out for her hand.

"Jones…" His voice was low and raspy and sent a delicious shudder racing through her as his fingers curled possessively around hers and he pulled her back down to the bench. She looked up to see him staring right at her, and she swallowed. Last time this had happened he had fixed her tie, but tonight she didn't have her uniform on.

"Yes?" Her voice was croaky, even to her own ears, but instead of answering, he lowered his mouth to hers, and before she knew what was happening, Curtis was kissing her. The feel of his lips on hers, his skin touching hers, his fingers entwined in hers… it all made her feel something that she hadn't felt in a very long time. Happy. He deepened the kiss, and Emma felt her whole body start to tingle. However, too soon it was over, and Curtis suddenly pulled away and leaned back against the bench, shaking his head as he looked up into the night sky.

"I shouldn't have done that."

OTHER BOOKS YOU MAY ENJOY

FAIRY BAD DAY

AMANDA ASHBY

speak

An Imprint of Penguin Group (USA) Inc.

SPEAK

Published by the Penguin Group

Penguin Group (USA) Inc., 345 Hudson Street, New York, New York 10014, U.S.A.

Penguin Group (Canada), 90 Eglinton Avenue East, Suite 700, Toronto, Ontario, Canada M4P 2Y3
(a division of Pearson Penguin Canada Inc.)

Penguin Books Ltd, 80 Strand, London WC2R 0RL, England

Penguin Ireland, 25 St Stephen's Green, Dublin 2, Ireland (a division of Penguin Books Ltd)

Penguin Group (Australia), 250 Camberwell Road, Camberwell, Victoria 3124, Australia
(a division of Pearson Australia Group Pty Ltd)

Penguin Books India Pvt Ltd, 11 Community Centre,
Panchsheel Park, New Delhi - 110 017, India

Penguin Group (NZ), 67 Apollo Drive, Rosedale, Auckland 0632, New Zealand
(a division of Pearson New Zealand Ltd.)

Penguin Books (South Africa) (Pty) Ltd, 24 Sturdee Avenue,
Rosebank, Johannesburg 2196, South Africa

Registered Offices: Penguin Books Ltd, 80 Strand, London WC2R 0RL, England

Published by Speak, an imprint of Penguin Group (USA) Inc., 2011

1 3 5 7 9 10 8 6 4 2

CATALOGING-IN-PUBLICATION DATA IS AVAILABLE.

Speak ISBN 978-0-14-241259-6

Designed by Jeanine Henderson
Text set in Granjon

Printed in the United States of America

ACKNOWLEDGMENTS

I would like to thank Jenny Bent, my fabulous Skittle-loving agent. This book wouldn't have existed without you. To Christina Phillips, Sara Hantz, and Pat Posner, only you guys know what this one was like to write—and I will buy you pretty shiny things if you promise not to tell! I would also like to thank my amazing editor, Karen Chaplin, who works so hard to find the story within—thank you, thank you, thank you! And to everyone else at Puffin, you have no idea how much I appreciate all that you do to make my dreams come true.

To Marie Zitney, Delia Lynch, and Vanessa Charters, I met you guys well before the Internet ever existed, yet somehow you've turned into my Facebook cheer squad—thank you! To my mum and my entire family, thank you for your excellent bookstore-stalking abilities! I'd also like to give a special thanks to Mandy, Claudia, Ruby, Niko, and Willie for being such amazing friends when we needed it most! An extra big shout-out to all the amazing YA bloggers out there who do so much to support writers. You guys are the best! And as always, nothing would exist without Barry, Molly, and Arthur. Thank you for ignoring the dust, the burnt meals, and the occasional vagueness.

CHAPTER ONE

D emon, definitely," Emma Jones whispered as another sophomore made his way from Principal Kessler's office to where everyone was waiting on the grassy quad. It was late afternoon and the sun was still lingering. Two seconds later the student lifted both his index fingers up onto his head to mimic demon horns and let everyone know that he was now a demon slayer.

"That's incredible. How do you do it?" Loni demanded, her dark violet eyes almost as wide as the large silver hoops that were hanging from her ears. (The same earrings that Loni had dragged Emma all around town searching for, before finally deciding to buy them from the first store they'd looked in.)

"It's a gift." Emma grinned and shrugged as she marked her chart. So far she had managed to correctly call the designation of eighty of their fellow Burtonwood Academy classmates. Though to be fair, it wasn't that difficult. For instance, Loni, with her small frame and sharp mind, was always going to be much better at killing wily goblins than brawny harpies, whereas their friend Tyler, who was long and lean, was perfectly suited to hunt the six-foot fire-breathing salamanders to which he had just been designated. Then there were the overbulked guys like the Lewis twins, who had ogre slayer written all over them.

"Well, it's a gift that should be harnessed." Tyler looked at the chart, his bright red shaggy hair poking out in all directions like an untamed lion's mane. "I mean, if you'd told me sooner how good you were at predicting this stuff, I would've gotten some bets going. We could've cleaned up."

"Tyler," Loni chided, "not everything has to be about making money and gambling."

"Want to bet?" Tyler grinned at his own joke as Loni rolled her eyes. "Besides, considering the amount you spent on that weird-looking purple coat the other day, I thought you would appreciate the extra cash."

"It's not weird, it's gorgeous," Loni corrected him in a stern voice. "Anyway, my horoscope said purple was my lucky color. What was I supposed to do? Ignore the sign?"

"Er, when the sign makes you spend a hundred dollars? Then yes, definitely just ignore it," he retorted, causing Loni to give him a swift punch in the arm.

Emma turned her attention back to her chart. Loni and Tyler had been bickering ever since they'd started Burtonwood Academy when they were eight years old (apparently it was because they were a Taurus and Leo, respectively), and so she hadn't really expected them to take a break just because they'd both received their dream designations. Of course the designations wouldn't be formally confirmed until the induction ceremony in six weeks, but everyone knew that once Principal Kessler had given you the all-important piece of paper, there was no going back.

"Earth to Emma." Tyler suddenly waved a hand in front of her eyes, causing her to blink. "So has anyone been given dragons yet?"

She shook her head. "Nope, not yet." Which wasn't really a surprise, since not only were dragons the hardest to kill out of all the elementals, they were also the creatures that the fewest people showed an affinity for. And there had never been more than one dragon slayer inducted in any given year.

"But of course that's going to change soon," Loni chimed in. "Since Emma's next to go in. Plus, she's an Aries, so it's only right that a fire sign should get a fire elemental to slay."

Emma couldn't resist smiling. She was one of those few people who did have an affinity for them.

While Burtonwood liked to wait until tenth grade before designating which of the twelve elemental creatures each of the sight-gifted students would spend their life tracking and hunting, there was no denying that Emma's natural talent for dragons had come out early. And even though Loni was convinced it was because of her star sign, Emma was fairly sure it was more due to the fact that her mom had been one of the greatest dragon slayers ever. Whatever the reason, from the moment Emma's sight had come through at the age of eight and she'd seen her first dragon (a bad-tempered yellow ridgeback that was terrorizing a camping ground over at the edge of the national park off State Highway 25), she'd been able to instinctively and silently track them.

Emma let her fingers skim the heavy crystal pendant that was hanging around her neck, neatly tucked under her school uniform. Her dad had brought it to her last week as a surprise. It had been one of her mom's favorites, and he thought she might want to wear it for good luck. He'd been right, and Emma, who still missed her mom every single day, hadn't taken it off since.

"Emma, he's ready for you." A voice shook her from her reverie, and she looked up to see Mrs. Barnes, Principal Kessler's right-hand woman, standing in front of her. She was about fifty and, as usual, her eyes were covered in purple eye shadow and topped off with a pair of green-framed glasses, which had led to her nickname "Barney."

Emma nodded and scrambled to her feet.

"Good luck." Loni reached out and squeezed her hand. "In less than five minutes, all your dreams will come true."

"And then we can celebrate," Tyler added in a low voice. "Glen and Garry are organizing a party behind the practice fields. Unless Miss Zodiac thinks the stars might not be in alignment."

"The stars are perfectly in alignment, thank you very much," Loni retorted in a prim voice, and Emma grinned. There was something ridiculously reassuring about their bickering that made her feel more relaxed.

"Thanks, guys." She smoothed down her skirt and walked inside behind Barney. The first time she'd come to

Burtonwood, she'd expected it to be some sort of Gothic castle full of turrets and winding corridors, maybe even on a treeless, gloomy hill. But instead it was a sprawling two-story Spanish Mission–style campus just north of San Francisco, complete with a bright orange roof and white stucco walls all perennially covered in piercing purple bougainvillea flowers—no turrets or winding corridors in sight. In fact, if it weren't for the large stuffed jungler demon in the reception area and the collection of antique slaying weapons on the walls, it could've been just about any other high school in America.

Which was probably lucky since, according to the outside world, Burtonwood was just a regular high school that specialized in languages and had a reputation for keeping to itself. Also, thanks to the fact that nearly all civilians were sight-blind and couldn't see any of the elementals that roamed the Earth, the deception was easier to keep up than most people might think.

Principal Kessler's office was just off to the left of the entrance, and Emma knocked first before going in. He was sitting behind his desk, his long gray hair pushed back off his tanned face and his thin lips tight, but Emma hardly noticed, as her eyes were drawn, as always, to the photographs hanging behind him.

She immediately honed in on the one of her mom. Apparently they looked alike, with matching green eyes, dark brown hair, and olive skin, but Emma was more excited about the elation that was spread across her mom's face as a group of Amazon villagers hugged her for slaying the ruchiac dragon that had been hunting in the area for years. Not that the villagers knew it was a ruchiac dragon. According to her mom, they had called it a sun god and thought it had been sent to collect human sacrifices. In fact, there were numerous names for what sight-blind people called elementals—ghosts, yetis, the devil. Still, it didn't really matter what people thought they were; all that mattered was that the elementals were stopped. And that's where the slayers came in.

"Emma, I hope you haven't been waiting too long."

Only three hours.

"Not really," she said as she sat down on the other side of the desk and forced herself to stop looking at the photograph.

"Good." He picked up a clipboard, then knitted his brow and coughed uncomfortably. "First of all, I just want to say that no matter how successful your mother was as a dragon slayer, this decision has been based on the numerous physical and psychological exams you've completed during your time at Burtonwood. You understand that, don't you?"

"Of course I do," she assured him, since everyone knew that nepotism was a big no-no at Burtonwood. Besides, she really did have the skill, speed, and accuracy to be a dragon slayer. Now all she needed was one small slip of paper and this would become the greatest day of her life. She took one last peek at the photograph of her mom on the wall and then allowed herself a small smile.

"Which is why, after careful consideration..." Principal Kessler continued, and Emma gave him an encouraging nod, "it's been decided that your designation is with . . . fairies."

"Thank you so mu—" she started to say, just the way she had rehearsed it for the last seven years, before she suddenly paused and wrinkled her nose. *"Um, excuse me?"* Okay, so obviously Principal Kessler needed to rehearse his part a little more because for a minute she thought he said fairies.

"Now, before you get upset, just let me say that this wasn't an easy decision." He pushed the clipboard away and handed over the results. For a moment Emma just stared at the word in front of her.

Fairies.

She slowly shook her head. This made no sense. No one slayed fairies. Fairies were dumb . . . *and small.* In fact, she didn't even know why they were listed as one of the twelve elementals that had come through the Gate of Linaria, since the worst she'd ever seen them do was change the food labels at the supermarket.

Which meant Kessler must be joking.

"I'm not joking," he suddenly said, as if somehow reading her mind. She carefully folded the slip of paper and put it in her lap before letting her fingers tighten around her mom's necklace.

"But you have to be," she finally said. "Maybe you got the name mixed up and you're thinking of Erin Juniper. I mean, we have the same initials. Just check again and I think you'll see it should say dragons. *My designation is dragons,*" she repeated in a firm voice.

He shook his head. "I'm sorry, Emma. It's no mistake. I've

discussed this carefully with the other training academies, and shown them your results, and they all agree that it points to the same thing. Fairies."

"Yes, but fairies are only ten inches tall and don't kill things. There's no need to slay them," Emma pointed out as she tried to make sense of a situation that quite clearly made no sense whatsoever.

"They're one of the elementals, and if they came through the Gate of Linaria, then they're dangerous," Principal Kessler said firmly. Then he softened his expression. "Look, Emma, no one knows more than I do how much you wanted to follow in your mom's footsteps, but my decision is final. You can't argue with results."

"Of course I can, especially when the results make no sense. Please, you can't do this to me. Aren't you always telling us that Sir Francis created those designation tests over four hundred years ago? I mean, if we did everything he said, we'd still be slaying things using arrows wrapped in sage leaves. Not everything he wrote has to be right," she pleaded, but she could tell by the stern expression that was morphing across the principal's face that he wasn't impressed with her argument.

Probably because Sir Francis was the man who had not only first seen the Gate of Linaria and then single-handedly closed it to stop any more elemental creatures from slithering and sliming their way onto Earth, way back in the seventeenth century. But he had also traveled the world to bring together those who shared his gift of sight and power, and then he set up the first training academy to teach them how to slay the creatures that had already made their way through the gate before it had been closed. Oh, and according to the records, he had also been the most powerful slayer that had ever existed, and since then, no one had even come close to matching his skill or strength.

In other words, as far as elemental training academies went, Sir Francis was God, and dissing him wasn't really such a smart move.

"Look, Emma"—Principal Kessler's lips went thin, which was a sure sign that the interview was over—"I've known you a long time, but I'm still the principal here and you're still the student, so I want you to accept your designation and get on with your training. Understood?"

No, not remotely, Emma wanted to yell. The ridiculous thing was that if someone had told her this morning that she would've guessed eighty out of eighty-one designations correctly, she would've been quite impressed. In fact, she probably would've even made a bet with Tyler, but now that she was the "one," she realized that being wrong definitely didn't feel so good.

"And can you please tell Curtis Green that I'm ready to see him," Principal Kessler said, but she hardly heard as she continued to stare numbly at the photograph of her mom's beaming smile. Then it clicked, and she quickly got up and left, realizing what she had to do.

Induction wasn't for another six weeks. So she had six weeks to get Principal Kessler to change his mind. She owed it to herself. She owed it to her mom's legacy. She didn't care what anyone said. She was a dragon slayer, because there was no way in the world that she was going to become the world's first fairy slayer. No way at all.

CHAPTER TWO

Five weeks later

E mma, really, it's not that bad," Loni said reassuringly.
"Of course it's that bad," Emma responded to her
friend from the other end of her cell phone. She took out
a tiny crossbow, which looked more like something that
belonged to Pocahontas Barbie than a slaying kit. "I'm stuck
in the mall hunting down a pack of ten-inch fairies, one
of whom is wearing an AC/DC T-shirt and leopard-skin
leggings. It couldn't possibly get any worse."

"You're joking." Loni was instantly distracted.

"I wish." Emma sighed as she glanced over at the fairy in
question. When she'd first seen the tiny air elementals just
after her sight had come through, she'd been taken with how
human they looked (except for the large gossamer wings that
protruded from their backs). But now all she noticed was
that they were arrogant, vain, and ate far too much junk food.

"But where do they even get that stuff from?" Loni wondered out loud.

"Well, judging by the amount of time they spend in the toy department and the Pets-R-Us counter, I'm guessing it's a combination of places," she retorted as three fairies came to a halt by the Sunglass Hut and started to throw ice cubes at her from a Starbucks cup.

Okay, so now it was definitely worse.

She rubbed her arm as three small blocks of ice hit her simultaneously, and she only just managed to move out of the way before another one went crashing into her forehead. It went rolling and bouncing along the marble floor, and a fat woman who was trying on some Dior shades shot her an evil glare as if it was Emma's fault.

The fairies howled with laughter as they high-fived each other before one of them flew down and hovered right in front of her face. *And that was another thing about them; they had no sense of personal space.*

"What's wrong, slayer? Why are you looking so grumpy? We just wanted you to chill out a bit." It smirked. "Get it. Ice cubes, chill out," the small creature said as its wings fluttered in a blurry pattern in front of her eyes. This one was wearing cargo pants and a plaid shirt and looked like it had come from the pages of a Gap catalog.

"Emma, are you still there?" Loni asked, sounding alarmed.

"It's the fairies." Emma sighed and tried to swipe the creature with her hands, but it lazily flitted out of her way before the other two joined it, just out of her reach. "They're mocking me."

"Mocking you?" a second fairy, the one in the AC/DC T-shirt, protested as it once again swooped close to her face. "My brother Gilbert might've been tormenting you, but I can assure you he was most definitely not mocking you. Isn't that right, Trevor?"

"That is correct, Rupert." A third fairy, wearing a miniature green hoodie and some baggy jeans now appeared. "Because we only save the mocking for those who are a real threat, not some two-bit useless wannabe slayer-girl."

"But don't worry," Emma continued to Loni in a tight voice as she once again tucked her cell phone under her ear and loaded up the tiny crossbow. "Because soon they're all going to be dead."

"Did you hear that? She thinks she's going to kill us. *With that thing!*"

"Oooh, no. Please don't hurt me. Last time you used that weapon, you only missed me by a mile." Gilbert pretended to shake with fear before suddenly scratching his chin. "Or was it two miles?"

"See, definitely tormenting," Rupert pointed out as he pretended to play some air guitar before darting right up to her face and wagging his tongue at her à la Gene Simmons. "Oh, and FYI, if you can't even scare Gilbert, then you really are doing a bad job, because he's the worrier of the group."

"It's true." Gilbert proudly nodded in agreement as he smoothed down his neat plaid shirt. "I guess it's an eldest fairy thing, because Rupert's the rebel, Trevor's the irresponsible one, and me? Well, I'm the worrier. I mean, the world's a scary place. But at least I don't have to worry about being shot by a pathetic slayer-girl." He grinned and then turned and gave his two brothers another high five.

Emma gritted her teeth as she held up the tiny crossbow, but by the time she released the arrow, the fairies had casually flown out of the way before turning so they could all watch the blunt skewer go skittering harmlessly along the marble floor.

"Er." Trevor gave a polite cough as he swooped down to where the skewer now lay. "I think you dropped something." Then without another word they all darted off, laughing like a pack of demented hyenas.

Emma reluctantly retrieved the skewer. Not for the first time she wished that the rules weren't quite so black and white about using lethal weapons when you were slaying elementals in public places.

Of course Emma could see the point of the ruling, since most sight-blind civilians tended to get freaked out when they saw a slayer with a sharp pointy weapon trying to fight what looked like, well... *nothing*.

It had actually long been a debate within the slaying community whether they should let the greater public know the truth about the elementals in order to make a slayer's job easier, but since most people refused to believe something they couldn't see, the idea had always been vetoed. Besides, most elementals stayed away from heavily populated areas, not by choice but because of the ever-increasing series of complex wards that slayers spent a lot of their time planting and maintaining in urban areas.

According to Loni, all elementals were filled with negative electrons and so the wards simply pulsed out positive electrons that shocked the creatures if they got too close. Apparently each elemental had a different shock point, so each ward was triggered to release a different voltage. While Emma didn't exactly understand the science behind them, she knew that the tiny nickel-size devices worked like permanent invisible force fields.

But, for whatever reason, the fairies seemed oblivious to all the known wards and instead chose to spend 24/7 at the mall. It was less than ideal.

"Seriously, Emma, what's going on? Did you kill any of them?" Loni demanded, yelling into the cell phone.

"No. How can such stupid things be so hard to kill?" she groaned in annoyance as she ran after the fairies, making sure not to let them out of her sight. They had an uncanny ability to blend into the background—not that she knew how, since between the bad miniature clothing and the glittery wings, they stood out like a sore thumb to anyone who had the sight. Yet the number of times she had lost track of them during her patrols didn't bear thinking about.

"It's just a matter of time," Loni said in a positive voice.

"I've had five weeks," Emma pointed out as the frustration came bubbling to the surface. "That's five Saturday patrols, not to mention the extra field days that Professor Vanderbilt has taken me on, and not one kill. Even Tyler's stopped taking bets on me killing one before Induction, and this is the guy who bets on cockroach races."

"Maybe you could try using the subsonic blaster I just finished making? I used it today, and the low-level frequency knocked out two goblins before they could even unsheathe their claws. Let me tell you, it made killing them a lot easier. I didn't even get covered in goblin slime this time."

"You killed two goblins today?" Emma tried and failed not to be jealous.

"Yes, but that wasn't my point. I just meant that maybe the blaster would work for you too. It's not like Sir Francis was very specific in how to kill fairies. It might be worth a try."

"I guess." Emma let out a halfhearted sigh as she managed to squeeze her way past two women pushing strollers and hurried after the fairies to the food court, before realizing that she'd once again lost them. "They're gone again. I think I'm just going to call the school minibus and get them to pick me up early. I might as well come back to Burtonwood and get working on my Plan C."

"Do I even want to know what Plan C is?" Loni checked in a cautious voice, brought about, no doubt, because Emma's Plan A (e-mail Principal Kessler every day until he changed his mind) had led to a detention and Plan B (ignore the designation and go dragon slaying anyway) had caused her to singe her eyebrows and get another detention. In fact, over the last five weeks there had been quite a few detentions.

"Plan C is to do something big to make sure Kessler knows how good I am before Induction next Sunday," Emma informed her, not that she was really sure what "something big" actually entailed, but she was confident she would figure it out. She had to since there was no way she could go through life chasing fairies in the mall.

She was Louisa Jones's daughter. Dragons were in her blood.

"Emma, are you really sure about all this? I mean, if Kessler was going to change his mind, he would've done it by now. And then there's the whole Curtis Green factor."

At the mention of Curtis's name, Emma narrowed her eyes. As it turned out, there were two designations that she'd managed to get wrong. Hers and Curtis Green's. Up until five weeks ago she didn't even have an opinion of Curtis. He'd first arrived at Burtonwood when he was eleven, which was late by anyone's standards, and for the last four years he had pretty much kept to himself. And while some of the guys had talked about how good he was at hand-to-hand combat, and a lot of the girls had made noises about his blond hair, dark chocolate-colored eyes, and broad shoulders, Emma had never really paid any attention to him.

In fact, she probably still wouldn't have noticed anything about him if he hadn't walked out of Kessler's office ten minutes after her own life had been ruined, with a dazed expression on his stupid face, and told everyone that he'd just been given dragons.

Even now the memory had the power to take her breath

away, and she clenched her fists in annoyance (before realizing that she still had the stupid crossbow, and if she clenched any harder it would probably snap with the pressure).

"Emma? Are you still there? Tell me you're not doing something dumb like buying a Curtis Green voodoo doll, because I thought we'd agreed that was a bad idea," Loni pleaded.

"There's no voodoo doll," she said wistfully. She had toyed with the idea, but Loni and Tyler had come together (for once) and talked her out of it. "But you've just reminded me why I need to get to work on Plan C."

"Look," Loni paused for a moment before continuing to speak, "I know you don't want to hear this, but maybe fairies are where you belong? I mean, for example, when I was trying to find a top to go with my blue skirt last Sunday, I kept going back to that gorgeous green T-shirt my mom got me for my birthday. Anyway, there was no way I was going to wear them together because of the whole blue-and-green-should-never-be-seen thing, but then I checked my horoscope and it said that Sunday was the perfect day for a Taurus girl to take a chance, and so I did and would you believe that it ended up looking awesome together? You even said so yourself."

"Okay, so are you comparing my life to an outfit?" Emma double-checked, and she could almost see her friend blushing from the other end of the phone.

"Of course not," Loni hastily reassured her. "I'm just saying that maybe this is a good match for you, even though it doesn't seem like it right now."

"But it's *fairies*," Emma wailed as she slumped down into one of the plastic chairs that were scattered around the food court and leaned forward onto the equally plastic table. "And you've seen what everyone's been like at Burtonwood. They're all laughing at me."

"I know and that sucks." Loni let out an empathetic sigh. "But that's mainly because everyone knows how much you hate your designation and because you've talked nonstop about how you're going to get Kessler to change his mind. But if you start accepting it, then I'm sure they'll lose interest and go back to concentrating on Brenda Vance's ridiculous night goggles that she insists on wearing when she's on patrol."

"You really think?" Emma said in a hopeful voice.

"I do," Loni agreed. "If you take the high road on this one and just concentrate on doing the best job you can with the fairies, I bet things will be back to normal before you know it."

Emma chewed her lip. The idea of giving up on her dragon dream seemed unbearable. But since it looked like it wasn't going to happen anyway, maybe Loni had a point. Maybe she should just make the most of what she had.

"Okay, I'll think about it," she finally said just as she caught sight of a quick flash of green hoodie by the Hong Kong Wong Chinese food counter. *"And there they are."*

"You've found them again?" Loni squealed in excitement. "That's great and most definitely a sign. So, are you going to go and try and kill them?"

Emma got to her feet and started to weave through the

tables. "Absolutely. These three particular fairies and their stupid outfits have been taunting me ever since I first started patrolling here. And now they're even starting to bring their girlfriends in on the mocking. Getting rid of them would make me very happy."

"See." Loni sounded like she was grinning. "It's not going to be so bad after all. Oh, but Emma, don't forget, you're at the mall, so you can't use any lethal weapons."

"Don't worry. I've got a few other tricks up my sleeve. I'll call you when I'm done," Emma said as she put away her cell phone just as the fairy darted behind the counter and disappeared to the kitchen out the back. *Okay, so that might dampen her plan a bit.*

After all, it was all right for the fairies to come and go as they pleased at the mall since no one but the sight-gifted could see them. Unfortunately, it wasn't exactly as easy for a regular-size human to do the same thing. Once again Emma longed to be out in the dark, cold forest hunting dragons instead.

Just before her mom had died five years ago, they had both staked out a troubadour dragon for three nights and hadn't even been able to light a fire for fear of giving away their location (which, for the record, she bet Curtis wouldn't have been able to handle). But on the fourth night the dragon had finally slunk out of its lair, and Emma's mom had instantly shot it through the soft scales at the base of its neck. It was the dragon's kill spot, and despite cold and tired limbs, her mom's first shot had been true and the dragon had died instantly, covering them both in thick, stenchy ectoplasm as its body disintegrated.

Right now Emma would give her right hand to be covered in thick, stenchy dragon ectoplasm instead of trailing a pack of belligerent fairies through the food court.

The Hong Kong Wong counter ran from wall to wall, but underneath, part of it was cut away and the countertop lifted up to let the workers in and out. Emma paused for a moment and was just trying to figure out how to get past the slim girl working the register, when suddenly a red-faced man came up and started to complain about the comment on his fortune cookie.

Yes. Thank you, red-faced man with ridiculous over-the-top consumer expectations.

Emma waited long enough for the slim girl to be drawn into his tirade before she slipped under the counter and through to the kitchen. The place was empty, though from a screen door at the back she could hear the soft murmurs of voices and the faint stench of cigarettes, which suggested whoever worked there had gone for a break.

Then she caught sight of about ten fairies all congregating around a large white door that looked like it led to a cold room. They were so busy staring at it, their stupid wings buzzing with rapid movement, that none of them even seemed to notice she was there.

Perfect. She reloaded the tiny crossbow and took aim.

Finally she would be able to get some credibility back. Then, without making a sound, she moved slowly toward them and pressed her finger down on the release trigger.

Good-bye, fairies, and hello—

But just as the tiny wooden skewer started to fly through the air, there was a large grating noise. And before she knew what was happening, the white door of the cold room blew open and the room was suddenly filled with smoke and flames and flying debris, which pounded against her face and arms.

Emma screamed and held up her hands to protect herself as the smoke continued to billow into the kitchen. She had no idea what had caused it or what had happened to the fairies, but she knew enough to know it wasn't good news. Burtonwood had instilled in its students from an early age that it was a slayer's job to be discreet and fly under the radar, and despite the pounding sensation in her head from where the debris had hit her, Emma was fairly sure that exploding cold rooms did not count as discreet.

Which was why she did the only thing any sane slayer would do. She pressed her hand to her aching face and ran.

CHAPTER THREE

O kay, so on a scale of one to ten, what are the chances
no one's heard?" Emma asked Loni on Monday
morning as they hurried across the dew-laden quad that
separated the dormitories from the rest of the school. As they
went, Emma smoothed down her uniform of a medium-
length box-pleated skirt, a navy blazer with a white shirt,
and a badly knotted dark green plaid tie. *Funny that she could
see and fight things that most people wouldn't even dream existed,
but ask her to knot a tie and she was all thumbs.* Not that she
really cared about her tie right now; she was more concerned
about being publicly humiliated in front of the five hundred
Burtonwood students who were currently sitting inside the
cafeteria eating their breakfast.

"I'd say about negative six hundred and five." Loni
puffed as she readjusted the heavy bag that was slung over
her shoulder. Her short black hair was gelled up so that her
heart-shaped face looked even more heart-shaped than ever.

"You do realize that wasn't the answer I was looking for,"
Emma noted as Loni shot her an apologetic wince.

"Sorry. But what do you expect? This kind of news travels fast around here."

"I know, but it's so unfair. I mean, the explosion wasn't my fault," Emma protested as she touched the horrible eye patch the school nurse had insisted she wear after making her spend all of Sunday in the infirmary. Apparently, a small speck of debris from the explosion had flown in there and it had to be removed by a large magnetized needle and a lot of freaking out on her behalf. "All I did was follow those stupid fairies, and the next thing I know—*boom!* The whole place exploded, the kitchen was toast, and my eye wouldn't stop aching. I just happened to be at the wrong place at the wrong time. Besides, it's not like anyone was hurt."

"Yeah, including any fairies," a voice rang out from behind them, and Emma spun around to see Glen Lewis.

"Did you miss that part in your handbook where it tells you that you're actually supposed to *kill* them?" his twin brother, Garry, added, like part two of a bad comedy act.

"Just ignore them," Loni advised as they both came to a halt in front of the large bronze statue of Sir Francis Edgar Hilary Mackay, who stood guarding the entrance of the cafeteria. Loni automatically reached up on tiptoes to touch Sir Francis's forehead. "You know what ogre slayers are like. Idiots."

"I know." Emma sighed as she followed her friend in pressing two fingers onto the cold metal face of their founding father. She had no idea where the forehead-touching-for-good-luck tradition came from, but with the way her week was shaping up, she didn't want to take any chances.

"After all," Loni said as she brushed past the twins and walked through to the cafeteria entrance, "you might not be slaying a lot of fairies right now, but you're stopping them from causing trouble. You should be proud, not embarrassed."

"I agree. You should let everyone know how great you are." Garry Lewis gave the statue a quick high five and followed them through, before raising his hands with a flourish. "In fact, allow me to do the honors. Ladies and gentlemen, can I please introduce Miss Emma Jones, the one-eyed, food-court-destroying, fairy-slayer extraordinaire."

Well, so much for hoping that no one had heard about what happened, and as the entire cafeteria burst out laughing, Emma futilely pushed forward her straight brown bangs to try to hide her eye patch. If she had been smart, she would've remembered to leave her long hair loose, but out of habit she had hastily tied it back into a low ponytail when she'd gotten dressed. Something she was now regretting.

"Look," Brenda Vance, an anally retentive demon slayer from Emma's year, called out. "Is it a bird? Is it a plane? Oh, wait, it's a fairy. Quick, let me blow it up."

The laughter increased and Emma tried to concentrate on her breathing. The worst thing was that she couldn't even blame them because it was true. After all, who had ever heard of a fairy slayer? It was stupid.

"Demon slayers are even bigger idiots than ogre slayers."

Loni bristled in annoyance as they both picked up orange trays and joined the line for their first meal of the day. "Just ignore the—" Loni continued, just as a voice called out from somewhere behind them.

"Yo, Curtis—nice job, man."

"Three kills in one night? You rock," another person added, and Emma spun around to see the lanky figure of Curtis Green standing at the cafeteria entrance propped up on crutches, his left leg covered in a fresh blue plaster cast. As the clapping continued, he raised an arm and shot the room in general a lopsided grin before he swung his way toward the back of the food line.

Right where they were standing.

Emma watched in horror as he joined them, the final confirmation she was having a bad morning.

"Hey, Jones. What happened to you?" he asked as he came to a halt and leaned forward on his crutches, studying her eye patch with interest. The top half of him was in a regular white shirt, blazer, and a tie (perfectly knotted, she might add, which didn't improve her opinion of him), but his gray trousers had been replaced by a pair of faded track pants that were slit up the side to accommodate his cast.

"Like you don't know," Emma snapped as she inched away from him. He might be only fifteen, but at six feet, with broad shoulders and blond curls that fell this way and that across his chocolate-brown eyes, Curtis Green took up far too much space. There should be a law against it.

"Fine." He shrugged as he awkwardly reached into his

backpack and started to pull out a yellow folder. "The thing is, we really need to start—"

"Oh, hey, Curtis." Loni suddenly stepped in between them and pointed over to the long table where most of the sophomores were sitting. "I think Tyler wants you. Why don't I grab you something to eat and you can go and see him."

"Um, okay," he said slowly, for a moment looking surprised before making his way through the cafeteria over to where Tyler was sitting. The minute he was gone, Emma spun around and stared at her friend in shock.

"Excuse me, but did you just offer to get Curtis Green his breakfast?" she demanded. "You *do* remember that he's my self-declared archenemy, don't you?"

"He has a broken leg," Loni defended as they shuffled forward in the line. "Besides, he had to deal with the embarrassment of getting caught in a fence while trying to fight a group of rogue dragons on his Saturday patrol. It isn't exactly the stuff comic book legends are made of. I thought he might be feeling bad."

Emma glanced over to where Curtis was now the center of attention and tried to bite back her bitterness. "Yeah, he looks like he's really suffering. Though I'm sure his pain has been eased by the fact that he took down three dragons before he passed out. What do I have? Nothing but mockery and a sore eye."

"It's not that bad," Loni insisted as she nudged Emma forward.

"In five weeks I haven't managed to slay one fairy. How is that not bad? And I really don't think Saturday's disaster has done me any favors."

"Emma, it's just breakfast," Loni defended as they finally reached the front of the line. "It's not a big deal."

"Of course it's a big deal," a red-cheeked cafeteria worker behind the counter clucked at them both. "It's the most important meal of the day. So, girls, how do you want your eggs? Scrambled or poached?"

"Scrambled, thanks," Emma forced herself to reply. She didn't feel remotely hungry, but she didn't want to face one of Kessler's a-slayer-slays-on-their-stomach speeches either, so she just plastered on a smile as the woman handed her a plate piled high with eggs, bacon, and toast and then did two more for Loni.

Her fake smile was put to the test even more when Loni proceeded to get two types of juice and *three* kinds cereal because she wasn't sure what Curtis would like. Emma helped herself to some granola, which she probably had a better chance of eating than a cooked breakfast. She watched Loni try to juggle the two trays and her large backpack before she finally relented.

"Look, give me that and I'll go get us a table while you take that over to 'poor' Curtis."

"Thanks, Em. I won't be long." Loni gratefully passed over her backpack and hurried to where the sophomores were all sitting while Emma hitched it over her other shoulder and picked up her tray from the counter. It didn't take her long to spot an empty table, and she sank as low as she could into her chair just as Loni reappeared.

"Turns out Curtis likes granola best. I would've thought he was a Lucky Charms sort of guy." Loni put down her tray and settled into her chair as Emma narrowed her one good eye.

"Oh my God, is that what this is about? Are you crushing on Curtis Green? Because we've been through a lot together, but I swear this could be the thing that breaks us."

"Of course I don't have a crush on Curtis." Loni busied herself with her breakfast. "I'm just saying that he likes granola and you like granola. Oh, and by the way I found out he's a Sagittarius, which means that you two are highly compatible. Don't you think that's interesting?"

"No." Emma put down her spoon with a clatter. "I do not. What's going on?"

"Nothing." Her friend shook her head. "Honestly, Emma, you're getting very suspicious in your old age."

"I'm fifteen."

"Yes, well, you were a lot more trusting when you were fourteen," Loni replied.

"Maybe my friends didn't act all weird when I was fourteen?" Emma countered. "Now please, Loni, tell me what's going on."

Loni looked at Emma and sighed. "Fine," she said, reluctantly reaching out for the heavy bag that was now sitting on one of the spare chairs. "At our Sunday afternoon meeting, instead of just recapping how our Saturday patrols had gone, Kessler gave out our new assignments for Alternative Slaying Practices. I was going to bring it over to your dorm room last night, but I ended up slaying until midnight."

"Since when do goblins stay up so late? And when did you start slaying on a Sunday?" Emma lifted an eyebrow in surprise since, as a rule, goblins were like fairies and tended to go out during the day. That, however, was where the similarities ended since everyone knew goblins were ruthless killers who didn't think twice about murdering humans and causing all kinds of havoc. Loni was so lucky.

"It wasn't goblins." Loni reached over and plucked a yellow folder off the top of the pile and handed it to Emma. "Kessler decided that we should team up with another slayer and study their techniques for the next month. And not just going out on Saturday patrols with each other. We need to shadow them, and there are all kinds of questionnaires and reports we have to do. Trust me—you haven't suffered until you've had Brenda Vance trailing around after you."

You got stuck with Brenda?" Emma shuddered, almost pleased she'd spent the whole day in the medical wing. Almost. She tentatively touched the eye patch.

"You have no idea. And then when I went out with her last night, it took her so long to mark out and scout the perimeter that by the time she deemed it okay for us to approach enemy territory, the demons had gone," Loni complained. "They could've rolled out on their bellies and Brenda would've been too busy filling in her paperwork and fiddling with her wards to even notice. I'd been hoping to test out my new laser too."

"So, did Kessler tell you who I was going to be paired with?" Emma asked, and Loni suddenly became very interested in her piece of toast. That couldn't be a good sign. "It's not one of the Lewis twins, right?"

"Okay, so the important thing is that you don't freak out." Her friend finally looked up. "This assignment is worth twenty percent of our grade, and—"

"Loni, just tell me who it is and put me out of my misery," Emma repeated as an uneasy feeling started to snake its way through her stomach.

Loni let out a reluctant sigh. "It's Curtis Green."

The breakfast cereal that Emma had been attempting to eat turned to cardboard in her throat while the loud drone of the other students faded away until all she was conscious of was the name that her friend had just said.

"You know, it makes sense when you think about it," Loni said in a rush, as if aware that she had to be quick before Emma's brain had a chance to digest the news. "He was off yesterday with an injury and so were you. And don't forget that you both like granola and are astrologically compatible. Honestly, once you spend time with him, I'm sure you'll have a great time."

Emma hardly heard. Instead, she forced herself to count her breaths until the jerky rhythm of her pounding heart finally started to return to normal and a wave of Zen-like calm washed over her.

She shook her head. This was a mistake.

All of it. Her mom dying. Principal Kessler thinking that she should be a fairy slayer, and in the process turning her into the laughingstock of Burtonwood. And now being told she needed to pair up with the guy who'd ruined her life? No, this was definitely all a big mistake. And she was going to fix it. Without a word, Emma got to her feet and scooped up the yellow folder as Loni looked at her in alarm.

"Where are you going? Why aren't you talking? It makes me nervous when you don't talk. Emma, say something."

"I'm going to see Principal Kessler," Emma said in a remarkably calm voice.

"What?! No, that's a very bad idea," Loni yelped as she jumped up and tried to block Emma's path. "And it's exactly the reason I was trying to avoid telling you. Just because you're a hotheaded Aries doesn't mean you can just go charging in and tell him that he's made a mistake with the assignments. What about the high road? Remember what a good idea you thought that was?"

"That was before I tried to kill a fairy and got caught in an explosion," Emma said in a dry voice. "Now I've left the high road and moved onto Desperation Avenue. And for the record, I'm not going to tell Kessler that he's made a mistake."

"You're not? Oh, thank goodness. Because for a moment there I thought you had gone completely crazy. Especially after all the trouble you've been in over the last five weeks, the last thing you want to do is annoy Kessler." Loni looked relieved for about a second before she realized that Emma was still standing up looking serious. *"You're still going to see him, aren't you?"*

"I am," Emma agreed in a tight voice. "But don't worry. I'm merely going to explain to him that I would rather die a long, slow, and horrible death at the claws of a lathium dragon—having my skin ripped off strip by pain-soaked strip while I writhe in agony—than work with Curtis Green."

Then without another word she turned and left.

CHAPTER FOUR

Emma ignored the snickers as she hurried out of the cafeteria. She reached Sir Francis, and after giving him another quick touch on the forehead, she went back along the cool terra-cotta tiles that paved the external corridor that flanked the quad. It was too much. First she had to suffer public humiliation, and now, *now*, she was supposed to be shown how to slay a dragon by Curtis Green?

Oh, she didn't think so.

As for the idea of taking him out and attempting to show him how to kill a fairy? No, no, and no. Anger churned in her stomach as she hurried through the main entrance of Burtonwood and turned left. As she went, the eyes of the people in the numerous photographs that graced the walls seemed to watch her. They were of all the graduates who had gone on to do great things in the slaying world, her mom being one of them, and ever since Emma had been a small child, this corridor had been one of her favorite parts of the academy. It made her feel connected to her past and excited about her future, but right now as she raced toward Kessler's office, all she felt was betrayed.

Well, it was going to stop here. Principal Kessler had been a friend of her mom's, and she would just have to keep talking to him until he finally understood why the whole fairy thing wasn't going to work. She was a dragon slayer. She was.

Once she reached his door, she paused for a moment to catch her breath. There was no answer when she knocked and so she knocked again, this time harder, but still there was no answer, and she was just wondering if she should poke her head in when the next door swung open and Mrs. Barnes appeared, her purple eye shadow making her look like she'd gone three rounds with a baritong demon.

"Emma, he's not in there."

"Oh." Frustration started to sting at her lip, and she had to bite it to stop from betraying her feelings. "Will he back before first period?"

The secretary took off her green glasses and shook her head. "I don't think so. Some people from the Department have been here since seven. He's still holed up with them now."

"Really?" For a moment Emma was distracted since the Department of Paranormal Containment was where most of the Burtonwood students would end up working once they graduated. It hadn't always been the case, but about fifty years ago the Department had realized the Academy slayers, with their sight and power, could kill the elementals better than any of their own agents, and so they'd started recruiting them. This meant after years of slayers just doing their job because of duty, they suddenly found they were getting a paycheck as well. Not surprisingly, sight-gifted parents were suddenly a lot happier to send their children to Burtonwood and the various other academies across the world. Sir Francis would've been proud. "What are they doing here?"

"I'm afraid I can't tell you that." Mrs. Barnes shook her head. "By the way, I heard about what happened to your eye on Saturday. Are you feeling any better?"

"I'm fine." Emma self-consciously touched the patch and wondered if there was anyone who didn't know about the explosion.

"Good, and you'll be pleased to know that you haven't been penalized for forgetting to hand back your pass-out, but I will need to get it from you now."

Emma sighed as she followed Mrs. Barnes back into the office and fished around in her school bag for the bullet-shaped piece of plastic that let her in and out of the school gate for her Saturday patrol. Sophomores got to spend ten field hours a week off campus slaying, and it went up to fifteen by the time they were juniors and twenty for seniors. However, the only way in and out was with a constantly changing security code that was embedded in the pass, and while no one could see cameras anywhere, Mrs. Barnes always seemed to know if someone tried to buck the system.

Emma handed the small pass back just as the bell rang,

and so she reluctantly made her way back down the half-empty corridor toward her first class of the day. Math. As if she hadn't suffered enough. Thankfully, her teacher wasn't there yet and Emma quickly slipped into the seat Loni had saved her.

"Well?" her friend demanded as Emma pulled out her math books. "What did he say?"

"He's in a secret meeting with some Department guys, but Barney wouldn't say what it was about. Probably telling them to make sure I get a desk job when I finally graduate." She made a face as she started to fiddle with her brown ponytail, which was hanging over her left shoulder.

"Stop it. First of all, you're not that important," Loni said in a stern voice. "And besides, you're breaking new ground. No one else has ever really tried to slay fairies before."

"Yes, that's because they're not worth slaying," Emma muttered.

"Hey, Em," Tyler said, leaning over Loni. "The explosion sucks, but don't let it get you down." He gave Emma a pat on the hand, which would've been comforting if he hadn't been wearing a pair of thickly spiked, flame-resistant gloves that he used when he was hunting salamanders.

"Ouch." She whipped her hand away.

"Sorry." Tyler shot her apologetic glance. "Someone bet me that I couldn't wear these bad boys all day. I forgot they were on."

"Just like you will no doubt forget your brain one day, Tyler Owens." Loni shook her head in disapproval. "My mom warned me what would happen if I became friends with a Leo, but would I listen?"

"Well you didn't complain when I helped you pass your tracking test the other day," Tyler reminded her, but before they could continue bickering, their math teacher walked into the room.

"As you know, there are twelve elementals. Three air, three fire, three earth, and three water," she said as she approached her desk. For a moment Emma wondered if it was a history lesson since learning about the elementals was fourth-grade stuff. "But it doesn't stop there. Take, for instance, demons. They might only be considered as one elemental group, but there are at least a hundred and five known subraces. So what if you were working on the Department's logistics team and had to decide how many agents you needed to send to clean up a newly hatched phoenix nest, two battling ogre tribes, and a problem on the East Coast with some krakens? How would you figure it out?"

Everyone except Tyler, who loved numbers, immediately started to groan as Professor Edwards held up a bunch of papers, which meant they were about to have a pop quiz. This day was just getting worse by the hour.

✷✷✷

By the time Emma walked into the cafeteria for dinner that night, she begrudgingly realized that, despite her inability to answer any of the questions (let alone understand what they even meant), the pop quiz was actually the highlight of an otherwise horrible day. Even now people were making explosive noises and giggling as she walked past them. Also, she'd been unsuccessful in her attempts to track down Principal Kessler.

"What are you doing?" Loni demanded in a confused voice as Emma suddenly slid down her chair halfway through eating her fettuccine.

"Hiding," Emma whispered as from across the room she caught sight of Curtis swinging his way into the cafeteria. The other thing she'd done all day was avoid her new assignment partner. She didn't care what Loni or anyone else said: there was no way she was working with him. It was a matter of principle. She watched as Brenda raced up to him, but after a brief conversation, the demon slayer went away and Curtis continued to scan the room.

"Yes, but why?" Tyler craned his neck in confusion. "Is there something I should know?"

"She's in denial," Loni explained before lowering her voice and mouthing, *"about Curtis."*

"Oh, is that all?" Tyler rolled his eyes before leaning across the table and swiping some of Emma's uneaten dinner. "At least you got someone who knows how to use a sword. I got stuck with Glen Lewis, and tomorrow I have to let him show me how to slay an ogre. Only problem is that he never finishes his sentences because he forgets that Garry isn't there to do it for him. Trust me, Curtis isn't so bad."

Emma kicked him in the shin.

"Ouch," he protested. "Why did you do that?"

"It's just, I thought you'd forgotten that Curtis Green is evil," Emma informed him. "And if you like him so much, then why don't you go and sit with him?"

"Because he's leaving the cafeteria," Tyler pointed out, and Emma let out a sigh of relief as she realized that after standing in the doorway and looking around for five minutes, he had indeed left the cafeteria and disappeared back out into the November evening.

"You know this isn't going to work, don't you?" Loni asked rhetorically as she pushed away the rest of her meal and Tyler instantly fell on it with a zeal she and Emma both ignored. "I mean, it's not like we even go to a regular school where you can miss a few classes. This is Burtonwood, Emma, and that means you can't run away from him forever."

"I can while he has his leg in a cast," Emma reminded her. "Anyway, until I change Kessler's mind, there's no way I'm going near Curtis in case he figures out my plan and tries to stop me."

"You have a plan?" Tyler finished the rest of Loni's dinner and looked up with interest.

"Well, it was to talk to Kessler, but since I can't find him, I might have to come up with something else, and when I do, I don't want Curtis nearby sticking his nose in it."

"That's it? Ruby, my five-legged pet cockroach has better plans than that." Tyler raised an eyebrow, but before he could say anything else, Ryan Duncan came up to him and they started talking about some football game that they'd been betting on. Loni and Emma rolled their eyes and both stood up.

"So do you want to go to the gym?" Loni asked, but Emma shook her head and yawned.

"Actually, I might make it an early night."

"Okay, well, I'll see you in the morning. And Emma, try to remember that, according to your horoscope, you're actually supposed to be having a good week."

"Remind me to take cover when my stars say I'm going to have a bad week." Emma only just resisted the urge to laugh as she said good night to her friend.

She jogged back toward her dorm. Normally she would've stopped and talked to the group of sophomores who were all sitting under an oak tree, but tonight she didn't bother since they were probably talking about her. Instead, she hurried back to her room and halfheartedly pulled out her homework.

An hour later she decided to call it a night since apparently staring aimlessly at her homework wasn't enough to get it finished. She was just about to turn off her laptop when her dad pinged her on IM.

She considered answering it for a moment before deciding to just call him in the morning. She'd promised after her accident that she'd update him every day about how she was doing, but she just didn't feel up to it. Especially since, no matter how much he tried, it was impossible for him to understand what she was going through. Not just about her sore eye or even getting stuck with fairies, but because he was sight-blind.

As a rule sight-gifted people tended to stick together mainly because it was frowned upon to talk about elementals with civilians. However, it wasn't actually illegal, and so when Emma's parents had met and fallen in love, there was nothing to stop them from getting married. Plus, her dad had briefly worked at Burtonwood, which had made any explaining her mom had to do a little bit easier.

The other reason that most slayers tended to stick together was that the children of mixed marriages were nearly always sight-blind. In fact, until she turned eight, Emma's biggest fear was that she would be as well and that all the amazing stories her mom had told her would just be that . . . stories.

But then it had happened.

On her eighth birthday, her parents had taken her out to the beach. It was April and the spring air had been warm and fresh, and the smell of salt had been dancing in her nostrils before it was suddenly replaced by something else. Something evil. Then, without even knowing why, Emma had dropped to all fours just before a large phoenix went swooping over her, missing her by mere inches.

In a second Emma took it all in: The heavy torrents of wind that gushed up as the creature went past her, its dark red feathers that almost seemed to blaze like fire against the blue spring sky. The small orange eyes that were filled with malice. And most noticeably the large beak, curved and deadly.

A second later her mom appeared with a crossbow in her hands and killed the creature before it could turn and dive a second time. Emma had instantly burst into tears, which her mom had mistaken for fear rather than joy. But how could she be scared when her mom was there to help her? And even better, now that she had the sight, she would be able to go to Burtonwood. It had truly been a perfect day, and together she and her mom spent the next two hours planting a series of tiny electromagnetic wards to stop any more phoenixes from returning to the area.

With that thought she shut her laptop and went to bed. Thinking of her mom just reminded her of how much was at stake. And as she drifted off to sleep, she desperately tried to come up with the perfect Plan C so that she could convince Kessler to change his mind. Her future depended on it.

CHAPTER FIVE

S o how much sleep did you get?" Tyler asked the next
morning as he carefully studied her face. "I bet it was
six hours. No, actually, make that five hours. Am I right? I
bet I'm right."

"Shut up, Tyler." Loni cut him off with a glare as Professor
Vanderbilt started to hand out a photocopied article on how
to dismantle a hand grenade. "But seriously, Emma, are you
okay? You do look a little tired. Maybe you should go and
get checked out again by the nurse."

"I'm fine." Emma yawned as she took one of the copies
and passed the rest of the pile just as Professor Vanderbilt
held up a hand grenade.

"Okay, everybody. I want you tell me three situations
when you might possibly need to use this weapon."

"When you're in the food court fighting fairies," Glen
called out from the back row, and the rest of the class
started to laugh. Emma sighed and slunk down in her chair.
Obviously her fifteen minutes of fame weren't quite up yet.

"Good idea, but remember we frown on hurting civilians,"

Professor Vanderbilt said in a mild voice—with a hint of sarcasm—before turning his attention back to the rest of the class. "Does anyone else have any ideas?"

Brenda immediately raised her hand, but before she could speak, Principal Kessler appeared in the doorway and nodded for Professor Vanderbilt to join him. Emma felt her mouth go dry as she studied the headmaster. His tanned narrow face was grim, and his straight gray hair was pushed back off the top of his forehead as he talked to Professor Vanderbilt in a low voice.

She turned to Loni and Tyler. "I bet this has something to do with his meeting with the Department yesterday. And maybe it will explain why I couldn't find him anywhere."

Loni nodded in agreement, but before she could reply, Principal Kessler finished his conversation and walked up to the podium.

"The Department's got word that a zombie virus has been released over in the western suburbs," he said, which instantly caused a murmur of confusion to go racing around the classroom. Even though there was some cross-training between Burtonwood and the other Departmental branches, zombie hunting definitely wasn't something that any slayer normally did. "However, their efforts to reverse the virus at stage two have been impeded by a clan of nearby crocus demons."

Ah. Emma and the rest of the room nodded in understanding. Now it made sense, since while some demons were solitary, crocus demons were notorious for hunting in large packs. And they were deadly as well, especially to zombie hunters.

"The Department's demon slayers are already stretched thin, so they've asked everyone at Burtonwood to help," the principal continued, his voice laden with authority. "The seniors and juniors have already been informed and will be joining us. People, this is serious. *It's code blue.*"

Emma turned to Loni in excitement. Code blue meant fighting. Finally something was going her way. She was going to get some real field hours *and*, more importantly, the chance to prove herself once and for all as a great slayer of things other than fairies. In short, the perfect Plan C had fallen into her lap, and Curtis had better watch out, because soon she would be back in her rightful spot as dragon slayer. The surge of relief she felt was overwhelming.

"So here's the drill," Principal Kessler said in a cool voice. "We'll be pulling out in an hour to launch a preemptive attack on the crocus demons so the Department can get on with their job of containing the zombies. In the meantime, there are agents waiting in the gym to brief you. Questions?"

No one raised their hand, but after the principal had dismissed the class and they all started to pour out the door for their briefing, Curtis finally coughed. "What about me?" he asked as he glanced down at his cast.

"I'm sorry, Curtis, but you know the rules. If you're injured, you stay here. No exceptions." Principal Kessler shook his head as he came over to where Curtis was sitting.

Emma got to her feet and shot him a smug look. She

normally didn't delight in other people's misfortunes, but she couldn't help but think that karma was starting to work with her on this one. However, before she could follow Loni and Tyler out of the room, Principal Kessler stepped in her way so that only she and Curtis were left in the room.

"Emma, we need to talk."

"We do?" She frowned. "Is this about the explosion on Saturday? Because I swear it wasn't my fault, and most importantly, no one was hurt."

"Except you," Curtis pointed out in an unhelpful voice from his chair.

"He's right," Principal Kessler said. "You're injured too, which means you have to stay behind. You and Curtis can start work on your assignment."

Emma felt like she had been hit by a truck. "But that doesn't make sense. There's a demon crisis about to unfold and you'd rather that I stay back here and do an assignment? Please, you can't leave me behind." *With Curtis.*

"I'm sorry, Emma, but it's not open for debate," Principal Kessler said.

"This is all because of my eye patch, isn't it?" She reached up and pulled it off her eye. Ouch. "Well, now it's gone. Does that mean I can go?"

"Just because you're not wearing the patch doesn't mean your eye's better. It's policy. I'm sorry."

"But I can help," Emma pleaded while secretly trying to refocus her left eye, which felt a little fuzzy. Not that Principal Kessler needed to know that.

"That's right," the headmaster cut in. "You can help. By doing your schoolwork. These questionnaires are based on field observations, so while neither of you is fit to slay, there is still plenty you can do. In the folders you can see how I want the reports written up, and Mrs. Barnes will issue you the passes. You know this is twenty percent of your grade, right?"

Emma couldn't believe it.

"Please," she tried again. "We all know that fairies aren't exactly the epitome of evil, and as for dragons, well, I think I know better than Curtis how to slay one. I mean—"

"Emma, I think you're forgetting yourself," Principal Kessler said in a commanding voice. "This assignment still has to be done, no matter what you think of it. End of discussion. Now I've got to go join in the briefing."

She stared in openmouthed frustration at the door Principal Kessler had just walked through. Up and down the corridors she could hear the sound of running feet as students prepared for the mission, which just made her feel even worse. But her pity party was interrupted by a coughing noise next to her.

Her eyes narrowed.

"This is all your fault," she said, spinning around and glaring at Curtis. Her eye was a little less fuzzy but it still hurt like crazy, and there were now all sorts of shadows dancing in front of it.

"My fault?" he started to say before he frowned and

studied her face. *"Hey, Jones, are you okay? Your eye looks really sore and your face is pale. Maybe you should see Nurse Reynes."*

"No thanks." Emma shook her head and immediately regretted it as the world started to swim, but she did her best to ignore it. There was no way she wanted to go back to the infirmary. Infirmaries reminded her of hospitals, and hospitals reminded her of her mom.

She shut her eyes to try to hold back the memories that were starting to seep out. The ironic thing was that after risking life and limb battling dragons every day, her mom had been in the hospital for a simple concussion and had ended up catching an infection that spread to her lungs and killed her. All within four days.

"Are you sure? Because it really doesn't look that good." Genuine concern seemed to be etched across Curtis's chiseled features, and for a moment she felt like he had read her mind and knew the real reason she didn't want to go.

"I'm fine," she said in a tight voice as she reminded herself that he was the person standing between her and her goal. "Besides, if you really want to help me, you can go and tell Kessler to change his mind about the designation."

Curtis tightened his jaw. "Look, I know you're bummed, but you can't keep taking it out on me. It wasn't like I planned this."

"Oh, really?" Emma narrowed her one good eye at him. "Well, it's funny that up until five weeks ago everyone thought it was my spot. I mean, for the last seven years, I've topped dragon studies, but you wouldn't know that because you didn't take any of the classes, yet suddenly you're an expert?"

"It's not that simple." As he spoke he leaned forward so that his brown eyes were staring directly into hers. His tanned face suddenly seemed far too close to her as she watched his white teeth bite into the fleshy part of his full lower lip.

"Is that right?" Emma blinked as she realized she had been staring at him. She dragged her gaze away, almost as annoyed with herself as she was with him. For a moment Curtis looked like he was going to answer, before he suddenly shut his mouth and clenched his jaw.

"Look. I know you're not happy, but this isn't the ideal situation for me, either."

"What's that supposed to mean?" Emma demanded, before realizing she knew exactly what he meant. How embarrassing to be stuck with the laughingstock of the entire Academy. As if reading her mind, he didn't bother to reply as he awkwardly got to his feet and flicked his tie back over his shoulder before reaching down for his crutches. As he did so, his white school shirt strained with the effort. Emma ignored it. Just because he had big muscly arms did not mean he was a better dragon slayer than she was. Once he tucked the crutches under his arm, he paused and seemed to study her for a minute before merely shrugging. *As if he was so above her that he didn't even owe her an explanation.*

"I've got to go and get changed for the assignment, but

then I'll meet you in the office so we can get our pass-outs, okay?" he said in a businesslike voice. Then, without another word, he swung his way out into the corridor, leaving Emma seething with indignation.

CHAPTER SIX

Y ou know, as much as I like to listen to you complain about Curtis, I've got to get ready," Loni said fifteen minutes later as Emma watched her friend race around her tiny dorm room, excitedly packing her slaying kit. "And if you're going to just sit there, you could at least make yourself useful and pass me that subsonic blaster."

"Yes, but it's so unfair," Emma insisted as she obediently reached over and handed her friend the small handheld weapon that was sitting on the dresser next to the bed. Then she returned to her brooding. "I mean, *why* is Curtis getting such special treatment anyway? Maybe he has some compromising photos of Kessler. Probably bought them on eBay and decided to use them as blackmail to get my spot."

"Yeah, that's definitely it," Loni said sarcastically as she continued to methodically pack her weapons, her brow knitted in concentration.

"Or, maybe his parents are mega rich and promised to

donate a new wing to Burtonwood?" Emma continued. "Oh. . . or the retinal-scanning machine that turned up last month? That could've been from them."

"Yes, or it could've been from the Department, like we were told when it first arrived," Loni said as she unsheathed one of her knives and held the blade up to the light. Once she was satisfied, she added it to her bag and turned her attention to a pile of wards that was sitting on her comforter, looking like metallic buttons. "I know you don't want to hear this, but you can't blame Curtis. Besides, we all know what an amazing fighter he is."

"Of course I can blame him. My life has turned to chopped liver ever since he was chosen to become a dragon slayer. Coincidence? I don't think so. And what's with all that hair? He should get it cut."

Loni put down the screwdriver she had been using to reconfigure the voltage on the tiny wards and blinked. "What's his hair got to do with anything?"

"It's just annoying."

Loni stopped and smirked. "Do you like him?"

"Like him?" Emma looked at her friend like she was crazy. "Of course I don't like him. Curtis Green is my archenemy— with emphasis on the 'arch.' Oh, and get a load of this. He told me that he doesn't want to do the assignment with me either."

"Really?" Loni marveled. "It's almost like he knows something."

"*Humph*. Whose side are you on?" Emma demanded as she gently scratched her sore eye and then got up and started to march around Loni's tiny dorm room, careful not to step on the tangle of wires and circuit boards that had migrated from the desk and were now scattered across the floor like a spaghetti explosion.

No one had been more surprised than Loni herself when she'd shown an aptitude for electronics several years ago, though after careful consideration she decided that it was because she was a Taurus and was therefore good with her hands. Plus, as a die-hard shopper, she loved the chance to pore over gadget catalogs. Personally, Emma couldn't see the attraction.

"I'm on the good side." Loni zipped up her kit bag and swung it over her shoulder. "And the good side is about to go and find some demons, so if you don't mind, I'll be off. And by the way, I don't think you should keep scratching your eye like that. Maybe you should put the patch back on?"

"My eye's fine. That nurse was totally overreacting," Emma said before letting out a long groan. "And I'm an idiot. I'm sorry. We shouldn't even be talking about me when you're about to go out on your first code blue. Are you scared?"

Loni turned and shot her a rueful grin. "A little bit. But apparently today is perfect for me to take risks and let the world see how much I can shine. *Oh, and for some reason I need to stay away from the color orange, so no carrots for me.*"

"Well, don't take too many risks," Emma lectured. "With

the demons or with the carrots." Then she gave her friend a big hug. "And don't let Tyler talk you into making any stupid bets like seeing who can be the first one to kill a demon and cut off their horns."

"Don't worry, I talked to Tyler just before you came in, and he sounded too scared to even think of betting on anything."

"Well, that's good. Make sure you both take care, and don't forget to text me as soon as it's all over."

"I will." Loni lost her stern expression. "And Emma, I know how upset you are about everything that's happened, but blaming Curtis isn't going to help. So please, try and be nice to him when you're working on this assignment? You might even find he's not so bad."

"You cannot be serious." Emma gave a stubborn tilt of her chin.

"I'm saying it for your own good," Loni pressed on. "Because the longer you obsess over the fact that Curtis has ruined your life, the tougher things are going to get. Besides," she wheedled, "when you think about it, this isn't about Curtis Green. The bigger issue is about you trying to convince Kessler to change his mind and make you a dragon slayer like your mom. Remember?"

Emma closed her eyes for a moment. She knew Loni was trying to understand, but she couldn't really. After all, her parents were alive and well and living in Idaho, and while they both liked their jobs with the Department, Emma never really got the feeling it was their calling. Ditto with Loni.

She said she wanted to be a goblin slayer, but Emma secretly knew her friend would've been just as pleased with whatever she was given, and as long as she grew up and married a nice sight-gifted Pisces guy (preferably on the cusp) her life would be happy. But it wasn't like that for Emma, and finding out she might lose dragons was just like losing her mom all over again. Even thinking about it left her feeling empty and desolate.

However, short of throwing herself in front of the bus and making Kessler take her with them on the mission, Emma knew she didn't have much of a choice. She gave her friend one final hug and reluctantly headed back to her room and got changed.

It was Burtonwood policy never to wear a uniform when you were doing any patrolling, and so Emma quickly slipped into a pair of jeans and the first clean shirt she could find. She was just checking to see that she had all her books when she glanced out the window and caught sight of Loni hurrying over to the bus that was parked in the second parking lot just in front of the woods that wrapped around Burtonwood like a comforter.

Another jab of disappointment went racing through her as she thought of Curtis and—*hey, what was that black shadow hovering over the bus?*

Emma's eye started to throb with pain and she snapped it shut, while acknowledging that ripping off the patch and trying to prove her point to Principal Kessler really hadn't been such a good idea. Especially since now, not only was her eye incredibly itchy, but it also appeared to be seeing big globby things.

She opened it again and peered back out the window, but instead of the dark shape disappearing, it had now taken on a definite form, and Emma felt a cold shudder go through her as she realized the shape had wings. This could not be what she thought it was. But after another look, it was confirmed.

A dragon!

She tried to focus her eyes to identify which breed it was, but everything was still blurry. She quickly grabbed her binoculars and raced back to the window, but even with a better view, she still didn't recognize the species. It was small for a dragon, a lot darker than they usually were, and it didn't seem at all affected by the fact that it was daylight. Even more disturbing, despite the fact that it was flying across the sky, no one on the ground below seemed to be paying any attention to it. Then, without warning, the dragon disappeared from sight, leaving Emma to wonder if she had imagined it.

Maybe she had? Nurse Reynes had said there was a small chance that she had mild concussion, so maybe it was all just a dream. After all, she was at Burtonwood, a place filled to the brim with sight-gifted students. So why couldn't they see it? And more important, why was the dragon on campus in the first place? There were wards everywhere. Not just for dragons but for all elementals. In fact, Loni, who spent a lot of her spare time helping the tech guys maintain the equipment, used to joke that there were wards on the wards, all of them pulsing out positive electrons designed to keep Burtonwood elemental-free.

Emma rubbed her aching eye, but before she could figure out what it all meant, the creature suddenly reappeared in the sky, like a dark angry blot. Then she watched in horror as it made a dive directly toward the bus, where Brenda Vance was standing. Emma dropped the binoculars onto the ground as she realized that not only was this very real, but that the dragon was hunting.

Without pausing, she raced to the door and out into the hallway. Her legs pounded on the ground, her chest started to burn, and her shoes rubbed as she forced herself to keep going. Finally, she burst through the building doors, past the overhanging bougainvillea, and along the gravel path to where Principal Kessler was checking equipment and ushering everyone onto the bus.

"Thank goodness I caught you in time." She panted as she came to a halt and tried to catch her breath. "There's a dragon on campus. And it's hunting."

Principal Kessler looked annoyed. "Emma, I thought we'd talked about this. Anything else can wait until after this operation is over."

"What?" She frowned for a minute before shaking her head in frustration. "No, you don't understand. There's a dragon. D-r-a-g-o-n. And it swooped so close to Brenda, it—"

"Oh my God. Emma Jones, you are so pathetic." Brenda appeared holding a box of sonar gear, her hair looking remarkably un-dragon-ruffled. "Not only are you pretending you can see an invisible dragon that can break through our wards, but you're trying to involve me in your delusions."

"Don't be ridiculous." Emma stared at her. "Why would I pretend?"

"Oh, let me think. Hmm, now, why would the girl who is *obsessed* with following in her dead mom's footsteps suddenly think she can see a dragon just days before the induction ceremony?"

"That's not true." Emma turned to Principal Kessler and shot him a pleading look. "I swear. I saw it. I've got a really bad feeling about this."

"Really, so where is it now? And why didn't anyone else see it?" Brenda retorted, and Emma twisted her head as she valiantly searched the skies. They were completely dragon-free.

"Okay, so I'm not quite sure where it went," she was forced to admit before she turned to Principal Kessler and shot him another pleading look. "But it was definitely a dragon. It must've broken through the wards somehow."

"Of course it did." Brenda rolled her eyes. "Because that's just so—"

"That's enough," Principal Kessler cut in as an angry scowl marched across his face and his pale blue eyes narrowed. "Brenda, you can get on the bus, and Emma, I can assure you that no elemental has ever broken through the wards, and if it had, the ops team would let me know."

"But—"

"But nothing." Principal Kessler cut her off. "I want you to continue with your assignment. *Now.*" Then, without another word, he climbed the stairs and signaled for the driver to start the engine.

"Wait—" Emma started to yell as the bus pulled away from the curb, but it was no good and she was forced to stand and watch it disappear out of the parking lot. Suddenly, there was a coughing noise behind her and she turned around to where Curtis was standing, leaning forward on his crutches. He had changed out of his uniform and wore a simple white T-shirt underneath a plain blue hoodie that stretched across his broad shoulders and seemed to make his tanned face look even tanner. He also had a very confused expression on his face.

"Um, Jones, did you just tell Kessler that you thought you saw a dragon on campus?" He knitted his brow.

"I *did* see a dragon on campus," Emma corrected as she continued to scan the skies. Then she turned to him and let out a reluctant sigh. "Unfortunately, it's gone now, and Kessler didn't believe me."

"But how is that even possible?" Curtis's face went pale. "It's daytime and we're in a built-up area that is warded up to the eyeballs. Not exactly ideal party conditions for a dragon."

"Thank you, but since I have studied dragon behavior for the last seven years and did actually grow up with one of the most famous slayers in the world, I do know that. However, I also know what I saw. It was a dragon. Why won't anyone believe me?"

"Oh, I believe you. For the last five weeks you've done

everything in your power to convince Kessler you should be the dragon slayer, so it doesn't really make sense that you'd suddenly try and make him think you're crazy."

"Exact—" she started to say before Curtis's words hit home. She frowned. "Okay, so it's not ideal that Kessler now thinks that I'm crazy, but if we can track down this dragon, then he will realize I'm telling the truth," she said before she noticed that Curtis was staring at her in disbelief. *"What? Why are you looking like this is a bad idea?* After all, you're the dragon slayer. I thought you would be jumping at the chance."

Curtis glanced down to his cast. "First, I'm not too hot in the jumping department right now. Second, I never track anything until I have my kit with me. And third, but most important, we've got an assignment to do."

"Oh, please. I don't think the world will stop if I don't show you how to slay a fairy. In fact, I can't believe you think a dumb assignment is more important than hunting this dragon. What kind of slayer are you?"

For a moment Curtis paused and looked like he wasn't going to answer her. Finally, he spoke. "The kind who still has three more years of study to go. Besides, Jones, we don't all have the luxury of being able to do whatever we want around here."

Emma was taken aback by his sudden change in tone, which almost sounded bitter and frustrated. She was about to protest when she caught the firm set of his jaw, which only served to cause his cheekbones to jut out.

She cleared her throat. "Okay, so since you have an

overwhelming desire to do everything Principal Kessler tells you, how about I tell you where to find some fairies while I go and find this dragon?"

"I wouldn't advise that."

"Why not?" Emma demanded. "Worried that I'll get your designation?"

"Actually, I was more concerned with the fact that Professor Vanderbilt's heading our way, and judging by the look on his face, I'm guessing that Kessler has spoken to him. Which means that your chances of going dragon hunting are slim to none."

"What—" Emma started to say before she spun around and realized that the old-fashioned armaments professor was bearing down on them with a grim expression on his face. She reluctantly acknowledged that Curtis was right. She could either stay there and get lectured or she could go and do the assignment.

"Fine," she mumbled as she felt the fight drain out of her. So much for her chance to try to find this dragon and prove to Kessler once and for all how capable she was. She was obviously destined to be a low-grade fairy slayer forever.

CHAPTER SEVEN

A re you sure you really want to trade all this in and become a dragon slayer," Curtis said as they both ordered a coffee and Emma directed him over to a table at the far end of the popular bookshop café on the second floor of the mall.

"What's that supposed to mean?" She couldn't quite hide her irritation. They'd already spent two hours looking for fairies, and if they didn't find any here at the mall, then Emma was going to call it quits. It was humiliating enough having to try to slay them in the first place, but having to spend all day with Curtis tagging along after her certainly wasn't helping matters any. Especially when they could be back at Burtonwood hunting for an elemental that was actually dangerous.

"It's just that all the dragons I've ever hunted tend to come out at night. Near cold muddy swamps. This seems a lot more civilized: books to read, food to eat, all in a nice temperature-controlled environment. In fact, I'm tempted to put in for a transfer myself."

"You're not going to change my mind," Emma informed him as she stirred some sugar in her coffee. "My mom used to tell me about all her hunting trips, and of course before you decided to ruin my life I did manage a few of my own."

She knew Loni had told her not to blame Curtis, but why couldn't he understand that his very presence was a reminder that all her dreams and hopes were dead? As in stone-cold and six feet under, never to see the light of day again. It was bound to make a girl bitter.

She was contemplating whether to suggest they go back to Burtonwood, but before she could say anything, a familiar sound of static started to ring in her ear, which meant fairies were nearby. Emma reluctantly glanced around and caught sight of two of them hovering over by the register, just near a large display of the latest book club selection.

She let out a sigh as she got to her feet. Next to her Curtis stiffened and turned toward the fairies, but instead of saying anything, he just stared blankly into the space where they were hovering. Then he rubbed his eyes. For a moment Emma tried to work out why he was acting so weird before she let out a long groan.

"Crap." She glanced up just as the fairies sprinkled a fine layer of glittery dust around the room. Well, that would explain why Curtis was looking blankly at the small fairies. "I think you just got glamour powder in your eyes. I should've warned you."

"Glamour powder?" He turned back to her, his dark eyes

now red-rimmed. Though somehow it actually made him look better than ever. Not that she cared, of course.

"Yeah, the little beasts use it all the time. As you know, most civilians are sight-blind, but there are a few out there who have the gift, so the fairies use glamour powder when they're in the mall. It also has the desired effect of concealing all of the man-made items that they touch. Imagine how freaked out people would be if they could see a bag of potato chips flying along in the air, apparently unconnected to anything. Anyway, it doesn't affect me, but when Loni came out with me once she went as sight-blind as a bat when it hit her." Then she perked up. "Oh well, I guess if you can't see them, then there's no point trying to slay them. Tomorrow maybe? And in the meantime we could get back to concentrating on the dragon."

"Jones, I told you, I don't have the luxury of just ignoring what Kessler tells me to do. You might not care about doing this assignment, but I do."

"Well, maybe you should've thought of that before you got hit with glamour powder," Emma retorted. "And unless you can see the fairies, there isn't much point in being here." For a moment Curtis was silent as he tightened his jaw. Then he muttered something under his breath before reluctantly digging around in his slaying kit.

"There might be one other way," he finally said as he pulled out what looked like...some white-framed Ray-Ban Wayfarers? She watched as he took a deep breath and slipped them onto his face.

"Um, do you always wear sunglasses at the mall? Not to mention the fact that they look like they're straight from the eighties. What's going on?"

"They're not sunglasses." He slid them over his nose, and Emma was forced to marvel at how the ugliest pair of glasses *in the world* still managed to look okay on him.

"Really, because they sure look like sunglasses—and ugly ones at that," she said, annoyed she'd even noticed how they looked on him.

He was silent, and for a moment Emma didn't think he was going to answer her, but finally he shrugged. "Kessler gave them to me. They've got special lenses. For when I need to fight Unseens."

"You need Unseen glasses?" she demanded, before narrowing her eyes and studying him as she thought of the giant dragons in question. Despite their name, they weren't actually invisible, but they did have the chameleon-like talent of blending into the background. "Why didn't I know about this?"

"Gee, I must've forgotten to send you the memo," he snapped in a sarcastic voice before letting out a sigh. "Look, it's not a big deal. Plenty of dragon slayers need help with Unseens."

"I don't. I was tested last year and have perfect vision," she retorted in a prim voice. Not that it really made a difference, since Curtis was right. There were plenty of dragon slayers who couldn't pick out an Unseen dragon when it went into camouflage mode at nighttime. Her mom had been one of them, though instead of using an ugly pair of sunglasses, she had relied on some special binoculars. But still, it was interesting that Perfect Mr. Dragon Slayer wasn't so perfect after all.

"Aren't you the lucky one," he said, his voice laced with bitterness, which if you asked her was overdramatic since it wasn't like dragon slayers came across Unseens very often. "Anyway, I just wondered if they would help me see the fairies. Despite the glamour powder." Then he craned his neck toward the roof, and over the top of the frames she could clearly see him raise an eyebrow. It looked like the ugly sunglasses were working.

"Wow, they really are little. Oh, but no pointy ears?"

"Shhh," Emma warned him. "Don't let them hear you say that. Or anything about their height. They have a Napoleon complex like you wouldn't believe. Once Professor Vanderbilt was out grading me on my tracking techniques, and all he did was mention a Danny DeVito movie he'd watched and you should've seen all the bite marks he ended up with."

"Got it. So what now?" he asked as he continued to write in the folder.

"I guess it's time to join me in some ritual humiliation," she said, just as another fairy flew in through the open door. As it got closer, it turned away from them and tugged at its tiny pants until they fell away to reveal a small white butt.

"Did that thing just moon me?" Curtis demanded as he readjusted the glasses as if checking to see if they were working correctly.

"Trust me, that's the least of what they do," Emma retorted as she flipped open her slaying bag and pulled out two packets of Skittles. She ripped both packets open and handed one to Curtis. "Now, the trick is to try and lure them over to the nonfiction section."

"Nonfiction? Skittles?" Curtis ran a hand through his blond curls and frowned. "Did I mention that none of this makes sense?"

Emma sighed. "They're all crazy about Skittles for some reason. I want them in the nonfiction because it's not as busy there, and as for why they come here? It's to read *OK! Magazine* as people flip through it. I guess they like their celebrity gossip. Now, if you're finished with the twenty questions, maybe we can continue?"

It looked like Curtis was about to say something, but at that moment one of the fairies spotted the Skittles, and after it let out a piercing whistle, six of them swooped toward Emma and Curtis like a swarm of bees at a honey convention.

"This way," she commanded as she quickly weaved her way through the tables toward the far end of the store. Behind her she could hear the sound of miniature angry voices.

"It's not going to work, you know," her "friend" from Saturday, Rupert, called out. "We're going to get those Skittles and then we're going to kick your sorry butts so bad that you'll be screaming for mercy."

"Yeah, and don't try any explosions this time. You know, we really should report you to the Commission of Ethical Treatment of Mortal Enemies," Trevor added, still wearing the green hoodie that was now charred around the hems from the explosion on Saturday.

"Do they always talk this much?" Curtis demanded as he swung his crutches in a two/two rhythm just behind her.

"More. In fact, they normally never shut up," Emma replied over her shoulder as she swatted one of the girl fairies out of her hair and turned into the art and biography aisle. "Okay, so when I say 'now,' I want you to throw a few Skittles on the ground—though not the red ones—you so don't want to see fairies after they've eaten red ones."

"That's right, buddy," Rupert called out as another fairy, dressed in tiny overalls, lunged at Curtis's arm and used its small (but very sharp) teeth to bite into his biceps. "Listen to what the useless slayer has to say, and no one will get hurt—too badly."

"Hey," Curtis protested as he shook his arm to get rid of the small fairy. It didn't work, and the thing remained clamped onto his flesh. "Emma, this is ridiculous. I need to get it off me now." As he spoke he thrust the candy deep into his pocket and instead pulled a slim-line laser gun from his slaying kit.

"No. Put that away and give them the Skittles," she hissed. However, Curtis—who up until this point had been showing signs of sanity—didn't seem to hear her as he pointed the laser in the direction of the small creature on his arm.

Emma groaned as she watched the red tip pierce the flesh and the fairy finally stopped biting Curtis's arm. It grinned in glee as its pale skin turned a glowing orange color and a bright beam raced out from along its fingers straight back toward Curtis's hand.

"Ouch," he yelped in pain as the laser fell away and one of his crutches toppled from under him. "What the—"

"You couldn't just give them the Skittles so that I could show you how to kill them, could you?" Emma demanded as she quickly emptied her packet onto the ground and jumped out of the way as six sugar-starved fairies sped toward them. "You had to do it your way. Make sure you put that in your assignment."

"Well, if you'd told me that my way would hurt so much, then maybe I would've thought twice," Curtis retorted as he cradled his singed hand. "So what happens now?"

"Now we kick your pathetic body into Timbuktu," Rupert said as he flew down and grabbed an orange Skittle straight out of Curtis's hand. "I mean, hello, you're even more useless than slayer-girl here, and that's really—"

"Gotcha," Emma yelled as she plunged her nail file deep into the fairy's wing and watched it wriggle on the ground in annoyance. She glanced back up at Curtis. "Lasers make them go all Incredible Hulk, but nail files render them pretty much useless. It's the steel. Apparently, they hate silver as well, but unfortunately my budget doesn't really stretch that far."

"Ha! That's a good one, calling us useless," the fairy yelled out as it continued struggling to break free of the file. "I mean, you haven't exactly had a great scorecard since you became a designated murderer."

"Well, I'd rather have a bad slaying record than be the one wriggling around on the floor with Skittle drool running down my chin," Emma retorted. "Now prepare to die, because... *hey*." Her eyes suddenly honed in on the tiny raglan T-shirt the fairy was wearing. She leaned in closer so that she could see it more clearly.

"Argh." Rupert tried to squirm away from her. "Gilbert, Trevor. Get her off me. She's trying to put her human cooties all over me. Please, brothers, for the love of evil, get her off. Get her off."

Emma ignored the squealing as she used the tip of her finger to smooth the tiny T-shirt out, much to Rupert's horror. Then she let out a gasp of surprise. "That's the dragon I saw."

"What?" Curtis leaned forward, his broad shoulder inadvertently grazing hers, and studied the black muscled beast that was printed on the minuscule shirt. "Are you serious?"

"Of course I'm serious. That's the same thing I saw before," she said as she inched away from him, since there was something disturbing about him when he got too close to her.

"What did you just say, stupid girl?" Gilbert, who had been scooping up Skittles into his pocket, stopped and narrowed its eyes.

"You heard her," Curtis growled as he glared at the fairy on the ground. "So why don't you start to tell us what's going on?"

"Rupert, don't tell them anything," the fairy commanded to his fallen comrade, all sense of humor gone.

"Please, Trevor, as if I'm going to spill my guts to a couple of pathetic kids." The injured fairy looked slightly outraged. "Besides, it's quite obvious that they don't have a clue what's happening."

"Aha, so there *is* something going on." Emma widened her eyes. "Curtis, go to my slaying kit and get the hairspray."

"I don't think now is really the time to worry about your hair, Jones. Besides, your hair always looks nice."

"It's not for me," Emma said between gritted teeth. "It's for Rupert here. He obviously knows something, and I need to find out what it is." *And did he just say her hair looked nice?* For a moment she was completely thrown as she stared at him, but Curtis didn't seem to notice her confusion.

"With hairspray?" he asked in a perplexed voice. "What did they put in your manual?"

Emma took a patient breath. "There is no manual for slaying fairies. Sir Francis's book only gave about three sentences, one of which basically said, 'Approach with caution.' Which is one of the many, many reasons why I want to become a dragon slayer. All of this stuff is what I've picked up as I've gone along. Hairspray totally screws up the oil in their wings and means they can't fly for at least a week. Oh, and apparently it makes them look ugly to the opposite sex as well."

Curtis handed her the can.

"It doesn't matter what you do to me." Rupert folded his tiny arms in a stubborn gesture. "I'm not going to tell you anything about the darkhel. Not a single—"

"Rupert. Zip it." Gilbert lifted his hand and made a slashing action across his throat, and the injured fairy let out an annoyed groan.

"What's a darkhel?" Curtis demanded.

"Darkhel?" Rupert fluttered his little fairy eyes in a blank expression. "I didn't say 'darkhel.' What I said was 'dark hell.' Dark. Dark. Dark hell. Which is exactly where you'll both be heading very soon. *You know, you should really get your ears checked out.*"

"You said 'darkhel,'" Emma corrected him.

"No, I didn't." Rupert shook his head.

"Yes, you did."

"No, no, no. I most definitely did not."

Emma, who found it hard enough to put up with Loni and Tyler's constant bickering, certainly wasn't going to bother with this for too long, and she finally arched an eyebrow and pointed to the tiny creature's shirt. "So the fact your T-shirt says 'Darkhels Rule the World' is a complete coincidence?"

"Man, Rupert, you had to wear that shirt?" Gilbert growled.

"Darkhel?" Curtis frowned as he turned to Emma. "I've never heard of it. I wonder if it's a new breed of dragon? Or maybe European?"

"Dragons?" Gilbert spat a crushed Skittle out of his mouth in disgust. "You insult us. The darkhels aren't dragons, they're fairies."

"That thing was a fairy?" Emma dropped the hairspray in shock. "But that's impossible. I mean, it was so big. And evil-

looking. And the size of its talons was like nothing I've ever seen before. There's no way it was a fairy."

The fairies all puckered in annoyance. "Size isn't everything, you know," Trevor growled. "And you should see Gilbert when he's in the middle of a job. You don't get more evil than that."

"Thanks, brother." Gilbert puffed his chest in pride. "I do like to bring a certain level of dastardliness to my work."

"I still don't understand." Emma scratched her head. "I mean, it looked just like a dragon."

Rupert growled in disgust, which was somewhat ruined by the fact that he was still squirming on the floor with a nail file poked through his wing and his T-shirt covered in Skittle stains. "Darkhels have more grace and evil in their little talon than a dragon has in its entire body. In fact, how dare you even mention them in the same sentence? It's sacrilege. Still, I guess it doesn't matter that you know, since there is nothing you can do to stop our glorious dark brother from regaining the Pure One. It has been foreseen."

"The Pure One?" Emma rolled her eyes. "Oh please, you've got to be—"

"Can I help you folks at all?" Someone coughed and Emma and Curtis both swung around to where a salesclerk was now standing with a helpful smile on her face.

"Er, no thanks, we're good." Emma jumped to her feet and tried to hide as many of the crushed Skittles as possible. Next to her, Curtis manfully scooped up the hairspray and thrust it behind his back.

"Are you sure?" The woman beamed at them. "We've got some great celebrity biographies here, and there's a special on right now that gives you twenty percent off your second purchase. I know. I know. It's a steal."

"Seriously, we're fine," Curtis said in a low voice as he did that thing with his eyes.

"It's just it seems such a shame to miss out on this wonderful offer. You could stock up for the holidays," the woman persisted, obviously indifferent to Curtis's low voice and his dark, velvety eyes. Which was a pity because, while Emma didn't approve of his using his charm when it came to stealing dragon-slayer designations, there was no denying it would've come in handy right about now.

"We're really just browsing," Emma repeated in a firm voice, and the woman started to deflate a bit.

"Well, if you're sure," she said, looking away, "then I guess I'll just let you get back to your . . . hey, did one of you drop a nail file?"

"Oh." Emma tried to stand in front of it, while wishing that the captured fairy wasn't quite so invisible. "That's mine. I'm just letting it . . . er, dry out. It fell in my coffee before and it got all wet, which of course meant that I couldn't use it and . . . well, I've got a nail emergency, and—"

The woman bent down and pulled it out of Rupert's wing, much to the delight of the fairy, who paused only long enough to poke his tongue out and straighten his T-shirt before immediately flying up to the ceiling to join his friends. "You can't just go around leaving nail files in the carpet like that. Someone could get hurt. And what are all these Skittles doing here? Do I need to ask you to leave?"

But before Emma could even open her mouth, she looked up to the ceiling and let out a long groan as she realized the fairies were gone.

CHAPTER EIGHT

I don't believe it," Emma said a few minutes later as they leaned over the railing of the top level of the mall and looked down. "We had them right there. All we needed was two more minutes and we could've found out exactly what this darkhel thing is."

"I'm sorry, Jones. Are you okay?" Curtis asked in a surprisingly soft voice, and Emma found the tension that had been building up between her shoulder blades start to ease.

"Yeah." She let out a sigh and turned to him. "Except for the fact that I can apparently see invisible fairies that are the size of dragons and that no one has ever heard of before. And here I was thinking my life couldn't get any weirder."

"Maybe you just haven't heard of this one before?" Curtis said in a hopeful voice, but Emma shook her head.

"When Kessler stuck me with the fairies, I made sure I read every single book I could find on them—not that there were many—and trust me, there was nothing remotely like a darkhel. Or even a fairy that stands over a foot high, for that matter." She rubbed her sore eye as her frustration started to mount again. "It doesn't make sense."

"I know," Curtis agreed, before pushing his ugly glasses up onto his wild curls and frowning. "First they talked about darkhels, and then they said all that mumbo jumbo about the Pure One. I mean, what was that about?"

Emma was immediately diverted as she studied his face in surprise. "You're kidding, right? You haven't heard of the Pure One?"

"Um, no." Curtis looked at her blankly. "What is it?"

"According to the legend, Sir Francis was so upset that a demon had killed his only brother that he decided to shut the Gate of Linaria once and for all to stop any more elementals from getting out. Because the gate disappears and reappears all the time, it took him ages to track it down, and then when he did he used some hocus-pocus spell to seal it. Apparently, part of the spell included five drops of blood from a nameless male child. The blood was meant to represent purity and innocence. Personally, I think it's a little gross. But the point is that ever since he sealed the gate, the elementals have been looking for the descendant of the nameless child so they can use its blood to reverse the spell, reopen the Gate of Linaria, and let all of their buddies who got trapped on the other side come through."

Curtis widened his eyes. "Okay, so I knew that the Gate

of Linaria disappeared and reappeared all the time, but I had no idea the spell could be reversed by using someone's blood. I thought it was sealed forever."

"It is," Emma assured him. "The Pure One is just a kid's story. And I can't believe you've never heard it before."

Curtis put his glasses back on, and for a moment his jaw tightened again. Emma looked at him in surprise. Up until today she hadn't taken him for being moody. Finally, he gave a nonchalant shrug as he studied his fingers. "My folks weren't big storytellers. So let's get back to the facts. How do you think the Pure One stuff ties in with this darkhel creature?"

"It doesn't." Emma shook her head. "The fairies were just trying to mess with us because they didn't want us to ask them any more questions about the darkhel. I guess they succeeded."

"I wouldn't say that. Look. Over there." As he spoke, he gave her a soft nudge and directed her gaze to the level below, where, sure enough, one of the fairies was hovering around a woman holding a Starbucks cup. Typical: fairies loved frappuccinos almost as much as they loved Skittles. The rest of them were just off to the side, and Emma felt a sense of relief go racing through her as she hurried toward the escalators, never taking her eyes off the tiny creatures. Despite his crutches, Curtis was right behind her as they made their way to the next level and discreetly squeezed through the crowd to where the fairy was still hovering.

"By the way, thanks for helping me find them again," she grudgingly said in a low voice as they carefully drew closer. "I really appreciate it."

"It's no biggie." Curtis gave a casual shrug before shooting her a lopsided smile that suddenly made Emma understand why so many of the sophomore girls talked about him. She shook her head as if to dislodge the thought from her mind as the fairies came to a halt and started to throw Skittles at them. However, Emma, who had been caught by this trick one too many times, let the raining candy fall harmlessly to the ground and watched as the fairies darted this way and that before they doubled back and made a beeline for the entrance of a Gap store.

"Gotcha." She grinned as she reached for Curtis's arm and nudged him to follow her toward the store. But just before they got there, Emma caught sight of a familiar-looking blonde-haired woman over by a perfume cart just outside the entrance.

What? No. Emma momentarily forgot about the fairies as her spine stiffened, and she only just resisted the urge to groan. Seriously, of all the perfume carts in the world, why did Olivia have to be at this one?

"Quick, turn around and run," she said in a low voice as she tugged at Curtis's sleeve and shot the entrance of the store one last look. Catching up to the fairies was her chance to prove to Principal Kessler that she hadn't made the darkhel up, but she couldn't let Olivia see them either. Talk about being stuck between a rock and a fairy bad place.

"Run?" He frowned as he glanced at his crutches.

"Okay, I'll run and you hobble," she suggested, but before she could go anywhere, Curtis caught her by the arm and narrowed his eyes as he pushed his glasses back into his mop of curls.

"Why are we running away from them? We've got them cornered. They're in the store. Besides, you just told me that we couldn't take our eyes off them or—"

"Emma?" Olivia's voice rang out from across the marble-floored court, and Emma reluctantly looked over to where the blonde woman was now waving at her.

Great.

Emma groaned as she watched Olivia make her way toward them. At the same time the fairy they had just seen flew over to the elevator and shot her a smug wink before melting away into the crowd.

"Do you know her?" Curtis sounded surprised.

"She's married to my dad, and I don't want to talk about it." Emma folded her arms and once again edged away from him. Why was it that everywhere she turned, she seemed to be touching his arm?

"She's your stepmom?" Curtis sounded like he was about to choke. "It's just, she looks so—"

If he said "young," Emma was going to kill him. She might have only a nail file and hairspray in her immediate possession, but she was sure she could figure out a way to make it slow and painful. She hadn't topped her class in Inventive Death for nothing.

"So pregnant," he said instead, which didn't remotely improve her mood. "I didn't know you were going to be a big sister."

"Still not wanting to talk about it," Emma muttered as Olivia made her way toward them, her blonde hair bouncing in a shampoo-commercial sort of way. Emma wasn't fond of having conversations with her stepmom at the best of times, but during the potentially worst week of her life, the possibility was even less welcome than normal. Especially since, despite Olivia's bulging stomach, her dad had only told Emma about the pregnancy when he'd come to Burtonwood and given her her mother's crystal necklace.

Now that Emma looked back on it, she shouldn't really have been surprised to receive fairies as her designation the following day. It had obviously been a sign of the impending apocalypse, and she just hadn't realized it at the time. Especially since her dad hardly ever visited Burtonwood anymore. Emma secretly wondered if it was because he was sight-blind and didn't like to be reminded of his old life with his slayer wife, which was the exact same reason why Emma didn't like going home much. And she doubted that would be changing anytime soon, especially if there was going to be a gross baby boy crawling all over the place.

"Emma, I thought that was you." Olivia beamed as she got closer to them, her giant belly poking out underneath a pale pink linen shirt. "What a lovely surprise."

"Hey, Olivia, nice to see you."

"You too. How are you feeling? I know your dad's been

worried about you. He'll be happy to hear you've got your eye patch off now." Olivia continued to smile in an overly sunny way.

"Oh, yeah. I haven't had a chance to call him back yet. School's been pretty busy." *What with being humiliated and left behind for the most exciting mission of the year, not to mention being forced to spend time with a guy she hated more than life itself.*

"Of course, I totally understand," Olivia quickly agreed as she unconsciously rubbed her stomach before she turned to Curtis and gave him an open smile. "So do you go to Burtonwood as well?"

"Yes, I'm Curtis."

"Nice to meet you, Curtis. I'm Olivia. So what do you specialize in?"

"What?" Curtis coughed.

"Oh, did I say the wrong word?" Olivia blushed as she shot Emma an embarrassed look. "I've always been hopeless with lingo. I just wondered if you're a fairy slayer like Emma."

"Oh, right. Sorry. I just didn't realize you knew what we did." Curtis pushed a blond curl out of his eyes and looked apologetic. Not that Emma could really blame him, since it wasn't often that a slayer came across a sight-blind civilian who not only knew what an elemental was, but talked about them (especially in the middle of the mall while holding her pregnant stomach). "Anyway, I'm with dragons," he said as he rubbed his hand.

"Oh, just like Emma's mom was; that's so nice. No wonder

you two are friends. By the way, is your hand okay?" Olivia's perpetual smile disappeared for a moment as she glanced at Curtis's hand, which was looking red and swollen from where his laser had backfired on him.

"Oh, this?" Curtis gave it a dismissive wave. "It's fine."

"Well, you should really get it checked out. You don't want it to get infected," Olivia persisted, and Emma looked at Curtis in annoyance. Why hadn't he said that his hand was injured? It wasn't like she wouldn't have bandaged it for him. She wasn't a monster. "In fact, I used to be a nurse. If you like, I could look at it now—"

"Actually, Olivia, we'd better get going. I'll make sure Curtis gets his hand checked," Emma interrupted as she tried to keep the impatience out of her voice.

"Oh, right." Olivia flushed as she glanced around. "Of course. I hope I didn't blow your cover. Anyway, I'd better go pick up the dry cleaning. I need it for Serena's wedding, and I meant to do it yesterday but forgot. I swear these baby hormones are turning me into a crazy person. Oh, but Emma, speaking of the wedding, I know Serena would love to have you there if you wanted to change your mind. I asked your dad to book you a ticket on our flight. Just in case."

"Well, I sort of have a lot of stuff going on. But I'll think about it." Emma plastered a smile onto her face.

"Please do, because my whole family is dying to see you again." Olivia held up both hands to show her fingers were crossed before giving Emma and Curtis one final sunny smile and heading off. "And happy slaying."

Emma rolled her eyes as Curtis turned and said, "Your stepmom seems pretty cool. It's nice that she wants you to feel like you're part of her family."

"Yeah. It's just great," Emma mumbled as she dropped her kit onto the nearby bench and pulled out some cream. Then she nodded for Curtis to sit down.

"You don't like her?" Curtis lifted an eyebrow in surprise as she reached out for his hand and inspected the wound while she tried to ignore how smooth the unburned part of his skin was. Did he moisturize?

"She's okay, I guess," Emma relented as she started to treat the burn just like she'd learned in all the first-aid courses she'd taken at Burtonwood. "Though she smiles way too much, and every time I go home for the weekend, she's always trying to help me polish my sword or patch up my clothes."

"I had no idea things were so tough for you," Curtis said, with a hint of sarcasm. He winced as Emma put some cream on his hand and it sank into the wound.

"Look, it's complicated," Emma was stung into replying as she carefully put some light gauze around the burn and avoided looking at him, since there was something about his deep brown eyes that she found unnerving.

"Why, because she and your dad are having a baby together and you think he's forgotten about your mom?" he said with more sarcasm.

"So what, now you're a dragon slayer *and* Dr. Phil?" Emma growled, finally looking up at him. However, instead of seeing an arrogant expression on his tanned, perfect face, her words seemed to sting him more than the cream, and she watched in surprise as two bright red spots of color blazed on his cheeks.

Okay, so she hadn't expected that.

"Hey, Jones. I'm sorry. I shouldn't have said that. She just seemed nice, that's all. But you're right. It's none of my business," he said in an apologetic voice. "It's easy to judge when you're standing on the outside and can't see what's really going on. But the truth is that even the most regular-looking families can be screwed up."

For a moment Emma blinked at him in surprise. She really hadn't taken Curtis for the sensitive, considerate type. And since when did he know about complicated families? "Yeah, something like that," she mumbled as she found herself returning his gaze, focusing on the smooth curve of his mouth as it swung up at the corners. It was a nice mouth. Why had she never noticed before? And suddenly Loni's words came back to haunt her. Perhaps she had been too hard on Curtis? After all, she didn't even know him, yet she had decided he was horrible, when really he was just as much a victim of this crappy situation as she was.

"Jones, are you okay?" Curtis suddenly asked as he studied her face, a bemused smile tugging at his mouth. "You're pretty quiet. And you're still holding my hand."

"What?" Emma could feel the heat rise up in her cheeks as she looked down and realized that she still had his hand in hers. She immediately let it go and busied herself putting everything away while making a mental note to avoid touching Curtis—it seemed to do strange things to her. "Yes, I'm fine. Anyway, your hand should be okay."

"Thanks." He gave it a wave in the air as if to check that the gauze would hold before he awkwardly got to his feet while Emma once again tried to ignore the way his blond curls hung over his eyes.

"Don't mention it." She shrugged, then took a deep breath. "And look, sorry I was a little rude. I don't really like talking about family stuff."

"I understand." For a moment the smile left his face and he gave a solemn nod, which caused his blond curls to scatter across his forehead in all directions. "So, do you want to look for the fairies one more time? We still have half an hour before we need to leave, and it might help us learn more about this darkhel of yours."

For the second time in as many minutes, Emma looked at him in surprise. First he seemed to understand her, and now he seemed eager to help her. Unfortunately, it was too late and she reluctantly shook her head.

"They'll be long gone, not to mention putting the call out to tell all the other fairies in the area to lie low. They make instant messaging look like ancient history."

"Oh." Curtis actually looked disappointed. "So we head back to Burtonwood, then?"

"I guess." Emma nodded. "I'll just give Kessler a call and let him know what's happened."

"You want to call Kessler?" Curtis's mood instantly

changed as a look of concern appeared on his brow. "Are you really sure you want to tell him about this? I mean, he seemed pretty pissed off when you called him last time."

"That was before I knew what it was. Now I have proof it's a fairy called a darkhel—"

"An invisible fairy that no one's ever seen or heard of before," Curtis reminded her in an enthusiasm-killing voice.

"That's not the point." Emma shook her head in frustration. And to think that a couple of minutes ago she thought they had reached some sort of understanding. Yet now he was acting like the arrogant dragon slayer that she had first thought he was. "You were there. You heard the fairies talk about it, and we already know it was hunting on campus. You do the math."

"I'm just saying it might be better to wait. Especially since Kessler's out on a code blue."

Emma folded her arms and glared at him. Why was he doing this? It was almost like he...oh! She widened her eyes. *It was almost like he didn't want her to let Kessler know that she hadn't been making it all up, in case it meant Kessler changed his mind about the dragon designation.* And to think that for one second she had thought Curtis was a nice guy. She narrowed her eyes.

"Really? Because it seems to me you're worried that he might be impressed with what I've found out."

"Jones, that's not what I meant," he said as a flash of annoyance went racing across his face. "Look, if there had been another way, don't you think I—" He suddenly bit down on his lip.

"Another way?" Emma narrowed her eyes. "Another way for what? What are you talking about?"

"Nothing," he quickly backtracked as he studied his freshly bandaged hand. "And look, if you want to call Kessler, it's your decision."

"Thank you," Emma said as she moved a few paces away and made the call. She didn't care what Curtis said, she was doing the right thing. Her mom would've done exactly the same. However, after several rings, the call went to voice mail. She hit redial but again there was no answer, so she left a detailed message explaining exactly what the fairies had told her, even going as far as to spell out the word "darkhel" in case the principal misheard. Then she slipped her cell phone back into her pocket.

She turned around to where Curtis was leaning forward on his crutches, his T-shirt and blue hoodie straining across his broad shoulders. Not that his obvious strength really gave him an edge over her as far as dragon slaying went, since that was as much about speed and stealth as anything else, but still—

Suddenly, he turned to her and she flushed.

She hoped he hadn't caught her looking at him. Not that she was really looking, she was just observing, and there was a difference. *A big, big, big difference.*

"He's not answering," she said in a matter-of-fact voice as

she headed for the taxi line and they made the trip back to Burtonwood the same way they had come. In silence.

"So did you have any luck with the fairies?" Mrs. Barnes asked half an hour later as they both handed back their passes and gave her the receipt for the taxi fare since the normal minibus hadn't been able to drop them off. Emma went to open her mouth when Curtis suddenly lifted his bandaged hand up and cut her off.

"Not so much. I learned the hard way not to use lasers around them. Slaying fairies is harder than I thought," he confessed.

"Yes, well, I did warn you, but would you listen?" Emma retorted, still annoyed that she had allowed herself to soften toward him, even for a moment.

"Trust me, I won't make that mistake again," Curtis assured her.

Emma turned back to Mrs. Barnes. "So what are we supposed to do now if everyone else is out on the code blue?"

"Professor Vanderbilt will supervise you both while you study. He's in the library. *And, Emma, Principal Kessler wants you to come and see him before class tomorrow. Apparently, there are some things he wants to discuss with you.*"

"Oh." Emma gulped as she took in the serious expression on Mrs. Barnes's face. "W-what about Curtis? Does he need to see him too?" But Mrs. Barnes just shook her head and shot her an apologetic look that told Emma all she needed to know.

Too late she realized Curtis had been right.

She should never have left the message for Kessler.

Emma only just managed to stifle a groan as it sunk in how stupid she had been. And the worst thing was, she had no one to blame but herself.

CHAPTER NINE

"...And then Loni jumped out on this huge demon and the minute she pressed her stunner into its spiky back, the thing crumpled like a pack of cards. Unbelievable." Tyler shook his head in wide-eyed excitement as they sat in the crowded, noisy cafeteria the following morning.

Those who had gone on the mission had returned too late for Emma to catch up with what had happened, which was why she had been drilling them for details ever since they'd all met up half an hour earlier. Plus, it was definitely helping to take her mind off her upcoming meeting with Kessler. Even the thought of it made her stomach knot with worry.

"Seriously, Em, Loni was incredible," Tyler continued before winking. "Our little girl is growing up."

"Shut up, Tyler. Stop being such an idiot." Loni blushed before relenting. "But it was totally insane. There must've been at least a hundred demons there and we took them all out. Oh, and you should've seen the Department guys. They were totally freaked because they couldn't see the demons that we were fighting. Actually, they looked just like the civilians in that training DVD we had to watch last year. You know the one that was supposed to make us realize why it's a bad idea to fight elementals in front of sight-blind people."

For a moment they all grinned, since the DVD in question was a bit of a joke. After all, the main reason slayers didn't fight elementals in public places wasn't that they wanted to avoid freaking out civilians (though that was true as well) but that thanks to the many wards that were in place, most fighting tended to occur in unpopulated (and more importantly, unwarded) areas.

"And then when it was over," Tyler interjected, "the Department guys were all like, *'Whoa, dudes, you were awesome. That was the best.'*"

"Okay, so now he's exaggerating." Loni laughed as she gave Tyler a gentle punch in the arm. "Absolutely none of them said the words 'whoa, dudes.'"

"Fine," Tyler conceded. "But all the same, not only did we save the Department guys from getting shredded, but the zombie virus got reversed, which meant no one got turned into bone-munching living dead. All with no injuries. Definitely a good day's work."

"Wow." Emma shook her long dark hair in awe as she soaked in every detail. Then she felt her mood start to plummet as she realized it might be the closest she ever got to some code-blue action. "You guys are so lucky."

"I know, right." Tyler reached over and grabbed a piece of Emma's uneaten bacon. "And did I tell you, three of the hot juniors were all over me in the bus on the way home?

Apparently they liked the way I handled myself."

"You might've mentioned it once or twice," Emma said diplomatically, since not only had he texted her about it, but on his way home in the bus last night, he had proceeded to draw diagrams and repeat the story every five minutes during breakfast.

"Or a hundred million times," Loni corrected, a lot less diplomatically.

"Sorry." Tyler shot them an unrepentant grin as he bit into the bacon. "But it was pretty cool. Anyway, now that we've told Emma all about the battle, I want to know what happened with this dragon yesterday? Did you seriously see one flying over—"

"Hey." Loni suddenly pointed over into the crowd. "Tyler, isn't that one of the girls from the bus? I think she's waving at you."

"Really?" Tyler was instantly distracted as he jumped to his feet and started to scan the room.

"Really," Loni agreed. "You know I bet that if you went over and asked her out, she would probably say yes. Especially since, according to your horoscope, love is in the air for Leo. You should strike while the iron is hot."

"Well, I was pretty awesome," Tyler agreed as he smoothed down his blazer and tried to pat his unruly red hair into some sort of order. "Okay, I'm going to do it. Wish me luck."

"Luck," Loni and Emma both chorused, but it wasn't until he hurried away from them that Emma rubbed her sore eye and frowned.

"I didn't see anyone waving to him. Where is she?"

"Oh." Loni shrugged. "I sort of made it up. It's just Tyler's on such a high right now from yesterday that I was worried he might ask so many annoying questions and we'd be forced to cut him up into tiny pieces and bury the body parts."

Emma nodded. They both adored Tyler, but there was no doubt that sometimes his testosterone took over his brain.

"Thanks," she said as she proceeded to fill her friend in on everything that had happened yesterday, from discovering that the dragon was in fact a fairy right up to her upcoming visit to see Principal Kessler in—*oh, about ten minutes*.

Once she had finished, Loni was looking more exasperated than ever, and her rosebud lips were scrunched together in two thin lines.

"I can't believe that Curtis just stood there and let you call Kessler and leave that message. And here I was thinking he was a nice guy. He's a Sagittarius too. You know I did not see that one coming, but you were obviously right about him. He's evil. One hundred percent, unadulterated evil." Loni bristled, causing Emma to reluctantly shake her head.

"Actually, Lon, Curtis tried to talk me out of it. In fact, short of tackling me to the ground, he did everything he could to convince me it was a bad idea. I should've listened to him." She groaned before narrowing her eyes in confusion. *"What? Why are you looking at me like that?"*

"Because," Loni informed her in a stunned voice, "I'm trying to figure out if this is the first time you've talked about Curtis without scowling or making a face."

"Okay, fine. You're right. He's not that bad." Emma held up her hands in defeat as she thought of the conversation they'd had while she'd treated his hand. It had been... unexpected.

"Oh, really? Like how?" Loni demanded, raising her eyebrows.

"I don't know." Emma flushed, suddenly not quite sure if she should mention that Curtis had dark velvety eyes and seemed to understand her. Instead she shrugged. "He just seems nice, that's all."

"I knew it." Loni clapped her hands in sheer happiness. "You like him. This is so exciting. I always secretly thought he liked you, but now that you like him too, it's just so perfect. You're an Aries and he's a Sagittarius. And then there is the whole granola breakfast cereal thing."

"What?" Emma's sore eye started to twitch. "Loni, no. I don't like him. I mean I don't *hate* him anymore. But it's not like I've suddenly developed a crush on him. That's crazy. *And please stop clapping. Everyone's looking.*"

"Yes, but—" Loni began, but Emma gave a firm shake of her head.

"Seriously, there's no crush."

"Oh." Loni's face fell. "So you're not going to invite him down to the practice range? I heard there are some new demons there and I bet Kessler would let you count the practice on your Alternative Slaying assignment."

"What? No, of course I'm not." Emma rolled her eyes. The practice range was down behind the second oval, and it was where the school kept a few captive elementals for training purposes. It was heavily warded and guarded except for three back stalls where students often went to make out. Not that Emma had ever been in them, and more to the point, she didn't intend on going there anytime soon.

"It was just a suggestion," Loni protested, but Emma ignored her.

"Well, it's one I can do without. Besides, I have more to worry about right now than that. I still can't believe I told Kessler that my dragon was an invisible fairy called a darkhel. What was I thinking? Especially since when Curtis and I went to the library yesterday we couldn't find a single mention of it. It's like it doesn't even exist."

"So the fairies made it up." Loni shrugged. "I mean, it wouldn't be the first time they've tricked you. Remember on your first patrol what they did with the melted ice cream?"

"Thanks for reminding me." Emma shuddered as she recalled just how long it had taken to get the ice cream out of her hair. "But I don't think they were tricking me. They actually seemed pretty annoyed that we found out about it. Ask Curtis, he saw it all."

"What?" Loni wrinkled her nose in confusion. "Didn't you tell me that Curtis got hit with some glamour powder? Because I know that when they got me with that stuff, it was like being a sight-blind civilian."

"Oh, right. I guess I forgot to tell you that he has glasses to fight Unseen dragons. Can you believe it?" For a moment Emma dwelled on the injustice of it all before realizing that

Loni was still waiting for an answer. "Anyway, the glasses worked on the fairies as well."

"What did they look like?" Loni was instantly curious as her violet eyes widened in a geeky way that Emma would never understand.

"They looked like some very ugly, white sunglasses that should've been destroyed along with leg warmers and Wham T-shirts back in the eighties. Why? What does it matter what they looked like?"

"I guess it doesn't." Loni rubbed her chin. "It's just I would be curious to see them. I've heard of Unseen glasses before, but I didn't know that their refracting lenses would work on glamour powder as well. It's intriguing."

"If you say so." Emma shrugged as she looked at her watch and reluctantly got to her feet. "Anyway, I better go and face the music with Kessler. I'm already in enough trouble without being late too."

Loni's violet eyes filled with worry. "Okay, well, good luck, and remember not to say anything to piss him off. Promise?"

"Don't piss off the principal. That's definitely my new motto," Emma assured her as she hurried toward the door while at the same time trying to smooth down her uniform. She'd had another bad night's sleep and hadn't really drifted off until just after her alarm clock started to buzz, which meant she'd been forced to get ready in a hurry, and now her hair was pulled up into a practical ponytail and her tie was more haphazardly knotted than ever.

As she went, she caught sight of Curtis glancing up

at her from across the cafeteria. He raised his hand and beckoned for her to wait for him. For a moment she paused and considered it, but as she watched him get to his feet she realized that unlike her own bedraggled appearance, Curtis looked as if he'd slept like a king. His blond curls were gleaming as they lay in a scatter across his forehead, perfectly framing his vivid brown eyes, while his navy blazer fell across his shoulders like it had been fitted by one of the designers from Loni's fashion magazines.

Suddenly Emma felt self-conscious and scruffy in her own hastily thrown-on uniform, and while half of her knew it was completely ridiculous to even worry about what she looked like, she did. So instead of waiting, she held up her arm and tapped her watch to let him know that she didn't have time. Then she turned and hurried toward her fate.

✳✳✳

"Emma, I'm disappointed. For most of your time at Burtonwood, your behavior has been exemplary," Principal Kessler said fifteen minutes later as he held up a slim file. Then he picked up a second (not so slim) file and shook his head. "Until five weeks ago when you suddenly started rivaling the Lewis twins as the student most likely to give me a coronary. Disobedience. Detentions. Your mother and I go back a long way, but trust me when I tell you that she would be the first to condemn your behavior."

Emma wished that she hadn't been in such a hurry to get to the principal's office as she clenched her jaw and leaned forward so that her bangs fell into her eyes. She knew this meeting was going to be bad, but it was worse than she ever could've imagined. *She would not cry, she would not cry.* Instead she concentrated on the bit of worn carpet near the corner of the desk. Anywhere was better than looking up at the wall behind Principal Kessler's head, where her mom's beaming face was still sitting in its frame, just like it always was.

Would she still be smiling if she knew that instead of being a dragon slayer, Emma was a fairy slayer. *A disgraced fairy slayer.*

"We all know how unhappy you are about your upcoming Induction," the principal continued in a grim voice. "However, as a student of this Academy, I expect you to follow whatever orders you are given. Understood?"

"Yes, sir," she forced herself to answer.

"There is a reason that we follow rules and regulations, and believe it or not, it has nothing to do with trying to ruin your life," he continued, as if warming to his task. "For example, yesterday we had a code-blue situation—something that I expect all the Academy students to treat seriously. Instead, what do I get? Someone who first insists that she's seen a dragon flying over campus, which I am compelled to take seriously, only to waste valuable time doing an EMR scan and double-checking all the wards. And then, she calls me *again* to say that the dragon wasn't a dragon after all but an invisible fairy called a darkhel. *Can you see what I'm getting at here?*"

Emma nodded as she tightened her grip on the arms of her chair, still refusing to look up in case she accidentally caught sight of just how annoyed Kessler really was. Besides, when he said it like that, it really did sound crazy. Ridiculous. Especially since, judging by his tone, he'd been doing some fruitless research on darkhels as well.

"Even worse, then I get a visit from another one of my students to confirm that what you had told me was true."

What? Emma's eyes widened. "Curtis came to see you?"

Kessler gave a sharp nod to let her know he hadn't appreciated the visit, and suddenly Emma felt a stab of guilt that Curtis had put himself in the line of fire on her behalf. She really had misjudged him.

"So if you were me, what would you suggest I do with you?" Kessler finally spoke in a subarctic voice.

Realize that I wasn't meant to be a fairy slayer and give me dragons instead? Emma longed to say in a hopeful voice, though she wisely realized that it probably wouldn't go over that well right about now.

"Well?" he prompted, but before she was forced to answer (what was clearly the trick question to end all trick questions), Barney poked her head around the door and gave a polite cough and then pushed her bright green glasses up onto her head, in what was obviously some sort of code. Principal Kessler got to his feet and made his way over to her.

"Excuse me for a moment, Emma."

"Of course," she said as he and Barney had a fast and furious conversation. She leaned forward to try to listen, but unfortunately they excelled at talking at subhuman levels.

"Right," he said as Barney left, and he walked back to his desk and picked up his phone. "Something's come up, so we're going to have to cut this short. But Emma, you're on detention for the next two weeks, and the only time you will be permitted to leave the grounds is when you're doing your assignment. And if I'm not fully satisfied with your behavior, I will have no choice but to expel you from Burtonwood Academy. Are we clear?"

Emma felt her throat tighten and her mouth go dry as she realized that Kessler had threatened her with the one thing worse than being a fairy slayer. Being a civilian who had to go and live at home. Surrounded by people who seemed to have forgotten that her mom had ever existed. Suddenly she felt sick as it sank in that this invisible fairy could've cost her everything that she held dear. What had she done?

CHAPTER TEN

Twenty minutes later Emma finished changing into her navy sweats and paused outside the simulation labs to press a hand to her burning cheeks. She'd known Kessler would be mad, but she had no idea he would be *that* mad. She couldn't even think of anyone who had ever been expelled from Burtonwood. Sight-gifted people were too few and far between to be treated like that. And yet he had said it. If she didn't get her act together, he would expel her.

It was unthinkable.

Unbearable.

And so not going to happen.

From now on she was going to do everything by the book. Not that there was a book for being a fairy slayer, but that was beside the point. She wasn't going to be expelled. Then she took a deep breath and pushed open the lab door.

The room itself looked more like a large warehouse than a classroom, with a giant projection screen at one end and a bank of computers at the other so that the teachers could control the virtual fights that students were put through to help train their mental and physical reactions. There were also a variety of fake elemental carcasses, tree stumps, and a clutter of other props that were sometimes used to help create the different battle environments.

However, today the students weren't going into a fully simulated combat, just a simple, virtual hand-to-hand battle. They would see their virtual opponent through their goggles, and during the fight, their endurance, agility, and stamina could be monitored by the specially designed equipment that they would be wearing. Personally, Emma would rather be fighting real elementals in real conditions, but at least it was better than doing math.

She scanned the room until she finally caught sight of Loni and Tyler over on a low bench against the wall. They both already had their gear on and were gesturing for Emma to join them. She hurried over.

"So?" Loni instantly demanded as she tossed Emma a large equipment bag. "Tell me everything now because I can't stand the suspense. Especially since your star sign said that today wasn't a good day for conflict."

"Well, I guess it was lucky that I didn't talk back to Kessler when he gave me a two-week detention," Emma said as she quickly slipped a vest over her head. Loni immediately leaned over and made sure that the wireless connection was switched on so that everything from Emma's heartbeat to her cholesterol level would be relayed back to the central computer. Once she was satisfied it was working properly, she handed Emma her goggles.

"Two weeks? That means you'll miss the induction party on Sunday afternoon." Tyler pushed his own goggles high onto his wild red hair so that it poked out in all directions. The induction party wasn't part of the official Burtonwood annual schedule, but for most students it was considered one of the highlights. It was the last chance to really let their hair down before the next stage of their training began. *It was also the least of her worries right now.*

"He also said that unless he was happy with my progress he would expel me," Emma said in what she hoped was an even voice. "There probably would've been more, but Barney came in and they had some top-secret talk and the next thing I knew Kessler put the whole I'm-disappointed speech on hold and couldn't wait to get rid of me."

"What?" Loni yelped. "I can't believe he threatened to expel you."

"Only if he's not happy with my progress in the next two weeks. *Which he will be.*"

"What else did he say?" Tyler leaned forward. "With particular reference to this invisible fairy of yours."

Sorry, Loni mouthed to her, and Emma guessed that Tyler had used what Loni liked to call his Leo persistence (and what Tyler called his Leo charm) to find out what had happened yesterday. Emma sighed.

"He hadn't heard of it, which I'm pretty sure is what led him to decide to give me a detention in the first place."

"So we still don't know anything about this darkhel thing?" Tyler looked surprised, but Emma merely shook her head.

"Nope, and I don't care. From now on my mission is to prove to Kessler that I'm a normal, sane Burtonwood student and not some nutcase who manages to get caught in exploding food courts and sees invisible fairies. I doubt it will be enough to get him to change his mind about Induction, but maybe by the time I graduate he might start to trust me again."

"It won't take that long," Loni assured her. "And besides, as soon as someone accidentally stabs themselves with their sword, sets their tutor on fire, or worse, everyone will forget all about you. Especially now that you're not wearing your eye patch."

Before Emma could comment, Professor Meyers stood up from the computer monitors at the back and clapped her hands. "Okay, class, sorry about the delay, but everything's ready to go. Now remember, I'm going to be focusing on your endurance, agility, and stamina."

Everyone spread out across the floor so that they were each standing in one of the specially marked circles that would help record all their vital statistics as the simulation fight took place. Emma pushed her goggles back over her nose and checked that her gloves were properly strapped just as a red light flashed in front of her eyes to let her know her test was about to start. Then she lifted her hands in a defense stance as a virtual cassock dragon made the first move. It was a predictable one, and Emma nimbly danced out of its way before sending in an uppercut. The fight was under way.

Twenty minutes later the red light blinked in her goggles to let her know it was over. She pushed them back on top of her head just as the bell rang.

"Okay, no class tomorrow," Professor Meyers announced, "but on Friday, as part of the Alternative Slaying Practices assignment Principal Kessler has given you, you're going to have a simulation battle with your assignment partners, and we're going to concentrate on strength and speed." Most of the class made a groaning noise as they put away their equipment and headed for the change rooms, where they had a quick shower.

"So you and Curtis will have to do a simulation battle on Friday." Loni raised an eyebrow as she rubbed her short spiked hair dry with a towel. "Interesting."

"Not as interesting as the fact that you'll have to fight Brenda." Emma grinned back at her friend as she stepped into her slightly crumpled skirt and pulled on her white shirt.

"Don't remind me." Loni made a groaning noise as they finished getting changed. Emma was just attempting to do something constructive with her hair when Loni asked, "Since we've got a free period, do you want to go to the library or study hall?"

"Library," Emma immediately said as she thought of all the course work she had been ignoring lately. If she wanted to show Kessler a new and improved her, she would really need to get it all done.

As they continued down the hall, she caught sight of

Curtis leaning against a wall, his crutches propped up next to him, his dark eyes serious and brooding. The instant he saw her, he straightened his spine in a way that let her know he had been waiting for her. Suddenly Emma felt guilty for snubbing him in the cafeteria earlier. She probably owed him an apology.

"Actually, Lon, do you mind if I talk to Curtis first?"

"Oh, interesting." Loni widened her eyes. "Is this part of the whole I-don't-have-a-crush-on-him thing?" she wanted to know.

"Actually, it's part of the whole he-went-to-see-Kessler-to-try-and-convince-him-that-I-was-telling-the-truth thing," Emma confessed.

"He tried to save your butt? I think I might love him myself." Loni let out a dreamy sigh before she caught sight of Brenda emerging from the locker room. "So, er, while you go and talk to him, I'll just wait for you around the corner. Possibly behind a very large book so Brenda doesn't corner me and make me do extra work."

"Nice disguise," Emma retorted as Loni scuttled away. She ran a hand through her long smooth hair, which was pulled back into a plain ponytail. Then she walked over to where Curtis was waiting for her.

"Hey, Jones. Hope you don't think I'm stalking you or anything. I was just worried about your meeting with Kessler." Curtis blew a stray curl off his brow, his face full of concern. "So how did it go?"

"Don't worry, I'm still here, so if you were hoping to get

a new assignment partner, I'm sorry to disappoint," she said as she caught sight of the hand he had burned yesterday when he'd tried to zap the fairies with his laser. It had a fresh dressing on it, and for an idle moment she wondered who had changed it for him.

"It's okay." Curtis gave a mild shrug of his shoulders as he started to fiddle with the handle of his crutches before he finally looked up. "I'm sort of getting used to my current one. Even if she is a little prickly."

"Only a little prickly?" Emma double-checked and noticed a surprised smile hovering around Curtis's mouth as he lifted an eyebrow.

"Did you just make a joke?"

"Definitely not," she assured him. "And sorry I couldn't wait for you at the cafeteria. I, er, didn't want to be late for Kessler."

"Wise move," he agreed, dropping his head slightly. "So what happened? What did he say?"

"You know, just the usual." She gave a cavalier shrug, but as Curtis's dark eyes drilled into hers, she somehow found herself telling him the truth. "Okay, so it wasn't quite the usual. He hit me with a two-week detention and the promise of expulsion if I didn't get my act together. So, I can safely say that I won't be trying to get him to change his mind about your designation."

"That's harsh." Curtis let out a long whistle and then reached out and gently touched her hand. "I'm sorry."

"You and me both," Emma replied in a faltering voice,

again thrown by his unexpected response, not to mention the unexpected sensation the brief touch of his fingers on her skin was causing her. She pulled her hand away and awkwardly coughed. "And by the way, Kessler told me that you went to see him."

"Yeah, about that." Curtis let out a frustrated sigh. "I hope I didn't make things worse."

"I think I managed that all on my own," she confessed as she tentatively peered up at him. "So why did you do it? I mean, I've been awful to you for the last six weeks. Why would you put yourself on the line like that?"

"Remember yesterday when you saw the darkhel and you wanted to go and look for it?" Curtis explained in an earnest voice. "Well, you asked me what kind of slayer I was. I guess I'd like to think I'm the kind who is there for his friends."

"We're friends?" The words were out of her mouth before she knew it, and Emma groaned at herself in annoyance. She had so not intended to say that.

"I, well... I'd like us to be." Curtis looked at her, his dark eyes piercing into hers in a way that caused an unfamiliar sensation to go racing through her body. She felt her pulse quicken and suddenly realized that she wasn't remotely in control of this situation. She coughed to cover her confusion and decided that a change of subject was required. Immediately.

"S-so, anyway, was there something you wanted to talk to me about before?" she stammered.

"Huh?" He blinked as if he were suffering from short-term memory loss.

"Before. At the cafeteria," she prompted him. "You were waving at me like you wanted to say something."

"Oh, right." He paused for a moment as if trying to understand what she was saying and then he suddenly shifted awkwardly on his broken leg, a guilty expression hovering around his mouth. "Well, this probably isn't the best timing, but after I went to see Kessler about you, Barney gave me our pass-outs for the next part of our assignment. Since we did fairies yesterday, tomorrow we're getting to look at some troubadour dragons. Two of them, to be exact. There's been a pair down by the lake for the last two weeks. But you know, I can just tell Barney that tomorrow isn't good."

She cut him off. "It's fine, Curtis. I'm up for it. Tomorrow night. Troubadour dragons. Should be fun," she added in what she hoped was a bright voice to match her new and improved attitude.

He looked more than a little confused. "Are you sure you're feeling okay? I mean, I just told you that I was going to show you how to slay a dragon and you didn't—"

"Bite your head off and read you the riot act?" Emma let out a rueful sigh. "Trust me, I'm riot-acting you on the inside. But the thing is that from now I have to do everything by the book, which means fully cooperating with you on this assignment. In fact, I'm going to put it into my cell phone right now so that I don't forget," she said as she made an exaggerated effort to punch the details into the calendar on her cell phone. "There, it's all done."

"Yup, there's definitely something wrong with you," Curtis said in a serious voice as he leaned forward, his face taking on the exact same expression that Nurse Reynes used when she did an examination. "I mean, I can see your lips moving but the words aren't making any sense. *Do everything by the book? Full cooperation?* Are you sure you haven't been body-snatched?"

Emma rolled her eyes while trying not to notice how long his sooty lashes were or how they framed his chocolate eyes so perfectly. *Or that he had been concerned enough about her to feel bad about the assignment.* "I'm serious. My future's on the line here. I'm trying to do the right thing."

"I see, so you're telling me that if I asked you to do anything, you would say yes?" he asked with interest, and Emma felt a reluctant smile sneak up to her mouth.

"Don't push your luck," she retorted as she gave him a light punch in the arm. Something she immediately regretted as it suddenly made her realize how close she was to him. And how hard his arm muscles were.

"Why not?" His voice was low and raspy and sent a delicious shudder racing through her. Emma bit the bottom of her lip as she studied the perfect sweep of his jaw, the way his eyelids were hanging heavy over his eyes. Then he tilted his head slightly and moved even closer to her, and it took all of Emma's self-control not to gasp.

Was Curtis Green going to kiss her?

The blood started to pound at her temples and her hands felt clammy. He was going to kiss her. And more important, she was going to let him. His face drew closer to hers. They were going to cross the invisible boundary that had been lying between them and—

However, before she knew what was happening, a group of juniors came clamoring down the hallway, and the moment they saw her, they made a banging noise to let her know that her food court explosion hadn't been forgotten yet. The minute they did so Curtis flinched, and instead of feeling his mouth on hers, she felt him gently lift his hands up to her neck and start to tug at her haphazardly knotted tie. She barely dared to breathe as his deft fingers tweaked it into submission.

"Sorry," he said in an unsteady voice. "But your tie's been driving me crazy. I hope you don't mind?"

"Oh, right. My tie, th-thanks," she croaked as she bit back her disappointment. How dare those juniors come along and ruin everything. Especially when she had wanted him to kiss her. *She had wanted Curtis Green to kiss her.* There, she had thought it. She had wanted to kiss her archenemy. Emma blinked at the knowledge, and then, before she could change her mind (or blush), she peered up him. "Y-you know, if you're not doing anything after dinner, maybe we could go to the practice range. I heard they've got some new demons in. We could use the fight training as part of our assignment and then . . . " She let the rest of the words hang, but instead of agreeing, Curtis took a deep breath and his face suddenly turned into a still mask.

"Actually, you know what?" He gave an awkward cough and studiously peered down at his leg cast. "Tonight isn't so good for me. I have something going on. And speaking of which, I should probably go, but I will see you tomorrow night at the gate with our pass-outs."

Then, without another word, he hurried off as fast as his crutches would allow him, and Emma felt a flush of embarrassment wash over her while something deep inside her stomach went plummeting to the ground. He didn't want to kiss her at all. He really had just wanted to fix her tie. *Oh, earth, please swallow her now.*

"Oh my gosh." Loni raced over with an excited expression on her face. "I was peeking around the corner...did he really just go to kiss you? That's so romantic. If only those stupid juniors hadn't come along and ruined it. So what happened? What did he say?"

Emma felt her face heat up all over again. "Well, he said he tried to help me with Kessler because we were friends. And then he sort of touched my hand and gave me a few of those hot, steamy looks. And I think there was some flirting, so I took your advice and asked if he wanted to go down to the practice range after dinner."

"You did not," Loni squealed in excitement. "I can't believe you have a date. I mean, this is huge. Emma Jones is going on a date with Curtis Green! I wonder if Barney would give us a pass-out so we could take you shopping at the mall? Because nothing says 'first date' like a new outfit, and—"

"Um, Lon." Emma coughed. "Before you get too carried away and start picking out names for Curtis's and my children, I should probably tell you that he said no."

Loni paused for a moment and blinked. "What? What do you mean he said no? Anyone can see he's crazy about you. I bet you didn't ask him the right way."

"I asked him the right way," Emma assured her as she filled her friend in on exactly what had happened. Then she shrugged to hide her disappointment. "Which means when he said he wanted to be friends, he really meant that he wanted to be friends."

"Yes, but Sagittarius guys aren't normally about the friendship, if you know what I'm saying," Loni persisted in a stubborn voice that Emma was well acquainted with.

"Well, this is one," Emma said drily.

"I refuse to believe that." Loni shook her head. "The only reason he pretended to fix your tie—which, for the record, is a complete disgrace—is because those juniors came along. And as for not going to the practice range with you, did it ever occur to you that he was actually telling the truth? Maybe he really does have something else going on tonight."

"Maybe," Emma agreed in a diplomatic voice while trying not to think about the frozen expression that had crossed Curtis's face as he had spoken to her. It had been dark. Like a shadow had fallen over him. And she didn't care what Loni said, Emma knew that Curtis had ditched her for a reason. Unfortunately, she had the feeling that whatever it was, she wasn't going to like it when she found out. And with that thought, she and Loni hurried to the library in silence while Emma tried to ignore the fact that, thanks to being brushed off by her archenemy, her life had just hit a new, all-time low.

CHAPTER ELEVEN

By three o'clock Emma realized that the humiliating encounter with Curtis was actually the least of her problems as she discovered that turning over a new leaf was going to be tougher than she thought. She'd lost count of the number of people who asked about her invisible dragons and whether Kessler was going to make a new designation just for her. And considering that it wasn't funny the first time someone said it, by the time the final bell rang, it was more than a little annoying. In fact, Emma almost missed being teased about the explosion in the food court.

It was actually almost a relief when she finally headed off to the detention room. At least Professor Meyers was supervising today, and she normally just let everyone do their homework.

"Emma," Professor Meyers called her over to the front desk and held up a piece of paper. "Before you sit down, I just wanted to talk to you about the results of the simulation fight you did this morning."

Emma groaned since she had been more than a little

distracted during the whole test. "Is it bad? Because the thing is that I've—"

"No." Professor Meyers shook her head, and a stray dark curl flopped onto her cheek. "It's actually the opposite. These results are a marked improvement on the test we did last week."

"Oh," Emma said in surprise as she studied the piece of paper.

"Anyway, you'd better take a seat and start on your homework, but I just wanted to let you know that I'm pleased with your efforts."

"Thanks," Emma said as she stuffed the results into her pocket and made her way toward the back of the room. As she did so, she glanced around. There were a couple of seniors she vaguely knew, plus a bunch of freshman who had been caught last week sneaking off campus without a pass. A few of them shot her curious looks, but she ignored them as she sat down, opened her laptop, and halfheartedly started working on her assignment for Kessler.

She reluctantly flipped open the yellow folder and randomly read one of the questions on the worksheet. *List ten things about your designated elemental that your training partner might not know.* Well, for a start, fairies were dumb. Annoying. Sarcastic. Ate too many Skittles and most definitely had bad taste in clothing.

Then she stopped herself, since she had a feeling that this wasn't exactly the sort of information she was supposed to use, and opened up her slaying guide. It was actually a copy of the original one that Sir Francis had written more than four hundred years ago. *A Complete and Utter Reference to the Vile and Evil Creatures That Have Spewed Forth from the Gate of Linaria and How They Shall Be Slain—In Three Volumes.*

Unfortunately, when she'd told Curtis yesterday that there wasn't a big section on fairies, she hadn't been joking, and she once again looked at the short paragraph in annoyance.

> *Fairies are the smallest and least dangerous of the air elementals and unlike some of the other creatures that came out of the Gate of Linaria, these beasts show a remarkable aptitude to adjust. Not only do they speak languages but they also cover their person in clothing. It is truly most remarkable. I have yet to discover an effective ward that works on them or where their kill spot is, though due to their unaggressive and somewhat docile nature, I don't think this is of much importance....*

Emma shut the book and pushed it away from her. Sir Francis might be considered the greatest slayer who ever lived, but it was blindingly obvious that he didn't know jack about fairies. What was even worse was that if she wanted to have even a chance of staying at Burtonwood and then moving on to the Department of Paranormal Containment when she graduated, she was going to have to accept that from now on she was stuck with them.

There, she had admitted it. The thing she had been skirting around all day.

She was Louisa Jones's daughter and she was a fairy

slayer. Even in her head she could hear the sound of canned laughter. She was making a mockery of her mom's legacy. She moodily thought about the U-turn her life had made. Unfortunately, that led to her thinking about Curtis.

Despite what Loni said, Emma knew there was a reason for the way he had acted earlier that day. For a moment she wondered if it was because he was embarrassed to be seen with her. Or it could be that he was getting her back for how badly she had acted toward him when the designations had first been announced. Or... *or nothing.* She cut herself off as she realized how pointless the whole exercise was.

At the end of the day it didn't matter how nice Curtis was (or how cute it was when his blond curls splayed out across his tanned forehead in abandoned disarray), the simple fact was that he was still the guy who had taken the one thing she had wanted more than anything in the world. Which meant that once they had finished working on this assignment together, she would have to make sure she kept her distance from him. It would be the best thing for everyone (and by "everyone," she meant herself, since she wasn't sure she could handle any more humiliation).

Emma sighed and looked out the window. The November light was fading, and judging by the way the scattered students were hurrying across the quad toward the cafeteria for dinner, it was obviously getting colder as well as darker. Then she caught sight of Loni and Tyler standing over by the statue of Sir Francis, where they had agreed to meet her. It looked like they were bickering.

For a moment Emma smiled at the fact that while just about everything she had ever believed in was now dead in the water, at least some things never changed. A scraping of chairs brought her out of her thoughts as she realized that everyone around her in the detention room was leaving. She started to gather her books and her laptop when a screeching static sound suddenly blasted into her ears without warning.

Emma only just resisted the urge to scream out loud as she clasped her hands to her ears. It was several seconds before the pain subsided enough for her to glance around, and when she did, it was only to discover that everyone else was still casually slinging their bags over their shoulders and making their way out of the room as if nothing had happened.

Okay, so that was weird and—

But before she could even finish her thought, the static buzz increased and her sore eye started to tingle in agony. She bit back the pain and got to her feet. As she did so, she caught sight of a dark shadow up in the already gray sky outside. Emma gasped as she realized it was the same creature she'd seen from her window during the code blue. And the same creature that the fairy had been wearing on his T-shirt yesterday.

The darkhel.

Her first instinct was to yell out a horrified warning as she watched it swoop so low that it almost flattened Loni's spiked dark hair, but instead she quickly scooped up her stuff and grabbed her bag.

"Hey," someone protested as she elbowed her way past

him. "What's wrong, a fairy emergency?" But Emma ignored the sarcasm as she pounded down the hallway and went flying out into the quad while letting out a small prayer of thanks that she'd had an armament lesson that afternoon and therefore had her full slaying kit with her.

As she ran, she pulled out her sword and threw the rest of her kit to the ground. Thanks to the fact that most fairies were only ten inches long, it had been a while since she'd used it, but as soon as her fingers wrapped around the hilt, it once again felt like it was an extension of her arm.

"There you are," Tyler called out as he and Loni jogged over to where she was frantically searching for the darkhel. "You're never going to believe what... *er, why do you have your sword in your hand?*"

"And unsheathed," Loni added in concern. "I thought you were going for the sane and normal approach?"

"And, in case you didn't realize, walking around with an unsheathed weapon definitely isn't sane or normal," Tyler clarified before narrowing his eyes. "What's going on?"

"It's here," she hissed as she continued to crane her neck just as the screeching static sound rang out in her ears again. This time the pain was worse. "Can't you hear that?"

"Hear what?" Loni demanded as she leaned in to study Emma's face. "Em, what's going on? Did something happen?"

"The darkhel has—" But before she could even finish her sentence, the ringing in her ear subsided and she heard a flap of wings. She spun around just in time to see the dark shadow fly once around the quad before it moved into a vertical position and plummeted down like a fallen angel about thirty feet away from her, its enormous wings suddenly snapping back as it hit the ground.

As soon as it landed, she knew that the creature wasn't a dragon. Rather it was seven feet of pure venom poured into a manlike body and draped in black leather and studs like some sort of sadomasochist's armor. For a second it just stood motionless, like a decayed, long-forgotten statue, before it suddenly turned its head and focused in on Emma.

Instantly the creature's face was transformed into a terrifying mask of planes and angles that gleamed and glistened with menace as its sinister red eyes bore into her. Her stomach churned and her hands felt moist and damp around the hilt of her sword.

"Emma, talk to me," Loni demanded in a confused voice, but Emma hardly heard as she raced forward, determined to get between her friends and this abomination. "What about the darkhel? It's... oh no. It's here, isn't it?"

Emma didn't respond. All she could hear was the rush of air as the creature raced toward them, its red eyes never leaving her. She forced her terrified breath out from between her lips as she swung her sword back and forth in her hand, reacquainting herself with its weight as the beast finally reached her.

"So you can see me? Interesting," the creature hissed in a guttural voice as it came to a halt only a few feet in front of her. "That will make it more fun when I kill you." It grinned, revealing a set of razor-sharp teeth squished into a wide, misshapen mouth.

Emma kept her balance as she lifted her sword. Well, at least she definitely knew it was a fairy now since dragons were monosyllabic to the point of muteness. Especially when they were fighting.

"It's the fear, isn't it?" the darkhel speculated as it closed the distance between them and she could all too clearly see the dark pits of its eyes. "It's made you incapable of speech."

Emma ignored it, instead trying to focus all her energy on what she was doing. Every elemental creature had a kill spot. For dragons it was under the neck, for demons it was the spinal cord. For goblins it was the heart. Unfortunately Sir Francis, in his not-so-infinite wisdom, never bothered to mention a kill spot for fairies, and so she decided that she would start with the neck and go from there.

She licked her lips and tried to control her breathing as she waited for the darkhel to come closer. It took a couple more steps toward her, an evil grin on its face. Without hesitation, Emma lunged forward, driving her sword deep into the fleshy dark skin at the base of its neck. The vibration went racing back up her arm as the point of her sword bounced off it like a nickel on sidewalk and she felt herself reeling from the impact. She lunged again, this time harder, and let out a sigh of relief when she managed to pierce the surface and a gush of dark, fetid blood started oozing out. For a moment the darkhel reached up and touched the open wound before it grinned at her. Okay, so the neck wasn't the kill spot.

Before she could regain her composure, the darkhel casually lifted one taloned hand and swiped it across her face. Emma managed to duck out of the way just in time. Then she drove her sword straight into its heart. She felt like she had struck iron and her muscles screamed in protest. Ignoring the pain, she pressed forward with all her might. The darkhel staggered back, which gave her time to regain her stance.

"Okay, no more Mr. Nice Guy," the darkhel droned as it ignored the blood that was now flowing freely down its torso. Instead it came toward her with lightning speed and sent her sword flying from her hand. The weapon landed on the manicured grass with a thud and Emma felt herself go crashing to the ground. The skin across her brow immediately split open, and the blood started to trickle into her eye. She quickly wiped it away with the back of her hand before realizing that the darkhel was leaning over her. She only just managed to roll out of the way to save herself from having her windpipe slashed by its long talons.

She groggily started to raise herself up, but before she could, the darkhel again loomed over her, this time pinning her down with a heavy leather boot. The boot pressed into her chest and she struggled to catch her breath. Emma glanced up and found herself staring into dark eyes that were full of rage. She shut her own eyes and tried to wriggle her hand onto the hilt of her sword, but it was no good.

"Well, my small brothers didn't really do you justice when they told me about your skills," the darkhel hissed, its stinking breath sending goose bumps racing up and down Emma's skin. "But still, I guess they were right about one thing. You're only human and humans just break so...*argh*."

Argh?

For a moment Emma blinked before realizing the creature had stiffened and raised its giant, corded hands up to its ears. Then she caught sight of Loni standing directly behind it with the subsonic blaster she'd just spent the last six months building. Tyler was next to her, clutching the thin rapier that he preferred, ready for action. As the darkhel continued to clutch at its ears, obviously trying to cut out the low-frequency noise that Loni's invention was emitting, Emma had all the time she needed to roll away and flip back up to her feet just as the creature turned and raised a giant arm at the unsuspecting Loni.

"Run!" Emma screamed as she realized her friends didn't have a clue about where the darkhel was attacking from. At the same time she reached down and grabbed her sword before thrusting it deep into the creature's hamstring. The impact almost sent her reeling again, but she balanced herself and pulled the sword out. The darkhel seemed to sag as it spun back around to face her, its eyes blazing.

"You know," it said in a low, guttural voice, "you really are your mother's daughter."

Emma, who had just been about to plunge her sword into

its arm, felt her weapon drop away as a sense of disbelief washed over her. "Wh-what did you just say?"

The beast needed only that one second of hesitation to get to its feet, and before Emma could even open her mouth, it had spread out its gigantic wings and lifted off the ground into the air.

CHAPTER TWELVE

Your mother?" Loni shot Emma a blank look half an hour later as she handed her another ice pack. "Are you definitely sure that's what it said?" Loni asked as she stood up and started to pace the cramped space in her dorm room.

"Absolutely, one hundred percent positive. It said I am my mother's daughter." Emma put the pack on her aching arm and tried not to groan out loud from the pain. She and Loni and Tyler had decided to go back to Loni's room in case anyone had seen Emma's one-sided fight and told Kessler about it. Of course, if they had, it wouldn't take long for him to find her. All he needed to do was follow the blood trail. At least they had managed to clean up the cut on her head, but it still throbbed in protest.

"Okay, so we've got a creature that no one has ever heard of and no one can see except you," Tyler said from over by the window as he ticked off the words with his fingers.

"You forgot to add that it fights like a ninja. Honestly, you guys, I feel like my arm is going to fall off. The darkhel's skin is thicker than a dragon's. How is that even possible?" Emma asked.

"How is any of this possible?" Loni rubbed her forehead in bewilderment. "I mean, you have no idea how weird it was that I could see you fighting and talking to something but there was nothing there. I don't know how sight-blind people deal with it."

"They don't have to deal with it, because for the most part they don't even know it's out there," Tyler reminded her. "So don't be feeling sorry for civilians, feel sorry for us. I mean, we know how dangerous elementals are, yet there was nothing we could do to help."

"Trust me, you helped. And besides, you definitely don't want to see the darkhel. I've fought brentton demons that are better-looking than this thing." Emma put down the ice pack and rubbed her sore eye. "The problem is that I have no idea where to go from here."

"I'll tell you where we go, straight to Kessler." Loni finally stopped her pacing and sat down on the bed. Emma instantly shook her head (remembering too late that head shaking, along with everything else, hurt).

"I hate to say it, Em, but Miss Zodiac's right," Tyler agreed.

"I can't go to Kessler," she told her two friends. "I've tried that already and managed to get myself stuck with detention. I think I've become the girl who cried wolf. Or in this case, the girl who cried invisible fairy. I can't risk being expelled."

"Yes, but Emma, I think you're forgetting something here," Tyler said.

"What?"

"That thing tried to kill you." Loni took over, and Emma realized that her two friends were so busy agreeing with each other that they were forgetting to bicker. "I mean, granted I couldn't see it happening, but I certainly saw you being flung around the quad like you were a rag doll."

"Yeah, I've never seen you have your butt whipped like that since . . . *well, never.* I mean even when you had to take on that mammoth Department guy who came to teach us some hand-to-hand combat techniques last year, you totally beat him. I actually made a lot of money on that fight," Tyler reminisced for a second before Loni jabbed him in the ribs with her elbow. "Which is entirely beside the point." He coughed. "The point is that thing was totally taking you down."

"I know." Emma rubbed her bruised arm. "And the worst thing is that so far I have no idea where the kill spot is."

"Did you try the neck?" Tyler asked, instantly curious, since like dragons, the huge salamanders that he fought were fire elementals and so they shared the same kill spot (not to mention the same love of roasting their victims in flames).

"Neck, heart, and spinal cord, and I swear each time I got a clear strike." Emma paused to rub her still-aching shoulder. "Yet it just looked at me like I was some sort of annoying mosquito. I have no idea what's going to happen the next time I have to fight it."

"Next time?" Loni's voice started to turn high-pitched. "You think there's going to be a next time? Because that's even more reason why we should go to Kessler."

"I promise, if I thought there was any chance Kessler would listen to me, I would go and see him, but aside from all of my aches and pains, we have no proof—"

"Wait." Tyler cut her off and suddenly darted over to Loni's laptop and started to tap away at the keyboard. "That's it!"

"What's it?" Loni demanded.

"We get proof that you were fighting the darkhel and then Kessler will have to believe you," he said as his fingers continued to fly across the keyboard.

"How?" Loni demanded.

"Okay, so this is completely off the record, but I might happen to know how to get into Burtonwood's security system. They put out an EMR pulse every two minutes to make sure all the wards are working and that no elementals enter the grounds."

Loni widened her eyes. "Tyler Owens, how exactly do you have the security clearance to get into that system?"

He grinned. "Let's just say I know someone who was dumb enough to bet against Ruby the cockroach, and then when they couldn't pay what they owed me, they offered me the code in lieu of cash."

"You know how to hack into the surveillance system because of a bet you made on an insect?" Emma double-checked to make sure she was hearing right.

"That's correct. I mean, it's not my fault if people continue

to underestimate the speed of a five-legged cockroach."
He gave an unrepentant shrug. "Anyway, the thing is that
Emma was fighting the darkhel for at least ten minutes,
which means there should be some sort of image, and maybe
we can get some clues from the thermal resonance. *Of course
it would help if I knew what I was looking for*," he added with
a frown.

"You get us in and I can do the rest," Loni assured him
as she leaned over his shoulder. "And Tyler, I'm going to be
wanting these codes. I still can't believe you held out on me
like this."

"Most girls want flowers and chocolate, but you want a
security code," Tyler quipped as he continued to tap away at
the keyboard, pausing only to wince as Loni hit him on the
arm. "Ouch. Anyway, Miss Zodiac, here's your EMR. Make
of it what you will."

"So what does it say, Lon?" Emma watched as her friend
intently studied the computer screen.

"It says…oh." Loni frowned as she nudged Tyler out of
the way so she could sit down and start tapping something
on the keyboard. Then she softly swore under her breath.
"According to this, there was no elemental activity at all." She
scrolled down the page. "And this is going back until ten
yesterday morning when you first saw it. Okay, that idea is
officially a bust. So how did it get through the wards and
through an EMR scan undetected?"

"And more to the point, why can Emma see it?" Tyler
added as the frown lines continued to gather on his face like

a storm. "You know, this is one bet that I wouldn't back."

"I know. It makes no sense." Loni continued to stare at the screen.

"Preaching to the choir," Emma assured them as she gingerly got to her feet and walked over to the window. "Problem is, that thing is out there. Somewhere. And we don't know anything about it. What if it's hunting right now?"

"All the more reason to tell Kessler," Loni persisted.

"Can't. Expelled, remember?"

"I don't like it." Loni shook her head so hard that her silver hoops started to jangle. "In fact, sometimes I think you're the Taurus and not me because you have one hell of a stubborn streak."

"Not stubborn, I just don't want to get kicked out of Burtonwood. Especially since right now all I want to do is find out how this thing knew my mom. I think we should go to the library and see if we can...what?" Emma paused as she realized her friend was looking at her like she had just suggested they both fly to Paris and jump off the Eiffel Tower together. *"Just because I'm not a fan of studying doesn't mean I can't do it when I need to."*

"It's not that." Loni reached over and picked up a hand mirror that had been sitting on a pile of astrology books. "But you might want to have a look at yourself before you think of going out."

Emma held up the small mirror and flinched as she realized what her friend meant. Her bottom lip was puffed up like Angelina Jolie's, while the rest of her face was a picture of cuts and bruises. Not that it was uncommon for Burtonwood students to walk around sporting worse injuries, but right now, after everything that had happened, she didn't really want to draw too much attention to herself.

"Look," Loni said in a diplomatic voice. "How about Tyler and I head over to the library and see what we can find on darkhels while you have an early night and try and stop looking like you've just gone ten rounds with some unknown elemental. Deal?"

Emma wanted to say no, but she recognized the determined gleam in Loni's eyes. Besides, normally after a fight, she either felt exhilarated or despondent, depending on the outcome, but right now all she felt was numb. So maybe, she decided, having some time to herself would help her process what had just happened.

An hour later she was back in her own room and she had extracted a promise from Loni and Tyler that they would call if they found anything. *"And I mean anything,"* she had repeated to ensure that her friends understood how important it was. After they left, Emma sat down and started to methodically clean her sword. It wasn't her favorite part of being a slayer, but there was something strangely soothing about falling into a routine that her mom had first taught her almost seven years ago.

She carefully put some oil on a soft cloth and ran it along the smooth surface, determined to remove all of the dark black blood that was smeared along on it. As she cleaned she tried to figure out what was going on.

What was the darkhel?

How did it know who she was?

How did it know who her mom was?

And finally, what did it want?

However, the more she thought about it, the more it felt like she was doing one of Professor Edwards's pop quizzes, where the questions all swirled into one and there was more chance of her growing horns and a tail than there was of figuring out the answers.

She finished with her sword and carefully slipped it back into its sheath; then she went through and checked that all her other weapons were in order. Finally, after sending both Loni and Tyler yet another text to see if they'd found anything (*no* and *no* were the synchronized replies), Emma reluctantly got ready for bed and turned off the light.

She half expected to have problems keeping her eyes shut, after everything that had happened, but instead, the minute her head touched the pillow, she fell asleep.

Unfortunately, with sleep did not come peace, and her dreams were dotted with visions of her mom. Her long brown hair, so like Emma's own, was dragged away from her forehead, while her lips were pursed in concentration as she showed Emma the best way to hamstring a dragon. Emma's own attempts were clumsy and ineffective, and she was just about to ask her mom to show her again, but before she could, the injured dragon suddenly morphed into a darkhel.

In her sleep Emma jumped at the sight of the dark, vile

creature, and she turned to her mom for help. But instead of fighting it, her mom just shrugged her shoulders and put down her sword so she could walk over to where the creature was standing.

What are you doing? Emma screamed. *Get away from it!*

It's fine, darling. I just need to talk to it for a moment. If it hurts me, then you can just kill it.

What? But I don't know how to kill it. Where's the kill spot? Why do you need to talk to it? Mom, what's going on?

But her mom didn't answer. Instead she stretched out her hand toward the darkhel, and Emma watched in horror as the creature opened its hideous misshapen mouth to reveal its sharp white teeth. Emma tried to race toward them, but she suddenly felt like the weight of a hundred bricks was pressing down on her limbs and her chest, pushing her deep into the bed and—

But whatever was about to happen next suddenly dissolved in her mind like the tide washing away a sandcastle as the sound of the alarm rang in her ear. For a moment she just lay there in a tangle of sheets and sweat. The alarm rang again and this time she jumped out of bed, eager to push away any remnants of the dream. The dream where her mom seemed to be hiding something from her. She quickly got dressed so that she could join Loni and Tyler and see if they'd had success in finding answers to the question that had been going around in her mind like a carousel. What exactly was a darkhel?

CHAPTER THiRTEEN

For the first time since the explosion in the food court, Emma realized that all eyes weren't on her as she hurried across to the cafeteria to where her friends were both sitting. Which in turn meant that her fight last night must've gone by undetected. Thank goodness for Northern California's early-evening fog and gloom.

Tyler shook his head so that his red hair scattered in all directions. "Well?" she demanded the minute she sat down. "Did you find anything out?"

"Sorry, Em. There was nothing. I even tried sweet-talking Gretchen, but unfortunately she appears to be completely unbribable."

"You tried to bribe Gretchen the librarian?" Emma said.

"'Tried' being the operative word." Tyler let out a disappointed sigh. "I figured since Brenda is always walking around with old-fashioned-looking leather books, there must be some secret stash that was reserved for really brainy people, or really sneaky ones. But apparently not."

"But don't worry," Loni added, no doubt catching Emma's

look of frustration. "Because I have an idea. It's been really bugging me all night about how the darkhel even got into Burtonwood. Twice. I mean, this place is warded up to the hilt, so technically it shouldn't have been here."

"Hence the conundrum." Emma tapped the table in frustration. "Since that's the reason why Kessler doesn't believe me—well, that and the fact that this thing apparently doesn't exist. But then again, the little fairies don't seem to be affected by wards either, which is why they can come and go so freely at the mall."

"Yes, but we have a lot more wards at Burtonwood than they have at the mall," Loni pointed out. "The double Windsor alone pumps out so much voltage that it should fry any elemental within a three-mile radius, and we have twenty of them dotted around the boundaries, which is why I'm wondering if the darkhel has managed to interfere with one of them."

"Is that even possible?" Emma frowned and tried to remember everything she had learned in her Ward Building class. I mean, aren't the wards designed so that elementals can't tamper with them?"

"Yes, as a rule," Loni said, "but since we don't know anything about the darkhel, we really don't know what it's capable of. You said it had talons, but it also sounded like it was pretty dexterous. I don't suppose you noticed if it had opposable thumbs?"

Emma stared at her blankly.

"No, I didn't think so," Loni quickly added. "Anyway, I thought I should go and make sure that everything's okay with all the wards."

"You can do that?" Now it was Tyler's turn to look surprised.

"I can." Loni grinned as she pulled out a small map of what looked like the entire Burtonwood grounds. "Who knew it would be so handy that I spent all that time tagging after the tech guys watching them do their maintenance. Anyway, all I need to do is slip into the workroom at lunchtime and get my hands on an analyzer. It will tell me if the electromagnetic field is still working and at what voltage it is pumping out the positive electrons. As long as it's over fifty volts, then the wards are working. Simple."

"You know, I've said it before and I'll say it again: Loni's just a bucket of plutonium away from being an evil genius." Tyler grinned.

"Ignore him," Loni advised as she gave Tyler a friendly shove. "Because the important thing is that we're going to get to the bottom of this. I know we are. We've just got to stay positive."

✳✳✳

By the end of the day Emma realized that just because a person wanted to figure something out didn't mean the person *would* figure something out. Not that she'd really had much of a chance, since between going to classes and her after-school detention, her time hadn't exactly been her own. But if she didn't get some answers soon, there was a strong chance that her head might explode.

Thankfully, after two long and laborious hours, a grim-looking Professor Vanderbilt finally got to her feet and said that everyone in the detention room could go. Emma didn't need to be told twice, and she hurried over to the library, where Loni had been researching the darkhel. Her friend was waiting outside the entrance idly flipping a tiny ward up and down in the air.

"Tyler's stuck with Glen Lewis talking about their assignment but he's going to meet me at the cafeteria in half an hour so he can help me check the wards," Loni told her as she pocketed the ward. "How are you dealing?"

"I'm fine, aside from the fact that I'm going completely and utterly insane—of course," Emma added as the light started to fade and the temperature felt cool against her cheeks. "Still, at least I managed to get my homework done. Though why a slayer needs to learn accounting I'll never know."

"Yeah, I've never seen anyone kill a goblin by knowing how to depreciate an asset over a ten-year period," Loni agreed as she reached out and gave Emma's hand a comforting squeeze. "And hang in there. We'll find something out. I know we will."

"Will we?" Emma paused for a moment, her frustration descending like the surrounding fog. She thrust her hands into her blazer pockets to keep them warm. "It just makes no sense, Lon. This is my mom we're talking about. So how does this...this...*thing* know anything about her? I can't bear the thought of her having any sort of secret, separate life. I need to find out what went on."

"And you will," Loni insisted before she thoughtfully bit her lower lip. "But you know, there's something we haven't considered. I mean, if the darkhel knew your mom, maybe your mom knew the darkhel?"

"Except my mom's dead, so we can't exactly ask her," Emma reminded her friend.

Loni shook her short, spiked hair. "No, that's not what I meant. It's just...remember when you first took me back to your house just after we both started at the Academy?"

Emma nodded. Loni had been homesick like crazy and her parents had both been off on a mission in Africa, trying to hunt down a rogue demon, and so Emma's dad had invited her to come over on a Saturday. Something that had been repeated many times over the years until Emma's mom died and Emma had stopped going home herself, preferring to spend most of her weekends and holidays at Burtonwood.

"Well," Loni continued, "your mom took me into her study and she had a zillion ancient-looking books, and I clearly remember her telling me that some of them were the only copies available in the whole world."

"You think that one of them might mention the darkhel?" Emma asked as a sense of hope started to swell up in her.

Loni was right: her mom had a seriously big collection of books, and while she hadn't been what Emma would call a meticulous note taker, there had been times when she had seen her mom scribbling in a small leather-bound book. However, another thought suddenly occurred to her, and Emma felt her hope slide away like a leaf down a stream. "But I can't get them." She groaned. "I'm on detention, remember? I can't leave campus."

Just then the alarm on her cell phone beeped and she absently stared at the screen. It was the reminder that she had put in yesterday. The one to tell her she was supposed to meet Curtis in fifteen minutes to work on their assignment.

Emma was just about to delete it, but before she could, Loni, who was leaning over her shoulder to read the message, let out a little squeak of excitement. "That's it. You already have your pass-out. You just need to ask Curtis if he minds if you swing by your house on the way the back from doing your assignment."

"What?" Emma yelped in surprise as her last encounter with Curtis suddenly flashed into her mind—with particular emphasis on the fact that she had mistakenly thought he was going to kiss her.

"It's perfect," Loni insisted in an excited voice. "You're allowed off campus for your assignment. So, just make a pit stop afterward. Tell her it's perfect, Tyler."

"It's perfect, Tyler," Tyler dutifully repeated as he approached them with a bulging backpack slung over his shoulder. "I'm not sure what we're talking about, but she's got her Taurus-girl face on and you know what she's like when she gets like that."

Loni ignored him as she turned her attention back to Emma and softened her expression. "Look, I get that you probably don't want to speak to him after what happened yesterday, but—"

"Yesterday? So what happened yesterday?" Tyler piped up. "Oh, I bet you told Curtis that you never wanted to speak to him again. Ten bucks says I'm right. Yes?"

However, the two girls just ignored him as Loni lowered her voice and squeezed Emma's hand. "The thing is, despite how you feel, this is your best chance of finding out about the darkhel. Besides, it's not like you can get out of doing the assignment. Not unless you want to make Kessler even more mad than he already is."

"I know, you're right," Emma reluctantly agreed. Not because she thought it was a good idea to spend any more time than was necessary with Curtis—or because she really wanted to face going home—but because Tyler was right. Loni's normally placid, heart-shaped face was pinched into a stubborn, bullish expression that Emma had long come to know, and she quickly realized that the chances of her friend dropping the subject were slim to none. And at least on the positive side, she wouldn't be wearing a tie, so Curtis wouldn't be tempted to straighten it again.

"Good." Loni grinned.

"But," Emma added, "if I'm going out with Curtis, then you guys need to promise that you'll be careful when you're checking those wards. The last thing I want is for either of you to get in any trouble. One dysfunctional, out-of-favor slayer is probably enough for now."

"We'll be careful," Loni promised as she gave her a fierce hug. "And good luck with your mom's books. I have a really good feeling about this."

Emma nodded. But she wished she shared her friend's confidence that it would all be okay.

CHAPTER FOURTEEN

Jones, I'd almost given up on you," Curtis said fifteen minutes later as they swiped their pass-outs and the security guard ushered them through the gate. Curtis looked like he didn't have a care in the world. In fact, he was probably congratulating himself on managing to escape her tacky and humiliating invitation to join her at the practice range yesterday.

He was dressed in standard slaying clothes, and the black, well-fitted top seemed to mold to his chest. Emma found herself unconsciously smoothing down her own matching black top as she tried to remember if she'd brushed her hair this morning.

However, the sight of the Burtonwood minibus parked just in front of them caused her to forget about her appearance as she realized that this was a fatal flaw in her plan. For some stupid reason she was thinking they would be catching a taxi and it would be a simple matter of just paying the driver to make a detour. But now that was clearly impossible, since whatever she said to the driver would go from his mouth to Kessler's ear. Which meant that she would have to text Loni and get her to arrange for a taxi to pick her up once the minibus dropped her off. *Not to mention asking Curtis to cover for her.*

It will be easy. Loni's words came back to her just as Curtis pushed back the sliding door and ushered her in. There was a group of seniors already spread out across the backseat of the bus, on their way to a selkie scouting mission farther past the lakes at the river's head. They shot Emma a curious glance as she made her way to a window seat as far away from them as possible. Curtis followed her in and awkwardly lowered himself down, propping up his crutches on the spare seat just as the bus drove off into the night.

"Hey, are you okay?" he suddenly asked as he unzipped his slaying kit and pulled out the familiar yellow folder that they were using for the assignment. "You've hardly said a word, which—no offense—isn't like you at all."

"I'm fine," she quickly assured him while taking great pains not to look at him, since no good ever seemed to come from doing that. "It's just been a long day. That's all."

"And going out dragon hunting with me isn't your ideal way to spend the night." He finished off her sentence in a dry voice, his jaw clenched slightly.

"Something like that," she mumbled, still managing to avoid his gaze. Then, as much to distract herself as anything else, she pulled out her cell phone and sent Loni a quick text, telling her about the change of plans and asking her to arrange for a taxi to meet her at the parking lot where the minibus would be dropping them off.

Loni replied immediately. *Done. And don't 4get 2 b nice 2 C.*

Emma rolled her eyes, put her cell phone away, and turned her attention to the darkening skies outside the bus. She and Curtis made the rest of the trip in silence.

A while later, the minibus slowly pulled up to a small tree-lined parking lot at the edge of a large lake just off the highway. There was a tall streetlamp and an overflowing trash can next to some badly maintained public restrooms. There was also a taxi parked by a tree, its engine idling. Emma glanced out the window at it as she waited for the minibus to come to a stop. She was just congratulating herself on successfully ignoring Curtis for most of the trip when he suddenly made a clicking noise with his tongue, while behind them the seniors were busy discussing the best thermal imager to use when scouting selkies.

"Okay, Jones, so are you going to spill it?"

"Spill what?" She blinked in what she hoped was an innocent expression.

"What's going on," he suggested in a mild voice.

"Nothing," she said. "Why would something be going on?"

"Because you've been acting weird the whole time in the minibus, and now you keep looking out the window over at that taxi, which I don't think is sitting there by accident. Is there something you want to tell me?"

No, Emma longed to say since he already knew far too

much about her life, thanks to their trip to the mall the other day. And it didn't matter how kind he seemed to be; it didn't alter the fact that he had the one thing she wanted.

She sighed.

"Okay, fine. I sort of have a favor to ask. I need to go and pick up some stuff at my dad's house, but because I'm on detention this is the only chance I have to get it. I hate to ask." *Like really, really hate to ask.* "But would you mind covering for me? I promise I'll be back before twenty-two hundred hours."

"What stuff?"

"Um, just stuff."

"Hello, back there, anytime tonight would be nice." The bus driver coughed, and they realized he was waiting for them to get off. Curtis retrieved his crutches and they made their way to the front while the driver studied his schedule. "Okay. It says here that you're doing observation and reconnaissance only, so no slaying. I'll be back for you at twenty-two hundred hours on the dot. Are we clear?"

"Yes, sir," Curtis and Emma both said as the bus pulled back out onto the highway. Once it had gone, Emma turned back to Curtis and shot him a hopeful look.

"So? Will you cover for me?"

"You want me to cover for you, but you don't want to tell me why?" he asked with a hint of annoyance.

"Curtis, please. It's complicated."

"I'm a smart guy, Jones. I'm sure I'll keep up. What's going on?"

Emma gritted her teeth and regretted that she had ever allowed Loni to talk her into this. Then, catching the way his jawline was as tight as a guitar string, she let out a sigh. He wasn't going to give up. "Okay, fine. Remember the darkhel? Well, he sorta attacked me last night and—"

"What?" The words exploded out of his mouth like a bullet, and Emma almost expected to hear them echoing around the otherwise silent parking lot. She looked at him in surprise but the easy, lopsided smile that normally hovered close to his mouth had disappeared and was replaced by a tight slit of a line. "Why didn't you tell me sooner? When did it happen? Are you okay?"

"I'm fine, and I didn't tell you because there was nothing you could do about it," she retorted, and instantly regretted her words when his whole face turned into a mask of stone. He tightened his jaw and turned away for a second. However, a moment later he turned back to her and the darkness had gone, though his knuckles were snow white and strained as they gripped his crutches.

"You still could've told me," he finally said.

She softened her voice. "Look, I'm okay. It attacked me last night in the quad. Thankfully, almost everyone was at dinner and it was pretty foggy, so I don't think anyone saw. *Well, I don't think anyone saw me,*" she corrected as she explained that once again the darkhel had been invisible to all but her. "The thing is, it's not like any other elemental I've ever fought. If Loni hadn't come along with her subsonic blaster, I'm not sure what would've happened."

Curtis paused for a moment and rubbed his hands through his blond curls, his face looking suddenly tired. "I guess it was lucky she was there to help. So what did Kessler say?" But when she didn't answer, he let out a long groan. *"You didn't tell him, did you?"*

"You know why I couldn't." She looked at him before taking a deep breath. "The thing is, the darkhel spoke to me. It told me that I fought just like my mother."

Curtis's dark eyes widened, and for a moment as he looked like he was having some sort of internal battle with himself, but whatever he had been wanting to say seemed to be lost, and instead he straightened himself to his full height and said in a businesslike voice, "So what can I do to help?"

"Loni and Tyler spent all last night at the library but still couldn't find a thing on the darkhel. That's why I need to go back to my house. My mom had a really big collection of one-of-a-kind elemental books. I'm hoping there will be something there." Her voice probably sounded a bit gruffer than she had intended, but it was only because his own change of tone had caused such an overwhelming sense of relief that she suddenly felt like crying. However, she quickly jabbed her nails into the fleshy part of her palm and managed to regain her composure. Slayers didn't cry. She didn't cry.

Curtis started to swing his way toward where the taxi was still waiting. "So you need to get the books and get back here before the minibus comes to pick us up."

"That's right...*and Curtis, thanks*," she said as she

swallowed hard. She seemed to be saying that a lot to him lately.

"It's no big deal." He gave a dismissive shrug as he came to a halt next to the taxi and held the back door open for her. She slid in and had just given the driver her dad's address when she realized that Curtis had made his way around to the other side of the taxi and was trying to maneuver himself, his crutches, and his slaying kit into the cramped space next to her. Finally, he was settled and he reached to put on his seat belt.

"What are you doing? You don't have to come with me. I'll meet you back here," Emma assured him as she rubbed her sore eye.

He shook his head. "Nope, I don't think so."

"But, Curtis—" she started to explain.

"Yes, Jones?" He cut her off with a serene smile, which reminded her why he was so annoying. She took a deep breath and tried again.

"Can't you just go and look for the troubadour dragons and do the assignment?" she urged, but he merely shook his head.

"Strangely enough, I'm not really in the mood for doing my assignment. Probably because you got attacked by something that no one else can see, and part of me thinks it might not be the best thing to let you go there alone." He turned to the driver. "Okay, we can go."

"But I'm the only one who can see the darkhel, so even if

it did attack me again, you couldn't help," she pointed out, and for a moment Curtis's face froze again before he gave her a tight shrug.

"All the same, I'm coming," he replied. Then he paused. "Actually, there's something else I wanted to talk to you about. It's about what happened yesterday outside the simulation labs."

"Oh." Her face started to heat up. "You mean with the tie?"

"I mean, how you asked if I wanted to go to the practice range," he clarified.

"R-right." Emma suddenly decided that it might be a good idea to study the handle of her slaying kit, since reliving humiliating experiences wasn't exactly her number one hobby.

"The thing is—" He paused for a moment and cleared his throat. "It's not that I didn't want to go with you, it's just the practice range isn't really my thing. I find it easier to fight in the simulation labs."

Emma looked at him and blinked in surprise, since of all the things she thought he might say, that wasn't one of them. "So that's why you said no?"

"Sure." He nodded, then his expression turned confused. "Why else?"

"Er, no reason." She blinked as she realized that Curtis must be the only student at Burtonwood who didn't know what "going to the practice range" was code for, but before she could say anything else, the taxi suddenly turned onto a quiet suburban street and too late she realized that she had been so focused on her conversation with Curtis that she was now woefully unprepared for her visit.

The taxi slowed down and came to a halt. Emma felt something catch in her throat as she stared out at the pale wood veneer and teak trim of the house on Larnark Road. It was the place she had grown up, but it no longer felt like home.

"Are you okay?" Curtis asked from beside her.

"I'm fine," Emma said, a little bit too quickly, as she busied herself getting out of the taxi, hoping he couldn't see her reaction. Curtis followed. She didn't even like telling Loni about her dad, so she was hardly going to talk to Curtis about him, even if they were friends now. Especially because to the outside world her dad was a pretty decent guy. Cheerful, happy, supportive. *Capable of transferring his affections from her mom to Olivia less than a year after her mom had died.*

Then without saying another word she hurried up the path and knocked on the door of the place she had once called home.

CHAPTER FIFTEEN

Emma. This is a wonderful surprise. We didn't expect you." Olivia appeared at the door wearing a soft green sweater to hide her baby bump, while deeper in the house Emma could hear the faint sound of music and smelled roast pork wafting through to the front. Turning up here unannounced suddenly didn't seem like such a good idea, and she felt a flood of emotions catch in her chest.

"Er, yeah. Sorry, I didn't mean to interrupt anything." Emma reluctantly stepped out of the cool autumn evening into the warmth of the house. Curtis followed.

"Don't be silly, you're not interrupting anything," Olivia assured them before ushering them into the living room, which had once been papered in sky-blue stripes but had now been painted a pale yellow, while the old comfy sofas that Emma had bounced on as a child had been replaced by stiff brown leather ones. As for the floor, the white carpet that she remembered had been ripped up, and in its place were polished hardwood floors and large Turkish rugs.

"You've redecorated?" Emma felt a lump form in her

throat as she tried very hard not to notice that her mom's antique console table was no longer under the window and there were no signs of the silver-framed photographs that used to sit on top of it.

"Oh yes, I forgot you haven't been here in a while. I know there's still two months to go, but we thought we'd better start making the house baby-proof. Do you like it?" Before Emma was forced to answer, her dad came into the room.

"Ah, so you haven't been eaten by swamp monsters. I was starting to wonder when I didn't hear back from you." He crossed over to her as he undid the frilly apron that he insisted on wearing when he cooked.

"Hey, Dad. Sorry I haven't been in touch. I know I promised I'd call every day after the accident. It's just, well . . . it's been a weird week."

"Well, at least you're here now," he said as he hugged her before stepping back so he could inspect her face. "So how's the eye? I see the patch is off, which is a good sign. Does it still hurt?"

"No, it's better now," Emma hastily assured him, feeling guilty that she kept forgetting to return his calls. Despite how awkward things sometimes felt, she knew he probably had been genuinely worried. Then she realized her dad was looking at Curtis with interest, and she reluctantly nodded toward him. "Anyway, this is Curtis. He goes to Burtonwood with me."

"Ah, the dragon slayer. Olivia told me she met you at the mall." Her dad held out his hand. "So have you had any luck with a kreplin yet? Most of the time I'm happy to be sight-blind, but I must admit when Emma's mom used to talk about the green kreplins, I had a longing to see them for myself."

"Hey, Mr. Jones." Curtis stretched out his hand. "I actually managed to slay my first kreplin the other day. As you can see, it left me with a souvenir." He nodded down to his cast, and her dad instantly lost his easy smile.

"I'm sorry to hear that, Curtis." He started to frown. "Any parent who has a child at Burtonwood worries about injuries. Thankfully, except for her sore eye the other day, Emma's been lucky."

"I'd hardly call it lucky. I just haven't had anything decent to slay," Emma mumbled as she picked up a weird-looking plastic thing on the mantel and started to fiddle with it before realizing it was actually a blue baby toy that said IT'S A BOY across the front. She instantly put it back down and tried not to think about the fact that she was going to have a half brother.

"Well, call me an old-fashioned sight-blind civilian but I'd rather you be safe than injured," her dad merely said before shooting her a hopeful glance. "So can you both stay for dinner? Olivia always teases me that I make too much food, but the advantage is that there is always plenty for extras."

Emma shook her head. "Sorry, but we're kind of in a hurry. We have a taxi waiting outside. Actually, the reason I'm here is because I need to look at some of Mom's books. Is it okay if I go up to the study?"

"Oh." A flash of guilt ran across her dad's face. "Do you

mean all the old ones with the brown leather covers?"

"Yes." She croaked as a stab of panic raced through her body. "Why? Is there a problem?"

"It's just—Well, we decided to turn the study into a nursery." He shot her an apologetic look. "Right now the only books in there are of *The Very Hungry Caterpillar* variety."

"And you have no idea how long it took him to set up the crib," Olivia teased as she put an affectionate hand on his arm.

"Hey, those things are hard to do," her dad protested as he returned her embrace, and Emma stared at them in horror.

"S-so what about Mom's things? You didn't..."

"What?" He looked at her blankly for a moment before shaking his head. "Oh sorry, honey, I didn't mean to scare you. Of course I didn't throw anything out; they're just up in the attic. Do you need them right away?"

"Yeah, it's kind of important," she said, just as a timer went off in the kitchen.

"Bill, I'll check that and you can go get the books for Emma," Olivia suggested in a sunny voice before heading for the kitchen while her dad went upstairs.

"Are you okay?" Curtis whispered to her when the room was empty. "You went a little pale for a minute."

"I'm fine. I was just worried they threw out my mom's books and then we would be back at square one."

"Why would they throw them out?" Curtis looked surprised.

"Same reason they've changed the furniture and put away

all the photos." Emma shrugged as she glanced around the room and tried to connect it with the home she had once known. "Out with the old and in with the new, I guess."

Before Curtis could answer, her dad reappeared with a weathered-looking cardboard box, and Emma felt her shoulders sag in relief.

"Thanks." She hurried over and took it from him.

"Did you find them?" Olivia reappeared from the kitchen with a matching frilly apron tied around her large bump, her face flushed from the heat of the kitchen.

"Yes. Anyway, we've got a taxi waiting outside, so we'd better get going, but thank you so much for these." Emma protectively gripped the box while next to her Curtis looked like he was trying to figure out a way to carry a box and use his crutches at the same time.

"Emma, you don't need to say thank you. They're as much yours as they are mine," her dad corrected as he took the box from her and followed her over to the front door. "And if you're sure you can't stay, why don't I drive you back to Burtonwood?"

"No." Emma quickly shook her head, thinking of the minibus that would be waiting to take her and Curtis back to the Academy. Then she caught her dad's hurt look. "I mean, your dinner's ready. And you don't need to come outside. It's cold."

"Nonsense," Olivia said as she followed them down to the taxi while the driver put away his cell phone and started the engine. "Being pregnant is like suddenly finding yourself on a tropical island, just minus the sand and the sun. I'm boiling. Plus, it will give me another chance to convince Emma to change her mind about not coming to Serena's wedding this weekend. I know she would love to have you there, especially now that your induction ceremony has been canceled."

"I'm sorry, but I really don't think I can. I've got a crazy amount of schoolwork to get done," she said as she ignored Curtis's pointed glance and hopped into the taxi. She rolled down the window to say good-bye, but it wasn't until the vehicle had pulled away from the curb that Curtis turned to her and raised a surprised eyebrow.

"So why do they think Induction's been canceled?" he asked in a low voice so the driver wouldn't hear. "Don't you want them to come?"

"Oh sure, I'm just dying for them to see me be inducted as a fairy slayer. Maybe we can even get the local paper to run a story about it," Emma retorted as an annoying pop song blared on the radio.

"Sorry, I wasn't trying to rub it in." Curtis flushed. "I just meant that maybe you should've given them the chance to decide if they wanted to go or not."

"I didn't tell them it was canceled in the first place," Emma quickly replied since Curtis obviously thought she was the kind of person who lied on a regular basis.

"Oh. I guess your dad just didn't strike me as the sort of guy who would miss it."

"You don't give up, do you?" Emma glared at him, then sighed. "Okay, so here's the thing. For whatever reason,

Olivia's family is big on weddings. Very big, and her sister is getting married in New York on Sunday. Only problem is that at the start of the school year, Principal Kessler changed the date of Induction from last weekend to this weekend, which meant my dad started to freak out because Olivia's a really bad flier. Anyway, he kept calling and texting me about it, and in the end I told him it was no big deal if he didn't come. As for why he told Olivia that it was canceled, it was probably because he didn't want her to worry. So now you know. Not only am I a stupid fairy slayer, I'll also be the only sophomore without any parents at the induction ceremony. Laughingstock once again. Go, me."

Curtis stopped and studied her. "Look, I'm sorry, Jones. That sucks." He paused and looked down at the books. Then he studied her face before finally speaking. "Why didn't you just ask your dad outright if your mom had ever mentioned the darkhel?"

"You think I should've asked him about an invisible fairy?" Emma folded her arms in annoyance, but when Curtis just raised an eyebrow at her, she finally sighed. "Fine, so the reason I didn't ask him is because I don't like talking about my mom with him. He's got a new life and a new wife now. Talking isn't really our thing."

"That's a shame."

"It's fine. Look, my mom's been gone awhile now, so it's not like this is new territory for me. Now, can we please just forget it?"

"Yes, but—"

"Seriously, Curtis. I know you're trying to help, but since you have no idea what it's like to be—"

"My folks won't be there either," he suddenly blurted out. However, the moment the words were out of his mouth, he winced, as if regretting his decision to say them.

She looked at him. "What? You're joking."

"Look, I didn't mean to say that, I just didn't want you to think that you were on your own. Now can we please just drop it?"

"Oh no." She shook her head. "You're not getting out of it that easily. If you know something about me, it's only fair that I know something about you. Spill. What are the parents of the famous Curtis Green doing that is so important that they can't make Induction?"

For a moment Curtis looked down before letting out a reluctant sigh. "My dad isn't exactly a fan of what we do at Burtonwood."

Emma stared at him blankly. "I don't understand."

"That's because you've grown up in a house where it's completely normal to talk about kreplin dragons and sword fighting." Curtis seemed to be clenching his jaw. "The first time I told my dad that I thought there was something *evil* in the room he didn't believe me. The second time I did it he smacked me around. The third time, well, I had enough sense to keep my mouth shut."

"What?" Emma studied his eyes to see if there was any hint of joking in them, but he merely returned her gaze in a steady, unflinching way.

"The thing is, my dad's spent most of his life working in a wood mill during the week, drinking his body weight in beer on the weekend, and hoping that the Vikings will win the Super Bowl. No one in my family has ever had the sight before, so it's not exactly an easy thing for them to accept."

"Your family's sight-blind? Curtis, I had no idea." She hadn't been quite sure what he was going to tell her, but it certainly wasn't this. She'd never even heard of someone being born to two sight-blind parents, and as far as she knew, she was the only one who had been born with just one sight-gifted parent.

"There's no reason why you should." He looked down at the cast on his leg. "Anyway, my dad pretty much disowned me when I came here, so I'm sort of on a scholarship. Now, seriously, can we please drop the subject?"

Emma ignored his request as she realized how wrong she had been about him. It also explained why he hadn't even known what the Pure One was.

She softened her voice. "What about your mom? And do you have any brothers or sisters?"

"My mom left when I was just a kid and we haven't heard from her since. And my younger brother died a few years ago." He bowed his head and seemed to be studying his hands.

"Curtis," Emma whispered, feeling her throat tighten.

He cut her off. "It's fine, Jones. Can we just forget it?"

"Sure." She quickly nodded.

"Right, folks, here we are," the driver interrupted as the taxi came to a halt. "So how do you want to pay for that?" he asked as Emma glanced up to realize they'd arrived back at the parking lot by the lakes. For a moment she just blinked as she tried to digest what Curtis had told her, before the taxi driver started to tap his hand impatiently on the steering wheel.

"Um, cash," she quickly said as she pulled some money out of her pocket and passed it over before getting her stuff together and getting out. Once the taxi had disappeared from sight and they'd made their way in silence over to a wooden picnic table, Emma started to carefully transfer the books into her slaying kit. She was fairly sure the minibus driver would want to know how they had managed to find a box of old books when they were observing troubadour dragons.

She had just finished when the minibus pulled into the parking lot. The group of seniors was already inside, looking a bit wet and worse for wear. All Emma longed to do was start reading her mom's books, but instead she was forced to spend the whole trip back listening to what the older slayers had been through on their selkie patrol. However, the trip was made easier by the comfortable silence that had descended between her and Curtis. It was . . . nice.

Finally, the minibus pulled into Burtonwood and they both made their way back into the dark, silent Academy.

"So what now?" Curtis asked as they came to a halt at the entrance of her dorm.

"Now I go back to my room and start going through these books and hope I can find some mention of the darkhel," she said as she hitched her slaying kit, weighted down with books, higher over her shoulder.

"Well, I'd offer to come and help you but I guess the last thing you need is to risk being caught with a guy in your room," he said as he leaned forward on his crutches so that his face was almost level with hers. For a moment Emma found herself staring at his dark, velvety eyes, temporarily mesmerized at the intense swirling colors. She wasn't sure how long it was before suddenly realizing he was waiting for her to answer. She felt her face start to heat.

"Oh yeah. It's probably best if you don't," she agreed, her voice sounding breathy, even to her own ears. "And, look, I'm sorry I've been such a . . . well, less than nice to you. I guess I was so caught up in my own problems I didn't really think anyone else had any."

"Hey, Jones, we've talked about this. You know it freaks me out when you're too nice to me. It makes me think you're going soft," he teased as he shot her a lopsided grin.

"Hardly." She found herself grinning back at him, her mood lighter than it had been all day. "As you will discover when we do our virtual tests tomorrow. Because, Mr. Green, I hate to inform you that I plan to whip your dragon-slaying butt."

"Really?" His lips twitched in amusement. "I'll have you know that just about the only time this stupid broken leg doesn't hold me back is when I'm doing a simulation test."

"Uh-huh. Sure." Emma smiled and turned to walk away. "Oh, and Jones?"

"Yes?" She turned back around for a moment to see that he was still grinning.

"Try not to stay up all night reading that stuff, because if you want to beat me, you're going to need your sleep."

"In your dreams," she retorted as she watched him swing his way back toward his dorm. But it wasn't until he was gone that she realized she was still smiling.

CHAPTER SIXTEEN

Thank God you're back," Loni announced fifteen minutes later as she walked into Emma's room and collapsed on the chair by the window. "I swear I would rather listen to one of Professor Edwards's boring lectures on why you will no doubt need to use pi every single day when you're an adult than have to spend one more minute with Brenda. Especially since I just found out she's a Scorpio." She gave a dramatic shudder. "Anyway, now I completely understand why you were so upset about getting stuck with Curtis. There is *nothing* worse than working with someone who drives you insane."

Emma looked up from the book she had been reading and smiled slightly. "Actually, turns out that Curtis isn't so bad. Did you know that he's from a sight-blind family and that his dad used to hit him just because he was different? Even worse, his mom left them and his brother died. It's sort of hard to imagine, isn't it? I mean, he seems so together, what with the hair and the attitude."

For a moment Loni didn't answer as she silently studied Emma's face. Then she suddenly sat up bolt straight and widened her violet eyes. "Oh my God. You like him again. I knew it. I just knew you would change your mind. *Man, I so should've taken that bet with Tyler.*"

"What?" Emma demanded as she tried not to flinch under her friend's piercing gaze. "Of course I don't. Why do you think that?"

"Because I'm all-knowing and all-seeing," Loni retorted. "Plus you're doing that thing with your fingers which means you're preoccupied. So what happened to the practice-range fiasco?"

"Don't laugh, but he thought I was asking him to actually practice fighting demons and the only reason he said no was because he prefers to do his practice in the simulation labs," Emma explained as she examined her fingers to see what thing she was supposedly doing.

"What?" Loni was momentarily distracted. "Who likes to fight pretend elementals when they can fight real ones?"

"I think you're missing the point." Emma coughed as she gave up studying her fingers. "The important thing is that he wasn't blowing me off."

"That's true." Loni clapped her hands in excitement. "And it also means I was right. There was a simple explanation for it. You know, I just never get sick of feeling right. *Er, so why don't you look happy?*"

"I am happy," Emma quickly assured her as she thought

of Curtis's gorgeous face. However, her mood dampened as she recalled the dark shadows that seemed to overtake it from time to time. "But—"

"There's a 'but'? Why's there a 'but'?"

"I'm not sure." Emma wrinkled her nose. "When I hated him, I thought his attitude was merely because he didn't want to hang out with a fairy slayer. Like it was beneath him. But since I've gotten to know him, I don't think it's that. But there is something. I just can't put my finger on what."

"Yes, it's called a Y chromosome," Loni retorted. "Guys aren't supposed to be like girls because otherwise they would take up too much room at the mall and steal our makeup. I think you're reading too much into this. He explained why he went all weird outside the simulation labs, so now you have nothing to worry about. You like him and I'm sure that he likes you. It's perfect."

"Well, except for the invisible fairy who knows my mom," Emma corrected as she realized that she had let herself get sidetracked, and so she forced herself to push aside the conundrum that was Curtis Green. "How did you and Tyler make out with the wards?"

"Nothing." Loni's face instantly dropped and she shook her head in disappointment. "I checked every single one and the voltages were correct on all of them. I can't believe it. I really thought our problems would be solved. But instead, we're right back where we started."

"Yes, but hopefully not for long." Emma nodded to the

heavy, leather-bound volumes that were stacked up on her desk.

"Wow, look at all of these," Loni said, instantly reaching for a slim book called *Elementals Through the Ages.* "I just know we're going to find something in one of them."

"I hope so. And thanks for helping." Emma shot her friend a grateful smile before turning her attention back to the book in her hands. It was so dumb, but even the sight of something that her mom had once touched made Emma catch her breath.

She'd had five years to get used to the idea that her mom was gone, but it still hadn't happened, and secretly, in the back of her mind, Emma kept thinking she was just on a really long mission and one day she would walk back through the kitchen door. Of course if she did, the kitchen wouldn't exactly be empty...it would be filled with Olivia and her giant bump, not to mention all the new furniture—

"Are you okay?" Loni asked, interrupting her thoughts. "Because you're looking kind of weird."

"No, I'm fine. I just want to find some answers." Emma shook her head and forced herself to push her memories away and get back to work.

However, by the time she had gone through three incredibly boring textbooks that had far too much information about how riddick demons liked to relieve back itch in winter, she was starting to wonder if she'd made the whole thing up. After all, the school nurse had mentioned a possible concussion. Maybe the last few days had just been one big crazy dream?

"Found it," Loni suddenly interrupted, and Emma felt her heart start to pound in excitement.

"What? Really?" She leaned over to see what her friend was reading. "What does it say about the darkhels? What are they? What do they want, and more importantly, how do you kill them?"

"Sorry." Loni shot her an apologetic look. "I didn't mean to get your hopes up. I just meant that next to this picture your mom wrote the words *'found it.'*"

"She did?" Emma said, her disappointment giving way to surprise.

"See." Loni held up the book so that Emma could clearly see her mom's loopy writing, and she had even underlined the words three times and then drawn an arrow toward a black-and-white pen sketch of a dragon curled up around a chest full of gems and jewelry that looked like they were glittering and gleaming, judging by the thin pen lines that were radiating out from them. Emma chewed her lip as she studied the picture, but she had no idea why her mom would've written *found it* like that.

It wasn't big news that all dragons liked treasure. Especially since half of their kills were motivated by the wish to steal people's wealth. And dragons were fire elementals, not air elementals like fairies, so her mom's words couldn't have anything to do with the two kinds of creatures being related. Plus she knew dragons and fairies didn't share the same kill spot.

She turned the page to see if there were any more clues, but the book then went on to discuss things to avoid when dealing with an enraged banshee.

"At least it's a start." Loni was trying to sound encouraging.

"But how? I mean, what does a maskret dragon and its hoard have to do with a darkhel? It's one impossible thing after another and the more I think about it, the less my brain seems to be working. I feel like I'm swimming upstream in a river of mud."

Loni stifled a yawn and looked at her watch. "That's probably because it's almost two in the morning."

"It is?" Emma yelped. No wonder they were both having problems trying to figure it all out.

"So what do you want to do? Should we reread all of these books now in the hope we've missed something or start fresh in the morning?" Loni asked, and Emma reluctantly started to pack away the books.

"We'd better call it a night. The last thing I need is another detention for falling asleep in class. At least tomorrow's Friday, so it's almost the weekend. Then we'll have more time to try and figure this thing out."

"Except that it's induction weekend, which means a dinner tomorrow night, an open day at Burtonwood on Saturday, and the ceremony on Sunday," Loni reminded her as she got to her feet and headed for the door.

"Induction." Emma finished stacking the rest of the books onto her desk and followed her friend over. "I can't believe I forgot. Still, I guess I've finally discovered the one thing that is actually worse than being inducted as a fairy slayer—finding out that my mom had some sort of secret that I don't know anything about."

"Emma, we *will* get this figured out," Loni said in a stern voice as she stepped out into the empty hallway. "And in the meantime, try and get some sleep. This whole thing will make a lot more sense tomorrow."

Emma shot her friend a doubtful look before closing her door. She was tempted to keep working, but she knew that Loni was right and so she got ready for bed. She took one final look at her mom's familiar handwriting, then shut the book and climbed into bed. After a few minutes of tossing and turning, she fell into a troubled sleep, which was full of dreams.

This time she was already fighting the darkhel, and after striking it in every kill spot she knew, she was still no closer to destroying the vile thing.

Is that the best you can do? Its voice was a sibilant hiss that made Emma long to fall to her knees and cry. But before she could do so, her mom suddenly wandered over and looked at them with interest.

Unlike in Emma's last dream, her mom wasn't dressed in her slaying clothes but in some freaksville 1950s housewife dress. Even her straight brown hair had been piled up in some sort of conservative mom hairstyle. The only thing

Emma recognized about the woman in front of her was the familiar crystal necklace clasped around her slender throat.

Mom. Emma raced over to her. *I don't know what's going on with all your weird clothes and hair, but please, you have to tell me what you know about this thing. I can't kill it. You have to tell me what to do.*

Darling, if you can't deal with one measly fairy on your own, you don't deserve my help, her mom said as she idly reached up to the necklace and touched it with her long fingers, callused from years of holding a sword. Then, before Emma even knew what was happening, the creature was on her, its giant talons aimed straight at her heart, slicing their way through her chest before she could even open her mouth to scream, and—

Emma woke up with a start as she realized it was a dream. *Just a dream,* she repeated as she sat up in bed and glanced around. But there was no darkhel there, just the morning sunshine filtering in through her half-drawn curtains. She quickly got up and flung them open, eager to push the dream out of her head, but despite her best efforts, the vision of her mom refusing to help her played over and over in her head.

How did she know the darkhel? What was the connection?

Emma felt a lump rise in her throat. When had things gotten so difficult? She thought that nothing could've been worse than losing her mom, but these dreams and the discovery that her mom somehow had a secret life was a million times more painful. How many other secrets did she have?

For a moment she toyed with the crystal pendant that

was hanging forlornly in the window. She had put it there almost six weeks ago, promising herself that she wouldn't wear it again until she was inducted as a dragon slayer. The fact that her mom was wearing the necklace in the dream was still disturbing her, and Emma let her fingers run along the smooth, cool surface of the crystal as it threw a weak rainbow of light that radiated out in lines around the room.

Emma froze.

Radiating out in lines? She had thought that same expression last night when she was looking at the drawing of the dragon guarding its hoard. Emma lunged for the textbook and flipped through it until she came to the right place and once again studied the dragon, though this time she wasn't looking at the beast itself, she was looking at the jewelry hoard that was spilling out of the chest at its scaly feet. Then she held the crystal up next to the picture and studied one of the necklaces that was in the far corner. They were identical. It couldn't be a coincidence. Her mom had given her the necklace for a reason. Now she just had to figure out what the reason was.

CHAPTER SEVENTEEN

S o what are you supposed to do with it?" Loni asked half an hour later as she and Emma hurried toward the cafeteria, stopping only to touch the statue of Sir Francis on the way. The large room was full not only of students eating breakfast but of Burtonwood staff starting to make the preparations for the formal dinner that would be held there tonight to kick off the induction weekend celebrations. The two girls ignored the bustle completely.

"I have no idea." Emma tucked the crystal back into her pocket as they each grabbed an orange tray and joined the end of the line.

"What if it's just a coincidence?" Loni asked. "Maybe we're overthinking this?"

"I'm sure it's connected," Emma said in a firm voice. She hadn't told Loni about her disturbing dream or how it had led her to the necklace in the first place, but the fact that her mom had also highlighted it in one of her old books was all the proof that Emma needed. "We just have to figure out how."

"Maybe it gives you some kind of luck?" Loni pondered.

"Yes, except I wore it on the day Kessler gave me my designation and all I got then was bad news. Not saying that I wouldn't like some good luck, but if that's what it does, then it hides the power really, really well," Emma said as the woman behind the counter passed over their plates, piled high with food, and they made their way over to where Tyler was waiting for them. Emma couldn't help but notice that there was no sign of Curtis next to him.

"Okay, so cross that one off the list. I wonder if any of the teachers would recognize it?" Loni suggested as she jumped out of the way before two giggling sophomores went crashing into her.

"Good idea." Emma nimbly sidestepped the girls without spilling any of her breakfast. "I'll start asking if anyone knows anything about it."

"Knows anything about what?" Tyler asked as he finished reading a text message and looked up with interest.

"About this," Emma said as she put down her tray and handed him the crystal necklace. "There was a picture of it in one of my mom's books, and the words 'found it' written next to it."

"Yes," Loni continued. "That's why we think it's a clue; we're just not sure what it means. I'm thinking good-luck charm."

"Or it could be superpowers," Tyler offered up as he eyed their breakfasts with interest.

"Thank you, Tyler. And anytime you're ready to actually help, just let us know," Loni said sarcastically.

"I'm serious," Tyler insisted as he stole a piece of Emma's toast and took a bite. "You said the crystal was in a picture of a meskret dragon's hoard. Why was it there?"

"Because it's shiny and pretty?" Loni blinked at him, looking none the wiser.

"Because it has power." Emma widened her eyes as she realized where Tyler was going with this. It was true that all dragons liked gold and gems, but most of them liked objects of strength as well. Especially mystical ones. "So you're thinking that maybe the dragon had it because it was more than just a crystal?"

"You might actually be on to something," Loni marveled before she turned to Emma. "So from now on you need to keep that crystal on you at all times."

"That's right," Tyler agreed. "Because... *hey, Em, are you listening?*"

"What? Oh, um, I, um, yes, I'm listening," she stuttered as she realized she had actually been scanning the cafeteria for Curtis.

"Do you have a neck cramp?" Tyler asked as he flexed his fingers. "Because I know this amazing Thai massage thing that is guaranteed to get rid of all cramps. In fact, I bet that if your sore neck hasn't gone in five minutes, then—"

"Oh please." Loni rolled her eyes at him. "Since when can you do massage?"

"Wouldn't you like to know?" Tyler waggled a finger at her, which only caused Loni to roll her eyes some more, but their bickering was interrupted by the bell. Emma and her friends jumped to their feet and hurried to their first class.

***

By fourth period Emma was starting to get despondent. She had stayed behind to show the pendant to Professor Vanderbilt, but he had thought it was merely some sort of key ring.

Even worse, she was late to the simulation labs, and by the time she got changed into her sweats, Professor Meyers had already arrived, along with most of the class. But instead of giving her a tardy (thank you, thank you, thank you), the teacher merely nodded for her to go and get her fight gear. Emma scooped up an equipment bag and was just about to head over to where Loni was standing when she remembered that today they were fighting their assignment partners. *Which would explain her friend's pained expression as Brenda was lecturing her about something or other.*

Emma shot her a sympathetic glance before heading over to the simulation circle that she had been allocated. There was no sign of Curtis, though. In fact, she hadn't seen him all day.

"Hey, Jones, don't tell me you were getting worried about me?" a voice suddenly said from behind her, and she spun around to see him swinging his way toward her, his simulation gear hanging around his neck as he handled his crutches.

"What?" she protested, a little too quickly, her voice

breathy as she still struggled to deal with the effect his presence was having on her. Then she realized he was looking at her expectantly, as if waiting for an answer. "O-of course not. I just figured you were too scared to fight today."

"Really?" He lifted an eyebrow at her as he came to a halt and leaned forward on his crutches so he and Emma were almost nose to nose. "Because I can assure you I've been looking forward to it. I just had to go and see Nurse Reynes about my leg. Speaking of which, she asked if I had seen you because apparently you had an appointment with her to get your eye checked."

"Oh, must've slipped my mind," Emma lied. There was no way she was voluntarily going back to the infirmary because it reminded her far too much of the hospital where her mom had died. Call her crazy, but she found denial worked much better when it was hidden away in a nice quiet corner of her mind.

"Well, she wants you to reschedule with her."

"There's nothing wrong with my eye," Emma insisted as she reached up and gave it a rub.

"I'm just the messenger." He shrugged as he pulled on his gloves, and Emma found herself marveling at how his navy T-shirt clung to his muscular arms and at the way he chewed his full bottom lip in concentration, which, in turn, seemed to highlight his strong jawline. "Anyway, you haven't told me if you found anything."

"Huh?" She stared at him blankly for a moment, trying to figure out what he was talking about.

"You know. Invisible fairy? The books we got from your dad's house last night? Ringing any bells?" he prompted as an annoying half smile twitched around his lips as if he knew that she had been checking him out.

"Oh, right." She felt her cheeks brighten again as she scooped the pendant out of the pocket of her sweatpants, showed it to him, and explained what she knew about it. "Loni thinks it might be good luck and Tyler thinks it might have some sort of mystical power."

"And what do you think?" he asked, his dark eyes drilling into hers, and for one stupid moment she almost felt tempted to tell him about the dreams she'd been having. How real they felt and how, as much as she wanted to think that this was the last they had seen of the darkhel, her gut feeling was that it was still out there. But before she could even consider putting any of her concerns into words, Professor Meyers clapped her hands.

"Okay, everyone, let's get started."

Emma quickly put on her goggles and laced up her gloves as she and Curtis moved into the simulation circle. Three days ago if she'd had to fight him she would've been determined to beat him at all costs, preferably in a humiliating way, but at that moment, as she lifted her hands into a defensive position, Emma realized that despite the trash talking they had done last night, she really didn't care if she won or lost.

She watched as he carefully got into position and then dropped his crutches outside the circle just as a red light flashed in her goggles to let her know the simulation had begun. Then she raised her hand to block Curtis's first virtual move and watched in appreciation as he easily anticipated her shot and countered with one of his own. After all the tension and stress of the last few days, Emma suddenly realized that this fight was just what she needed to burn off some steam. She held up an arm to block his parry and then the fight started in earnest.

Half an hour later it was over, and when they looked at the counter, Emma was surprised to see she had won. She shot Curtis a grateful look.

"Thanks for that." She took the goggles off her head and put them down on the bench.

"For what?" He pushed his own back up into his blond curls.

"For going easy on me."

"Jones, I didn't go easy on you. In fact, I was just going to ask you what you've been eating for breakfast because that was some fight."

"Yeah, right." She shook her head. "Anyway, something else I need to thank you for is last night."

"It was nothing." He shrugged as he busied himself taking off his simulation gear.

"Somehow I don't think Kessler would've seen it that way if he'd caught us. Anyway, I just want you to know that I'm really grateful for what you did."

"I helped you get some books; it wasn't like I fought the darkhel or anything," he said, his voice almost sounding gruff as a flash of annoyance went racing across his face.

There it was again. Emma frowned, but before she could figure out why his mood had suddenly changed, the look had gone and he shot her a rueful smile. "Besides, Jones. I told you it makes me nervous when you act too nice."

"I'll make sure it doesn't happen again," she promised as a reluctant smile hovered around her mouth, but before Emma could say anything else, Professor Meyers clapped again for everyone's attention.

"Okay, that's it for the week. Don't forget homework due on Monday. Oh, and try not to celebrate too much this weekend during Induction. Especially on Sunday afternoon at that student party that we don't know anything about." Professor Meyers winked, and most of the class started to laugh. However, Emma ignored them as she realized the simulation teacher was gathering up her bag and getting ready to leave. She put her hand into her pocket and let her fingers curl around the pendant before she hurried over to the teacher.

"Emma, that was another great test. Not only was your hand/eye coordination up but your strength has increased by thirty percent. Have you changed your gym workout?"

Emma shook her head. Between exploding food courts and invisible fairies, she hadn't set foot in the gym for over a week.

"Hmm." Professor Meyers chewed the tip of her pen for a moment. "Well, maybe it's the change in routine?"

"I guess." Emma shrugged as she carefully pulled the

pendant out of her pocket. "Actually, I wanted to ask you about something else."

"Of course. My virtual door is always open." The teacher grinned. "What's up?"

"I was wondering if you've ever seen anything like this? My mom gave it to me and I was curious to find out if it had some sort of power?"

Professor Meyers instantly pulled her glasses onto her nose and studied the pendant for several moments before shaking her dark hair. "Sorry. The crystal itself looks fairly regular but I don't recognize the engravings around the edge. Why don't you try Professor Yemin, since he specializes in enchanted objects?"

"I actually did try him but he wasn't in his office and apparently no one has seen him today." Emma sighed; Professor Meyers was the third teacher to suggest him.

"Really?" Professor Meyers wrinkled her nose. "That's strange. Bob...I mean Professor Yemin never misses our Friday-afternoon staff meetings. He really likes the Oreos."

Emma smiled politely. "Well, thanks anyway," she said as she put the crystal back into her pocket and hid her disappointment. She hurried to get changed.

A few hours and another detention session later, Emma found herself at the library, where Loni and Tyler were waiting for her. They'd told Curtis about their meeting as well, but he had to go to some special training session with the one of the gym instructors.

"So?" Loni demanded as they hurried across the quad. It was only five thirty in the afternoon but it was almost dark. "Did you find out anything about the pendant?"

"No." Emma let out a frustrated sigh. "And Professor Yemin, who is apparently the only one who might know what it is, hasn't been in today. This is just driving me crazy. I know this pendant links my mom to the darkhel but I don't know how. And if I don't find out soon I think my head is going to explode."

"Well, that would be a shame," a voice suddenly said. Emma turned around as Curtis swung his way toward them with a grin on his face. How he had managed to sneak up on them, she had no idea. Though suddenly she imagined just how lethal he could be tracking dragons when he wasn't encumbered by his crutches.

"Hey," she said, some of her frustration instantly leaving her. "This is a nice surprise. I thought you had a gym session this afternoon."

"I did." He nodded before he frowned. "But on the way back I bumped into your dad down by the bottom parking lot."

"My dad's here at Burtonwood?" Now Emma was most definitely distracted; although her dad used to do some of the computer work for the Academy a long time ago, he wasn't a frequent visitor anymore. In fact, before his trip to give her the pendant and the news of Olivia's pregnancy, Emma couldn't remember the last time he had visited. Especially not late on a Friday afternoon. "Are you sure it's him?"

"I only met him last night," Curtis reminded her as he turned and nodded for her to follow him. "Anyway, you'd better hurry because he said it was urgent."

Emma felt the blood drain from her face as she turned and started to sprint toward the parking lot. Whatever it was, she had a feeling it wasn't going to be good news.

CHAPTER EIGHTEEN

Emma hurried over to where her father was waiting by his late-model Volvo. The parking lot was next to the second practice field. People weren't allowed to come and go as they pleased at Burtonwood, but induction weekend was an exception, and the visitors' parking lot was already half filled with parents who had arrived for tonight's dinner. Down on the practice field itself she noticed several groups of students scattered around giving combat demonstrations to interested parents under the glow of the large spotlights that dotted the area.

Loni, Tyler, and Curtis stopped at a nearby wooden bench while Emma covered the rest of the distance on her own.

"Dad, what's wrong? What are you doing here?"

"Hey, sweetheart." Her dad hugged her before stepping back and catching her gaze with his pale blue eyes. "Sorry, I didn't mean to worry you; it's just, we're leaving for the airport in an hour and I really wanted to talk to you before we go. I was going to the office to find out where you'd be, but then I bumped into Curtis and he said he'd get you for me."

"What's up?" Emma felt her stomach start to churn. Her dad most definitely had his serious face on.

"It's about your visit last night. I'm so sorry I told Olivia that your induction ceremony was canceled. I know you said that you didn't mind if we weren't there, but ... well ... I guess I didn't want her to worry—"

Oh. Right. So that's what this was about.

"It's okay." Emma quickly cut him off, because while it was okay in principle, she wasn't sure she really wanted him to spell out how important his new life was. In fact, the words "salt" and "wound" made themselves comfortable in her mind. "I know why you did it, so I wasn't worried."

"Are you sure?" He seemed to be studying her face, and when she nodded, a look of relief washed over him. For a moment Emma thought about what Curtis had said about talking to her dad, and she felt a rush of guilt go racing through her. At least she had a dad she could talk to if she wanted to. But when she tried to open her mouth, she realized she had no idea where to start, so she just shrugged.

"I'm sure. But why did you come all the way over here just to tell me that? You know there are these crazy inventions called cell phones."

"Oh yes, those things. Problem is that while I know how to use them, my daughter seems to have a bad habit of not answering her calls or returning her messages. Must be a generation thing."

Emma winced. "Yeah, I really am sorry about that. I didn't realize you'd been so worried."

"I'm a dad. It's my job to worry. Anyway, the other reason I couldn't call you is because Olivia insisted that I come out and see you in person."

"But why?" Emma blurted out before she could stop herself. "I mean, she doesn't know that Induction isn't really canceled, so she would hardly tell you to come out and see me about it."

"No, it has nothing to do with that," he assured her. "It's just that last night at about midnight she suddenly decided that the baby's room was the wrong shade of blue—apparently duck-egg blue and sky blue are two completely different colors. The thing is, she got out of bed and started going through a box to find her color charts, but instead she found one of your mom's books."

"She did?" Emma felt her heart start to pound as her dad nodded.

"And to be honest, I thought it could've waited until we were back, but Olivia absolutely insisted that if the books were important enough for you to come out and pick them up last night, then it was important enough for me to bring this one straight to you." As he spoke, he pulled a slim leather-bound book out of his coat pocket and passed it over.

A lump formed in her throat as she took the book. The cover felt dry and cracked against her skin, and for a moment she let her fingers rest on it as she tried to imagine her mom doing the same thing. Finally, her curiosity got the better of her and she flipped it open. The wafer-thin pages crackled as if in displeasure at being disturbed, but Emma hardly noticed as she studied the contents. It was a textbook, and every now and then, in faded ink, her mom had written notes in her achingly familiar loopy handwriting.

Without even reading it, Emma instinctively knew that this was what she had been looking for.

"Thank you so much," she gulped in a raspy voice as relief and gratitude mingled together, before she impulsively added, "A-and thank Olivia for me too."

For a moment her dad almost looked surprised before he gave her a warm smile. "Anyway, I guess I'd better go if I don't want to miss my flight."

"Actually." Emma took a deep breath as she let her fingers trace a pattern on the cover of the book he had given her. "Before you go, can you tell me if Mom ever mentioned anything called a darkhel to you?"

"A darkhel?" He wrinkled his nose the way Emma remembered his doing when she was a kid. "It's not ringing any bells. Is it a dragon?"

"Not exactly. So do you remember her ever talking about any other elementals? Maybe one she was having a problem with? Different from her normal missions."

This time her dad instantly shook his head. "Never. Your mom truly was an amazing woman and she never had a mission that she didn't complete—okay, well, that's a lie, she was dismal at doing PTA baking duties in your old school before your sight came through and you moved to Burtonwood. That was when I first mastered my famous triple-layer chocolate cake."

Emma smiled. "I didn't know that," she said, surprised and momentarily distracted. She didn't tend to think of her life before Burtonwood much. Spontaneously she asked, "Was it weird being married to a slayer?"

"I don't know if 'weird' is the right word. It had certain challenges—none of which I would have changed. But let's say it's nice to not worry if Olivia is going to come home from a day at the hospital with her leg half eaten by an iganu dragon."

"Iigaanual dragon," Emma automatically corrected as she rolled her eyes. "And Mom's leg wasn't half eaten, just a tiny cut. It didn't even scar."

"And now you sound just like her."

"Rea—" Emma started to say, but before she could finish, a static buzz rang in her ear, and she only just stopped herself from crying out from the pain. Instead, instinct made her spin around just in time to see the darkhel on the far side of the practice field, black against the pale beams of the overhead lights. Her sore eye started to water and a stab of fear went racing straight to her heart.

"Dad." She instantly spun back toward him and all but pushed him into the car. "Sorry, I've got to go. I just remembered something that I need to do."

"Oh, of course. I didn't mean to hold you up." His eyes

widened in disappointment. "We'll be back from New York on Tuesday. But Emma, you call me if you need anything. Okay?"

She frantically nodded as she waited for him to start the car. "I promise." It seemed to take forever, but finally he carefully pulled away just as the darkhel raced toward the parking lot, passing oblivious students and parents alike as it ran along the practice field.

Emma's pulse quickened. Last time she had fought it, everyone was inside, but tonight there was a group of sophomore guys who were throwing a Frisbee around, as well as the combat demonstrations. And unfortunately the guys with the Frisbee were in between her and the darkhel, so she went racing over to where Loni and the others were waiting for her. Thank goodness that after her last fight she had taken to carrying her slaying kit everywhere with her.

"Are you okay?" Loni's face filled with concern. "You didn't have a fight with your dad, did you? Because—"

"It's here. Take this," Emma hissed, cutting her off as she thrust the slim leather book into Loni's hands and grabbed her slaying kit. She barely slowed her pace as she yanked back the zipper and pulled out her sword. Then she caught sight of the metal nail files that she used for the small fairies, and she grabbed a handful before letting the kit fall to the ground.

She shoved the files deep into her pocket of her school skirt and curled her fingers around the hilt of her sword as her breathing started to emerge in erratic gasps. She finally covered the distance between her and the darkhel at the edge of the parking lot. For a moment it paused before turning its attention to where the oblivious sophomores were throwing their Frisbee and talking about Sunday's Induction.

"Hey," she screamed at the group. "Get out of here now." But they didn't seem to hear her, and Emma watched in horror as the darkhel raced toward Garry Lewis, its razor-sharp talons stretched out in front of him, while Garry stood blindly by trying to spin the Frisbee on his finger. Next to him, Glen was equally unaware as he reached over and knocked the Frisbee away from his twin brother.

"Go," she yelled again as she desperately tried to close the distance between herself and the group before the darkhel reached them, but there was still no response until suddenly Tyler's voice boomed out at them.

"I'm offering double odds to anyone who thinks one of Professor Gregory's lab rats can beat Ruby the cockroach in a race." The moment he said it, the whole group started to swarm off toward where Tyler was holding his betting book.

Emma had no idea why they would find Tyler's offer so tantalizing, but right now she couldn't afford to think about it as she watched Garry Lewis inadvertently step away from the darkhel, giving her just enough time to block it.

"You," the darkhel accused, its voice low and full of venom as its dark red eyes fastened on her like a laser, but Emma ignored them. She was vaguely aware that if anyone looked over at her, they would either think that she was crazy or that she was doing some sort of solo combat demonstration.

She sincerely hoped it would be the latter. However, as the darkhel advanced toward her, she cleared her mind. She would have to worry about the fallout later.

Instead, she tightened her grip on the hilt of her sword before she sent it plunging into the darkhel's rib cage. This time she was prepared for the vibrations, and she forced herself to press harder so that her weapon could pierce the skin. She finally managed it and the darkhel looked up at her with annoyance.

She knew it was a long shot to aim for the same kill spot as a harpy, but until she knew where the correct spot was, she was just going to have to keep guessing. The darkhel pushed the sword away.

"You can't protect him forever. I know he's close. I can smell him." The darkhel shrugged before straightening to its full height, seemingly unbothered by the stream of black ooze that was now running down its side.

"What are you talking about?" Emma demanded, but instead of answering, the creature lunged at her. She managed to dance out of the way just in time to avoid one of the sharp talons from slicing through her flesh. However, she stumbled backward and landed awkwardly on her wrist. Pain lashed through her as the darkhel rushed at her again.

This time she held her sword up and managed to nick its flesh. For a moment it paused and winced, and Emma quickly got to her feet, at least grateful her injured wrist wasn't part of her sword hand. She had thought her first fight with the creature was hard, but this was even worse, and her muscles screamed in protest as she lifted her sword once again and sent it plunging deep through the ironlike skin and slashing at its windpipe. For a moment its red eyes widened and then it . . . *laughed*?

"Oh, did Mommy forget to mention that while she managed to *inconvenience me for a while*, I'm not that easy to kill?" It grinned to reveal a mouth full of razor-sharp teeth.

"How do you know my mother?" Emma demanded as she wiped the sweat away from her brow and tried not to panic.

The creature didn't bother to answer. Instead, it stepped toward her again, this time raising a giant talon. Emma only just managed to avoid it, her whole body burning up despite the cold, overcast weather.

"The pendant," Loni yelled from somewhere in the distance, and Emma immediately dug into her skirt pocket and pulled it out. She had no idea what she was supposed to do with it, but it had to be worth a try. The minute she held it up, the darkhel took a step back, which gave her a moment to collect her thoughts. *Maybe it was like darkhel kryptonite?* She held it toward the beast, but the fear had gone from its eyes and it started to laugh at her again.

"You don't have any idea what that thing is, do you?"

"I know you don't like it," Emma bluffed as the creature once again stalked toward her. *Okay, so there went the kryptonite theory.* She felt some of her confidence shrivel up and go racing back across the quad. The creature struck out at her again, and she went tumbling. She winced as her body jolted harshly against the ground. Pain lashed through her and her sword went flying out of her hand.

"Now," the creature continued, its mouth contorted as if it wasn't big enough to hold all of its teeth. "Time to die."

"I don't think so." A voice suddenly came from somewhere in the distance, and the creature swung around just in time to witness the brunt of Curtis's sword crashing into its skull. Never had Emma been more pleased to see anyone in her whole life. Even if the someone did have a broken leg, a burned hand, and was wearing the dreadful white sunglasses.

"You can see it?" Emma tried to drag herself up, but her leg refused to work, so instead she crawled over to retrieve her weapon. The pain threatened to overcome her, but she bit it back. She was her mother's daughter. Pain would not defeat her.

Before Curtis could answer, the darkhel steadied itself as it reached out and slashed at him. Curtis blocked the move with his sword before sending a second thrust into the creature's shoulder. He pressed forward once again, but as he did so, the single crutch he had been leaning on fell away, and Emma gasped as the darkhel delivered a blow that sent Curtis sprawling across the ground.

Emma was still trying to drag herself into a sitting position as the creature spun toward her, its red eyes full of fire and hate.

This time there were no fancy speeches or small talk; it simply lifted its giant arm, the sinewy muscles outlined against the leather sleeve. As she tried to roll out of the darkhel's reach, she considered trying the pendant again but then remembered the nail files in her other pocket and she let her fingers curl around one of them. It felt flimsy and inadequate, but as the creature brought its hand crashing down toward her, she used all her might to thrust the file deep into the fleshy palm before quickly rolling out of the way.

The darkhel let out a howl before opening up its gigantic wings and flying up into the gray early-evening sky.

Emma blinked and for a second was tempted to check to see if someone was holding a remote control and they'd fast-forwarded through half the movie, because seriously it didn't make any sense that a simple little nail file could chase off the darkhel.

"What's happening?" Loni screamed out. "Is it still there?"

"No, it's gone," Curtis said.

Emma looked up to see him reach out for his single crutch and swing his way toward her, concern written all over his face.

"Jones, are you okay?" he asked.

"I think so," Emma said as Curtis stretched out his hand and she found herself clasping it as she struggled to her feet, her legs still wobbly. "Well, I don't think anything's broken, though it might've been different if you hadn't turned up. I'm pretty sure I wasn't winning the fight. I can't believe your Unseen glasses actually worked."

At the mention of the glasses, Curtis suddenly reached up, took them off, and shoved them into his pocket. "Yeah, lucky. The thing is—" Before he could finish the sentence, Loni and Tyler came racing over.

"Okay, so is it definitely gone? And more importantly how come Curtis could fight it?" Tyler instantly demanded.

"It's the glasses," Loni exclaimed in a fascinated voice. "Emma said that they worked after the little fairies had glamour-powdered him and they obviously worked with the darkhel as well."

"Seriously?" Tyler ran a hand through his red hair and looked perplexed. "Are you saying that if we all get some glasses like that, we can see this thing as well?"

"Actually." Curtis coughed uncomfortably. "As far as I know, this is the only pair. They were made by some German dude. I think his name is Waffle. Apparently they're a prototype. But right now the most important thing is—"

"Wenshaffle?" Loni widened her eyes. "Your glasses are made by Wenshaffle?" Suddenly realizing that everyone was looking at her blankly, she elaborated. "He's an über-designer. He mainly works with recoding existing wards so that they can monitor just how many elementals are in a given area, but he's obviously branching out into lenses. I thought it was weird that some glasses would work on glamour powder, but this explains everything." She turned to Curtis. *"May I?"*

For a moment Curtis tightened his jaw and Emma widened her eyes. There was that weird look again, but before she could nudge Loni, the look had gone and Curtis was handing the glasses over.

"Incredible. I still have no idea how he did it." Loni reverently examined the glasses, making a low whistling noise every now and then before she finally handed them back. "But the main thing is that they worked and that you could help Emma. It's amazing."

"It's not amazing," Curtis corrected in a tight voice. "It was just a fluke."

"An amazing fluke," Loni added as she looked at Curtis with interest, but instead of answering, he just shrugged and slipped the glasses back into his pocket before turning to Emma.

"So how did you manage to fight that thing? It's so freaking strong. I feel like my arm is about to fall off."

"Probably the adrenaline rush from discovering that it wanted to kill me," Emma retorted in a dry voice. "Or the fact that I'm still not any closer to knowing how to kill it. I tried the pendant and for a moment it looked scared, but then it just laughed. In fact, the only thing that worked was the nail file that I use for the regular fairies."

"Okay, are you telling me that you made it go away with a nail file?" Tyler choked in surprise. "Because even though I couldn't see the fight, it didn't seem like the type of thing that would be stopped by a wooden nail file."

"Not wood, steel," Emma corrected. "But Tyler's right. I mean, the second I stabbed it with the nail file, the darkhel disappeared faster than Garry Lewis after he blew up the science lab last year. Yet my sword's steel as well, which means they are essentially the same thing. It doesn't make sense."

"Except for the salt," Loni added, and Curtis looked confused.

"What."

"Salt," Loni repeated. "Emma read on some Web site that fairies really hate salt as well as steel."

"Loni's right," Emma said. "I rub each nail file with salt. To be honest I've never really been able to figure out if it makes a difference or not, but guessing by the fact that my nail file did what my sword couldn't, it must be true."

"Okay." Tyler composed himself. "So we don't know how to kill this creature, but a combination of salt and steel will slow it down. I guess it's a start, but we still need to figure out what it's doing here."

"Well, maybe this can help." Loni held up the leather-bound book that she was still clutching. "This is the book that Emma gave me before she fought the darkhel. It's actually written by Sir Francis and there's a whole section on our invisible friend. Which means we might be able to finally find out something about the darkhel."

CHAPTER NINETEEN

S o, what's the verdict? How are they?" Loni asked Tyler twenty minutes later as they all sat in Emma's room. She knew she should be grateful that Loni had finally agreed not to drag both her and Curtis to the infirmary, but right now all she really wanted to do was look at the book her dad had brought her. Unfortunately, Loni refused to even open it until she was sure there were no serious injuries. Tyler, who had been in charge of bandaging, looked up and nodded.

"Curtis has some bruising," he observed, "and Emma's leg will live to see another long, hot summer wearing those cutoff jeans of hers."

"In other words we're fine," Emma translated as she flexed her leg and sore wrist. "So now can you please tell us what you found out?"

"Besides the fact that for a fairy slayer you're very stubborn?" Loni arched an eyebrow before relenting and flipping open the book. Then she pointed to an ancient wood-block sketch at the bottom of the page. "So is this your guy?"

Emma and Curtis both leaned over and studied it before they nodded simultaneously.

"That's him." Emma shuddered at the blurred image, which still managed to perfectly capture the appearance of the vile creature, from the strong hooked talons to the shimmering narrow eyes. "I can't believe we've finally found a book that even mentions darkhels."

"Well, you'd better believe it," Loni assured her as she started to read the text. "'Darkhels are related to the common fairy but are taller, stronger, and filled with raging evil. Their preferred method of killing is to slash at their victims with their lethal talons, injecting them with a deadly poison.'"

Loni wrinkled her nose as she continued to scan the page. "Okay, so that doesn't make sense. It says here that when Sir Francis finally shut the Gate of Linaria, the darkhels on our side of the gate died off. Apparently the air on Earth was too wholesome for their corrupted lungs and they could only survive while the gate was open and letting through all their bad, evil air."

"Well, obviously our guy never got that memo," Emma said. "Because it was definitely alive and getting bad, evil air from somewhere." Then she froze and stared at them all. "You don't think this means that the Gate of Linaria has been opened?"

"No way." Loni instantly shook her head. "Even though the gate moves around a lot, some science guy from one of the Academies in Europe put a sensor on it so we would instantly know if the gate had been permanently opened. I read an article on how he built the sensor and it was truly remarkable the way he linked up the—"

"Er, Lon." Tyler coughed as he tapped his watch. "Not that we're not all interested in how he did it but we're up against the clock here since we still don't have any idea how a thing that shouldn't be here *is* here."

"Well, Mr. We're-Up-Against-the-Clock, I was going to add that from time to time the gate has been temporarily opened but never for more than three seconds," Loni said. "So even if Emma's darkhel did manage to temporarily open the Gate of Linaria and get out within three seconds, we still don't how it is staying alive, or—*oh*." Loni's face turned a pale shade of white as she squinted and moved the book closer to her face. Finally, she pulled it away and looked back up to them. "Well, that can't be a good thing," she mumbled.

"What?" Emma demanded. "What does it say?"

"It's talking about the kill spot," Loni said in a reluctant voice before she let out a big sigh. "Apparently it doesn't have one."

"But that's impossible." Curtis shook his head. "All elementals have a kill spot."

"Not fairies," Emma amended.

"And especially not this fairy," Loni said in a hoarse voice. "According to this, the darkhel isn't just a regular run-of-the-mill garden-variety elemental. It's the first elemental. It's also the strongest, rarest, and completely impossible to kill."

Emma felt her throat tighten as Loni handed her the book so that she could study the page. The blood pounded in her temples and her ears began to throb, and for one terrible moment she thought she was going to faint. It took all of her concentration to push the dark, tingling feeling aside. She had fought some bad elementals before, but nothing like the darkhel, *and now to find out that there was no way to kill it?*

"Okay." Tyler started to tick points off his fingers. "So the darkhel is the first of all elementals. We can't kill it and apparently it is managing to survive on Earth despite the fact that the Gate of Linaria is shut. But the one big question that we still don't know the answer to is what is it doing here?"

Curtis suddenly looked up. "Actually, yes, we do. Well, I don't know how it got out or how it's staying alive, but I do know what it's doing here. It's looking for the Pure One."

"What?" Loni and Tyler both spluttered, but Curtis ignored their disbelief.

"When Emma and I were at the mall the other day, the fairies said that the darkhel was looking for the Pure One," he explained. "And if you think about it, it makes sense. If it can find the Pure One, it can use his blood to open the Gate of Linaria and let in all the other darkhels."

"And then it can go looking for Santa Claus to get some free presents." Loni rolled her eyes. "I mean, please, the Pure One? That's crazy. It's a story. I guess I can believe that Sir Francis used five drops of blood from a nameless male child to help seal the gate shut. But the idea that the nameless male child's descendant still has some magical blood that will reopen the gate is just ridiculous. For a start, the chance of the same blood being passed down from one male to another makes it, well ... improbable. Not only does it not take into account the fact that there might not be a male heir in any given generation, but what happens to the old Pure One? Does he suddenly lose his Pure One blood once it's been passed on? I mean, as far as theories go, it's just a big old mess."

"Actually," Emma croaked as she held up her mom's book and gulped, "I think I can answer that. Listen to this: "*The spell I did to close the Gate of Linaria ensured that the sacred blood of the Pure One shall be passed from the oldest son to the oldest son. If there are no male descendants, it jumps to the oldest son of the second oldest child so that the line is always continued. As long as the Pure One's blood is safe, the Gate will stay shut.*'"

"Wow." Loni blinked. "But even if it's true that the Pure One is still around, how on earth would the darkhel find him? And more importantly what would it do *with* him?"

Emma looked grim as she once again held the book up. "I'm afraid I've got an answer for that as well. It says here that to reopen the Gate of Linaria, not only does an elemental need the blood of the Pure One, but it also needs a special spell. And, oh—"

"What?" Curtis demanded, his voice tight.

"Sir Francis might've only needed five drops of the Pure One's blood to close the gate, but according to this, the only way to open the gate is to drain the Pure One completely."

Everyone was silent for a minute before Tyler finally broke the silence.

"Okay, so not only is there some poor, unsuspecting dude walking around with Pure One blood running through his veins, but if the darkhel finds him, he will kill him and open up the Gate of Linaria."

Emma didn't want to believe it.

After all, it was bad enough that there was one impossible-to-kill invisible darkhel on the planet—the idea that it could soon be joined by all of its friends made her feel sick to the core.

"Even worse," Loni added in a subdued voice, "we have no idea how to find the Pure One and stop it from happening."

"Hang on, I need to think about this." Emma shut her eyes and rubbed the bridge of her nose for a moment before finally looking up. "Okay, so when I was fighting the darkhel before, not only did it say that I couldn't protect 'him' forever, but it also said that it knew he was close." She widened her eyes. "Which would explain why I keep seeing the darkhel here, because it—"

"Because the darkhel thinks the Pure One is here. At Burtonwood." Curtis finished her sentence, his jaw clenched and his voice soft. For a moment no one spoke as the implications of what was happening started to settle in on them just like the heavy fog was doing on the quad outside.

"Here?" Loni finally croaked, and Emma couldn't help but notice that her friend's face was ashen.

"Look," Curtis eventually coughed, "I know that before you weren't so eager to tell Principal Kessler about this, but

I really think we should. I mean, we have no idea what this thing will do to get the Pure One. Let alone how to stop it."

"Curtis is right." Loni nodded. "Last time you spoke to Principal Kessler he hadn't heard of a darkhel, and since you had no proof, there wasn't much you could do. But now not only has it attacked you twice, but we've got your mom's book and that pendant thing, which means we can show that you're not making it up. Besides, he might not have heard of the darkhel before, but every slayer knows about the Gate of Linaria and the Pure One."

"I agree," Emma said.

"You do?" Loni's jaw dropped in surprise. "But I hadn't even got to my next part, which was all about you doing your duty as a responsible slayer. I had it all planned. It was very moving."

"Sorry." Emma shot her friend a rueful grin. "But you're all right. I was so freaked out about possibly getting expelled, but right now it's not really about me. Plus, the idea of this thing hanging around Burtonwood looking for the Pure One is seriously creeping me out. *Especially since there's one other thing . . .*

"What?" Loni looked alarmed. "You *are* injured, aren't you? I knew it."

"No, it's not that." Emma quickly shook her head. "It talked about my mom again. It said that she slowed it down but didn't stop it. What does that mean?"

"Well, we know she didn't kill it, but if she slowed it down, maybe she injured it?" Tyler wondered aloud.

"But that would have been over five years ago..." Loni looked skeptical. "That must've been some injury."

"Or... what if she managed to banish it?" Curtis said in a quiet voice. "And it's only just figured a way to get back through the gate?"

"Which is all the more reason to go and see Kessler about this," Tyler said in an urgent voice. "Because seriously, this whole thing is turning into the worst homework assignment ever. Plus, I think the induction dinner started an hour ago."

"We're in the middle of an invisible-fairy crisis and all you can think about is your stomach?" Loni demanded.

"What? No. Well, yes, but what I meant is, Kessler will be at the dinner. So we go there, grab some food, and tell Kessler about it all at the same time. It's a win-win," Tyler said as he got to his feet. Then he realized that Loni was looking at him. "*What?* I'm telling you it's a good idea."

"I know." Loni reluctantly nodded. "But somehow I can't see Kessler being pleased if we all burst in wearing our uniforms."

"So what are you saying? That we need to get dressed up for this thing?" Emma looked at her friend in disgust.

"She's got a point," Tyler agreed before Emma could open her mouth. "Especially with all the parents and ex-students around. The last thing Kessler would want is us running in there and freaking everyone out. Besides, it will only take two seconds to get changed and then we can meet down at Sir Francis."

Emma reluctantly agreed and she waited until everyone had left her room before she hobbled over to her closet. She pulled out a plain black dress that Loni had helped her choose. It was made of some sort of silky stuff and had a dipped neck and jeweled belt that wrapped around her waist. It also had deep pockets buried in the skirt that she could easily slip a handful of nail files into.

She quickly shrugged it on and then grabbed some makeup to cover the worst of her cuts and bruises. She was about to leave her hair pulled back from her head, but then she caught sight of another bruise just on her collarbone and so she reluctantly pulled out her clips and let it fall down around her shoulders, before adding her mom's crystal necklace around her neck. Finally, she grabbed a small purse and slipped a dagger in it. Now she was ready.

Ten minutes later she and Loni met up with Tyler and Curtis, who were both wearing suits. Emma couldn't help but admire the way Curtis's plain charcoal jacket molded to his shoulders. He had even taken the time to run a comb through his blond curls, and they were pushed down into a semblance of order. She also noticed the way his dark eyes widened at the sight of her in a dress, and she smiled to herself. They hastily touched Sir Francis and hurried into the cafeteria.

As part of the celebration, the plain veneer tables had all been covered with white starched cloths and gleaming silver cutlery while the china was all stamped with the golden Burtonwood emblem. However, Emma was more intent on finding Kessler, so she discreetly pushed her way through the crowds of students and their parents—most of whom were alumni and tended to treat induction weekend as an informal reunion.

Unfortunately, by the time they got to the other side of the room, there was still no sign of the principal, and Emma felt a stab of panic go racing through her.

"Hey, there's Barney." Loni nudged her and they instantly made a beeline for her.

"Mrs. Barnes," Emma said without preamble. "Is Principal Kessler here? We really need to speak with him. It's sort of important."

"Sorry." Mrs. Barnes shook her head as she headed back the way Emma and the others had just come, so once again they had to battle the crowds. "He's somewhere else. On business."

"Okay, so when I say 'sort of important,' I mean it's really, really important," Emma pleaded as she trailed after the secretary and tried to ignore her aching muscles.

"And yet he's still not here."

"So, will he be back tonight?" Emma pressed.

"Emma, I really don't know," Mrs. Barnes said in a pleasant voice that was laced with steel and more effective than any sword. "But I'm sure that whatever it is can wait until tomorrow morning." Then, without another word, she was gone. Emma turned to the others and groaned.

"Well, that was next to useless. Maybe I should try calling him?" she asked in a cautious voice since her last few phone calls to the principal hadn't exactly worked out that well, but Curtis shook his head.

"Actually, I already did," he confessed as he shot her a rueful look and waved his cell phone in the air. "I didn't want you to get into any more trouble over this, so I thought it would be better if he didn't see your name and number come up on the screen."

"You did?" Emma paused for a moment, touched by his consideration, before realizing that everyone was looking at her. "Er, so what did he say?"

"He didn't." Curtis let out a reluctant sigh. "It went straight to his voice mail, so I just left him a message asking for him to call."

"Which means until we can talk to him, we're on our own," Emma said in a tight voice. "We need to figure out who the Pure One is so that we can stop the darkhel from finding him. Not to mention finding a way to banish it back to the other side of the gate."

"And what if it comes back before we figure all of that out?" Tyler looked concerned.

"Then I'll fight it." Emma shrugged. "I'll keep patrolling, and if my eye hurts or I hear a static noise, I'll know that it's close by."

"As far as plans go, that's a pretty bad one," Loni said in a stubborn voice. "You've just fought this thing and you look exhausted. You shouldn't be out there alone."

Emma knew her friend was right. Between the fight and her lack of sleep over the last couple of days she had a feeling she was starting to resemble one of the zombies that had caused so many problems earlier in the week. But she also knew that there was no way she could sleep while that thing was still out there.

"She won't be alone," Curtis cut in before turning to Loni. "Jones and I will patrol, and you and Tyler can start trying to figure out who the Pure One is and how we can stop the darkhel. Deal?"

"I guess." Loni reluctantly nodded, and Emma shot them all a grateful look.

"Thanks," she said, turning toward the exit. "But I think we'd better hurry because my gut feeling is that we don't have much time."

CHAPTER TWENTY

By eleven o'clock Emma and Curtis had been around the grounds three times and there had been no sign of the darkhel, which, Emma was forced to admit, was probably a good thing. She was still feeling pretty exhausted from her earlier fight. At least they'd slipped back to her room and changed, so she wasn't forced to patrol in a dress and heels.

She came to a halt by the same bench where Loni, Tyler, and Curtis had waited when she had talked to her dad earlier that evening. It seemed like a lifetime ago now. She sat down and her throbbing muscles instantly let out a sigh of relief.

"So are you really okay?" Curtis sat down beside her and spoke in a low voice as if not wanting to disturb the night. Above them the moon was partly obscured by clouds.

"I'm fine." She sighed. "Though I probably wouldn't have been if you hadn't come along when you did. Thanks for watching my back."

"Sure." He shrugged as he started to play with one of his crutches, which were leaning on the bench next to him, before he peered at her from underneath his blond curls. "It's been a pretty crazy day."

"Make that a crazy week," Emma corrected as she paused to rub her eye. Ever since the fight it had been itching like a demon.

"Yeah, that too," he agreed. Then he paused for a moment as if considering something before finally speaking. "So, with everything that happened, you never said how it went with your dad?"

"It was fine. I mean, Olivia insisted he bring me that book in case it was important," Emma was forced to admit.

"Which it was," he reminded her.

She folded her arms and leaned back on the bench so that she was looking up at the inky-black night sky. "I know what you're trying to do, Curtis."

"And what's that?"

"You're trying to make the point that my dad and Olivia aren't as bad as I think they are."

"And?" he prompted as he cocked an eyebrow and let a small smile hover around his mouth.

She took a deep breath. "Look, I never thought they were that bad. It's just…well…" She paused for a moment then turned to him. "It's just that it's not how I want things to be."

"I know. I'm sorry," he said in a low voice as his broad shoulder grazed hers. "It sucks when things don't turn out the way you want."

"Thanks," she mumbled, the warmth of his shoulder making her feel at ease. "And by the way, don't get all gloaty, but I did that thing you suggested. You know, the talking thing."

"With your dad?" He sounded surprised.

"Yeah, and it was...okay. He said my mom had never mentioned the darkhel, but he told me some other stuff. Just dumb family stuff. Nothing big or world changing, but it was nice to hear it all the same." Then she flushed as she realized what she was saying. She never told anyone how she felt, not even Loni, because she knew it didn't make sense. After all, her mom was dead. She wasn't coming back, but even though Emma knew that, accepting it seemed to be another thing entirely.

Suddenly, she was aware of the silence between them, and after the embarrassing misunderstanding of the tie incident, she decided that she had better stand up before she made another stupid mistake. She started to get to her feet, but before she could, she felt his fingers reach out for her hand.

"Jones..." His voice was low and raspy and sent a delicious shudder racing through her as his fingers curled possessively around hers and he pulled her back down to the bench. She looked up to see him staring right at her, and she swallowed. Last time this had happened he had fixed her tie, but tonight she didn't have her uniform on.

"Yes?" Her voice was croaky, even to her own ears, but instead of answering, he lowered his mouth to hers, and before she knew what was happening, Curtis was kissing her. The feel of his lips on hers, his skin touching hers, his fingers entwined in hers…it all made her feel something that she hadn't felt in a very long time. Happy. He deepened the kiss, and Emma felt her whole body start to tingle. However, too soon it was over, and Curtis suddenly pulled away and leaned back against the bench, shaking his head as he looked up into the night sky.

"I shouldn't have done that." He groaned, still not looking at her. "I'm sorry."

Emma felt her cheeks start to burn. She might not be an A student when it came to guys, but she was pretty sure they didn't normally apologize for kissing. And unlike the tie incident, where she had given him the benefit of the doubt, this time there was no mistaking the pained expression on his face.

"Curtis, what's going on?" she whispered.

"Nothing." He gave an angry shake of his head as he refused to meet her gaze. "Look, can we just forget it ever happened? It was nothing."

"Nothing?" Emma blinked at him, the crazy emotions of the day starting to overwhelm her, and she heard her voice start to go squeaky. "How can this be nothing? I mean, first you're all nice and try and stand up to Kessler for me and say that we're friends with the whole big because-that's-the-kind-of-slayer-I-am speech. Then you almost kissed me outside the simulation labs. And then, when I asked you to come to the practice range—which, for your information, is code for kissing—you assured me that the *only* reason you didn't come was because you didn't like fighting live elementals for your training. And now this? I don't understand."

For a moment Curtis was silent, then he rubbed his hands across his eyes. Finally, he spoke. "I know you're really pissed off at me and I don't blame you. I'm pissed off at me as well. It's just there's stuff about me that you don't know—"

"So tell me," she pleaded while trying to avoid feeling like the biggest idiot in the world. "I want to understand, Curtis. I really do. Because this thing you're doing is driving me crazy."

"This thing?"

"Yes, this thing. I mean, sometimes you're so sweet and kind to me that I could almost cry, and then other times you get this look on your face like you can't bear to be near me. Is it because I was so horrible to you about the dragon designation? Because if so, then I want you to know that—"

"Jones, please. Can we just not do this?" Curtis looked pained as he avoiding making eye contact with her. "It's just something I need to deal with on my own. You can't help me."

Emma put her hand up to her still-swollen mouth, but before she could even think of what to say, there was a noise from behind them and Loni and Tyler suddenly came bursting out of the darkness, racing toward them.

"Man, there you guys are," Loni announced. "We've been looking for you everywhere."

"What is it, did you find something?" Emma composed herself and quickly scrambled to her feet, despite her aching limbs. How could she be kissing Curtis when they were in the middle of a crisis? Not to mention the fact that Curtis had pretty much told her that the whole thing had been a big fat mistake. Then she realized that Loni was looking at her oddly. "So, what have you got?"

"Well, at first we thought it was going to be useless," Tyler admitted. "Because everything we read only talked about how great the blood of the Pure One was. That it was untainted. That it had healing properties. That some people even thought it had magical protective qualities as well."

"What?" Emma looked confused.

"I know, right," Loni cut in as she rolled her eyes. "It was starting to sound like some new health drink or something. But then Tyler had the genius idea of not looking up the Pure One himself, but rather the spell that Sir Francis cast. You know, the one where he used the Pure One's blood to seal the Gate of Linaria."

"You found the original spell?" Emma widened her eyes, and Tyler blushed in a goofy way as he pulled out some printouts.

"Sure did. Even better, this guy in Florida tried to replicate Sir Francis's ritual to see if it would work. I guess he was worried that one day we might need to close the gate again. So, apparently some of the ingredients were hard to find and he was forced to use ground horse hoof instead of unicorn hoof. Not to mention he swapped cow tongue for dragon innards, but aside from the complete gross-out factor, the important thing is he had to try it five times with different blood types before he could finally get the spell to work. Which means—"

"Which means you found out what blood type the Pure One is?" Curtis widened his eyes as he leaned forward on his crutches, though Emma couldn't help but notice that he was studiously avoiding her gaze.

"That's right," Loni continued, oblivious to Curtis's reaction. "Well, the guy who did this only managed to seal shut his closet door, which isn't quite the same as shutting the Gate of Linaria, but still, the science makes sense. Not only that but the spell also has the ritual that the darkhel will have to do if he does try to open the gate. So we're looking for a male who has B-negative blood and who has somehow been connected to Burtonwood within the last thirty-two years, since that's when your mom would've first come here. And obviously it had to be more than five years ago because... well..." Loni trailed off, obviously not wanting to remind Emma of when her mom had passed away.

Emma shot her friend a grateful look.

"So I know that sounds good in theory, but how can we find that information?" Curtis asked, still not looking at Emma. "We can't exactly go around asking for blood samples."

"We don't have to," Tyler cut in with a grin. "Because thanks to the fact that Burtonwood is über-paranoid about security, every single student and staff member has to have a full medical exam before they come here. I'm talking everyone from the cleaning staff through to Kessler. And that's not even the best part. You know that security code I gave Loni the other day to get into the system? Well, apparently it lets her in everywhere. *Including medical records*," he added.

"What? So now you're a hacker?" Emma turned to her friend and widened her eyes.

"Of course I'm not," Loni protested before letting out a rueful grin. "But I must admit that it might make a nice side hobby. Anyway, Tyler's going to get his laptop since it's got better specs than mine and then we're going to get started."

"I can't tell you what a relief this is. Finally we've got something concrete we can work on," Emma said, but Loni shook her head and firmly took her by the shoulders.

"Oh, no, not 'we.' The only concrete thing that *you* will be doing is sleeping. You're going to bed. You can help in the morning."

"What? No," Emma protested. "There's no way I will be able to sleep. Aside from figuring out who the Pure One is, we also need to find a way to banish the darkhel. I'm still convinced that my mom's necklace is somehow involved, so we can't forget about that."

"Absolutely," Loni agreed in a firm voice. "Thankfully, we can do all of these things without you. So, say good night to Curtis and Tyler, and no more arguments."

Emma, who was just about to protest, noticed that Curtis was looking relieved, as if the idea of being able to work without her in the room was actually a good thing. She felt the fight drain out of her and nodded obediently.

"Fine. But I still could've helped, you know," she said in a defeated voice as Loni steered her away from Curtis and Tyler and back toward the dorms.

"Like I said, you can help tomorrow," Loni retorted. "Besides, for all we know, your salt-and-steel thing worked and the darkhel's already dead. Maybe that's why we can't find it. I mean, just because Sir Francis said it couldn't be killed doesn't mean it's not possible to kill it."

"Maybe," Emma said, though deep down she knew it wasn't true.

"So," Loni said as they reached Emma's door. "Are you going to tell me what's going on with you and Curtis?"

"Nothing." Emma shrugged a little bit too quickly, and Loni shot her a telling glance to let her know that she was all-seeing. Emma relented. "Okay, so yes, something happened, but it's hardly important. I mean, we're in the middle of a darkhel crisis."

"It still matters," Loni insisted in a firm voice. "So spill."

Emma sighed as she turned to her friend. "We kissed and let's just say that it didn't go well," she said before amending her statement. "Okay, so it went *really* well, until Curtis suddenly started to act like he had made the biggest mistake in the world."

"Are you sure? I mean, look what happened last time," Loni said in a hopeful voice. "There was a completely logical explanation for what happened."

"Remember Tyler's face when he ate twenty hot chilies in

a row just to win a bet that he made with Gary Lewis? Well, that was nothing compared to how Curtis looked."

"Ouch." Loni winced and wrinkled her nose. "So what's his deal? I mean, it's so obvious he likes you. There must be something going on."

"Does it matter?" Emma demanded as she recalled the humiliating experience with a shudder. "It seems pretty obvious he doesn't like me. In fact, he more or less spelled it out, so why would I want to torture myself on the reasons why?"

"Yes, but—" Before Loni could finish, Emma shook her head.

"I'm serious. Besides, we shouldn't even be thinking about this stuff right now. My mom wouldn't let herself get sidetracked like this."

"I guess you're right," Loni reluctantly agreed before putting her stern face on. "But this conversation is just on hold until after we've managed to beat the darkhel, okay? And speaking of darkhels. You've fought it twice in three days and there's a good chance you might need to fight it again, which means you need your sleep. Understood?" she said in a firm voice.

"Yes." Emma gave her a halfhearted smile as she shut the door and got ready for bed.

CHAPTER TWENTY-ONE

The next morning Emma scanned the crowded cafeteria until she caught sight of Loni and Tyler in one of the booths in the far corner. The chilly November weather had settled like a polar blanket over the campus, but thanks to all the visitors, the cafeteria was packed to the rafters and the long windows were steamed up with condensation.

"So how did it go last night?" Emma demanded as she slid into the orange upholstered seat and gracefully eased the lid off the coffee cup that Loni pushed into her chilled hands.

"Well," Loni said as she stifled a yawn, "the good news is that I'm now officially a hacker."

"Are you serious? You got into the medical records?" Emma felt a wave of relief flood through her, and she reached across the table and grasped Loni and Tyler's hands so that she could give them a grateful squeeze. "That's so great. In fact, I don't know what I would've done if my two best friends weren't an electronic genius and a guy who spends far too much time betting on his five-legged cockroach."

"For a start you could stop squeezing so hard," Tyler

complained. "I've been up all night. You need to be gentle with me."

"Sorry." Emma smiled and immediately released her grip. "I'm just so relieved. So where's the list? Is there anyone on it that we know?"

"Okay, so the thing is," Loni said as she gave her own hand a shake, "while I managed to get into the system, I didn't exactly figure out how to get what we wanted right away. In fact, I sort of accidently downloaded all the medical records onto Tyler's computer."

"And printed it out," Tyler added. "I think Miss Zodiac's going to have to plant about a hundred trees to fix this little carbon-footprint disaster."

"What?" Emma felt her relief start to sink. "So we don't have a list?"

"Not yet," Loni admitted. "But don't get freaked out because I've finally figured out a way to separate the people who have B-negative blood from the rest of the list and now we're just waiting for it to download."

"And let's just say that for a state-of-the-art computer system, not only is it very hackable but it's also very slow. It might still be a few hours before the list is ready."

"Okay, so no list yet." Emma paled before shooting them a hopeful look. "I don't suppose either of you have heard if Kessler's back yet."

"Negative," Tyler said. "I spoke with Barney this morning. Well, obviously she didn't know it was me, she actually thought it was Tony Weber, a new and enthusiastic sales rep from Good Knight Swords. But I found out Kessler's still away and probably won't be back until tomorrow morning before Induction."

"Okay. So I guess all we can do is hit the books and figure out a way to banish this thing, since killing doesn't appear to be an option," Emma said as she pulled her mom's pendant out of her pocket and put it on the table, as if hoping it would give her some sort of clue about what to do.

"Actually"—Loni brightened—"last night I suddenly wondered if I could make a ward that would work on the darkhel? After all, we now know that it really hates steel and salt, and remember I used my subsonic blaster on it the first time you fought it. Well, that got me thinking—why not include a subsonic pulse as well, then we can hit it three ways."

"You can do that?" Emma shot her a blank look.

"In theory." Loni nodded, then made a face. "Of course there's the slight problem that no one has ever added a subsonic pulse to wards before but I don't see why it wouldn't work. Besides, the ward I made for ogres had some chopped-up seagull feathers, which I just slipped it into the small space below the circuit boards, and it ended up working. Now I just need to go and hunt down some steel. Preferably as high grade as possible. I've been doing some research and silver would be better."

"Definitely." Emma nodded in agreement. "Because if the little fairies are anything to go by, they hate silver even more than they hate my nail files. That bracelet you gave me for my birthday touched one of them and it dropped to the ground like a dead fly."

"Unfortunately, time and money aren't exactly on our side, so I guess steel will have to do," Loni said.

"It's a shame you couldn't just use last night's fancy cutlery," Emma said idly while she glanced over to the cutlery tray that some of the kitchen workers had carried out to a large trestle table. For a moment Loni just stared, her mouth hanging open like in the shape of a Life Saver.

"Emma Jones, you're a genius," she finally said in astonishment.

"I am?" Emma blinked.

"She is?" Tyler seconded as he wrinkled his nose. "Because I know I zoned out of a few ward-making classes, but I don't remember cutlery ever being able to fit into something that only has a one-inch diameter."

"Most wards are small so that people don't notice them and so they can be easily placed. While normally I would prefer to melt the steel or silver down and fit it into a smaller casing, there is no reason why a ward can't be made out of cutlery." Loni picked up a knife and inspected it. "I mean the two circuit boards could clip onto the blade and I could just glue some salt on. Of course I'm not saying it will win a beauty contest or anything, but as long as it does the job, that's all that matters. So now I just need to go and pocket some knives and then I can get started."

"Do you want some help?" Emma asked. "Not that I'm an expert thief or anything but I have been taking extra napkins from this place for years to help clean my sword and I've never been caught once."

"Well, that certainly is a stellar track record," Loni agreed in a diplomatic voice. "But it's probably better to try to figure out the best way to banish the darkhel. We managed to get a whole bunch of books together. In addition to your mom's books, Tyler hit up everyone on his dorm floor. We now have the definitive elemental banishing collection."

"Thank you," Emma said before glancing around. "So where are they?"

"Curtis has them. He was going to look at them last night after he left us." At the mention of his name Emma felt her stomach drop. However, Tyler seemed oblivious as he glanced around the crowded cafeteria. "Actually, he should be here by now. Do you know where he is?"

"Of course not. I mean, it's not like we're joined at the hip or anything," Emma said a bit too quickly as last night's humiliating experience came flooding back to her. Unfortunately, the memory was accompanied by a vision of the kiss that had happened right *before* the humiliating experience, and as she felt her cheeks start to burn, she scolded her mutinous mind for even thinking about it.

"Interesting." Tyler shot her a grin. Emma sighed and Tyler turned to Loni. "You know, me thinketh the lady doth protest too much. Especially since I've seen the way her eyes seem to widen when he does that lopsided grin thing. I wonder if he'll teach me that trick."

"Hello, sitting right here," Emma reminded them while resisting the urge to touch her lips and re-create the feel of Curtis's mouth on hers. "And I do not widen my eyes when he does the lopsided grin thing." Then she caught sight of Curtis swinging his way toward them on his crutches and lowered her voice. "Okay, you guys can't leave me alone with him. I mean it. Oh, and Tyler, if you say one thing in front of him, I swear on all that is holy that I will kill you. And not in a nice way either."

"What's not in a nice way?" Curtis asked with interest as Emma shot Tyler a telling glare, in response to which he pretended to zip his lips, even going as far as to throw away an invisible key. *Great, now Curtis would think they'd been talking about him.*

"Nothing," Emma quickly assured him. "So I heard you've got the books on banishment spells for me to look at."

"Yes," Curtis agreed as he patted the backpack that was slung over his shoulder with casual ease. "So should I get them out here or are we all going over to the library to look at them?"

"Actually"—Loni slid out of the booth and grabbed Tyler before he could protest—"I'm going to try and make some wards that might work against the darkhel and Tyler's going to check to see if that program's finished running yet. So it's just going to be you and Emma on study duty."

Then without another word Loni and Tyler disappeared toward the exit. Emma glared at their retreating backs before turning to Curtis and studiously ignoring his face, since she definitely didn't want to have an encore performance of last night.

"It's okay. You don't need to help. I've got it covered," Emma quickly assured him. Curtis tightened his jaw for a moment and looked frustrated.

"Of course I want to help."

"I said it's fine," she repeated in a tight voice.

"Look," he finally said. "I know you're probably pissed at me for last night, and I'm sorry. I should never have let things get that far. I screwed up."

However, Emma, through lack of sleep and stress, suddenly felt something inside her snap as the events of the last week started to catch up with her.

"Oh, right. The big secret thing that you can't tell me about." She sniffed as she grabbed her slaying kit and slid out of the booth, careful not to touch him as he moved out of her way.

"Jones—" he started to say, but Emma cut him off.

"No, you know what, Curtis? I'm sick of everyone having secrets. My mom, the darkhel, and now you? It's too much. So whatever your stupid secret is, I don't care. Keep it to yourself because I've got bigger things to worry about." Then without another word she hurried toward the exit before he could see that her cheeks were burning like they were on fire.

CHAPTER TWENTY-TWO

O f course the main problem with a big, dramatic exit was that it made things awkward if you then had to sit in the same room with the person and go through a heap of books looking for ways to banish an invisible fairy. Emma reached for another one of the books that Curtis had unceremoniously dumped into the middle of the table when they'd arrived at the library half an hour ago. As she did so, she was careful to avoid his gaze since right now talking to Curtis Green wasn't on her agenda.

The book she picked up was one that she'd collected from her own house on Wednesday night, but since then Curtis had gone through it and flagged some of its pages with miniature Post-it notes, which were now sticking out in what appeared to be some sort of color-coded order. As she flipped to the first marked page, she discovered that in his small neat handwriting, he had jotted down the pros and cons of each banishment. She turned to another page and it was the same. For some reason she found this annoying, and she reminded herself that just because someone was organized didn't make him nice.

"So, Jones, do you have the pendant?" he suddenly asked as she realized he was looming over her. It was the first time he had spoken to her since her dramatic exit. "I want to ask Gretchen if she has any information on mysterious jewelry that could banish creatures back to the other side of the Gate of Linaria."

"Oh, right." Emma slid the pendant across the table, careful not to touch his hand. He picked it up and headed off, but returned ten minutes later with a frustrated expression on his face.

"She said no. Actually she said it five times. Twice in German in case I was having difficulty understanding her the other times." He eased himself down into a chair across from where Emma was sitting and put the pendant back on the table before he picked up *One Hundred Ways to Banish Elementals Beyond the Gate of Linaria* and opened it to one of his Post-it notes. "We're just going to have to figure it out on our own."

Three hours later, Emma shut the last of the books and let out a groan. "There's nothing in any of these," she said before remembering that she still wasn't speaking to him. She determinedly looked away from him.

"What about the other book?" Curtis suddenly asked.

"What other book?" Emma demanded while staring directly ahead of her.

"The one your dad gave you last night? Loni said you took it back to your room. I was just wondering if you'd found anything useful in it."

Emma realized that she'd forgotten all about the book after she'd thrust it into her slaying kit before she headed out of her room this morning.

"Er, no, I haven't found anything yet, but let me check again," she mumbled as she fished it out of her kit, still berating herself for having forgotten it. Her fingers curled around the old leather cover before she carefully opened it up, the ancient pages crackling as she did so.

Now she remembered why she had fallen asleep last night while she had been trying to read it. The typeface was tiny and the words blurred together and she had to squint to read it. However, after suffering through the first chapter, in which Sir Francis described (in great, great detail) how he had first stumbled across the Gate of Linaria, Emma had started to feel like she was in a boring history class.

She was just about to flip to the next page when something caught her attention.

Today I can rejoice because the Gate of Linaria is finally shut. My heart aches to realize that any of these foul creatures have been allowed to pollute our Earth but at the same time I am filled with joyful relief that some of the most vile ones seem to have died off completely. For this I am grateful. One such dark beast that no longer walks on our soil is the darkhel.

I have fought only the one. The beast was surrounded by some of the smaller fairies, who, if I'm honest, are more of an annoyance than a danger. However, this hideous creature was different, and our battle was great and long. My bones ached with weariness and still I could not defeat it. Eventually I fended it off, but I fear that if I had not managed to close the gate and banish these abominations, everyone would have felt their wrath. For not only are they the strongest and most evil of all the elementals, but as far as I can tell, there is no way to kill them. . . .

She stared at the words as the bile churned in her stomach. Loni had said last night that the darkhel couldn't be killed, but Emma had secretly been hoping there might be a loophole. Unfortunately, if Sir Francis, the most powerful elemental slayer who had ever lived said it couldn't be killed, she was going to have to accept that there was no loophole.

Emma turned her attention back to the page, and her eyes widened as she realized that down at the very bottom was her mom's writing, in ink so pale that it would soon be completely gone.

Emma squinted to read the faded words and then felt a shudder go racing through her.

Darkhel says Pure One is here. No mention of banishment. Must find; must protect Pure One.

So they had been right. The darkhel was hunting for the Pure One and it was hunting for it at Burtonwood. Just like it had been doing when her mom had fought it. And she knew her mom had succeeded since the Gate of Linaria was still shut. Now all Emma had to do was figure out how her mom had done it. The answer must be somewhere in the book.

Feverishly she flipped through the delicate pages, reading her mom's entries, always in faded ink, dulled by the passage of time. Most of them concerned various ways of killing or banishing the darkhel, all of which her mom dismissed as useless. But at the end, when Sir Francis finished talking about his hopes for a future on Earth that was free of elementals now that the gate had been shut, her mom had written in bright red pen.

Finally have way. Darkhel won't win.

I know how to banish it.

Emma turned the page to find the rest of the entry— especially the part where her mom explained in full detail (with perhaps some diagrams thrown in for good measure) exactly what she had discovered. But there was nothing except three words scrawled at the bottom of the back cover: *It is done.*

How was that possible? Emma rubbed her sore eye before carefully rereading Sir Francis's text in case she had missed something that her mom had discovered, but she came up blank. For a moment she just stared at her mom's writing. *I know how to banish it.*

"This is useless." She snapped the book shut as frustration gnawed at her. "We might as well go and help Loni make wards. At least they might have a chance of working."

Curtis looked up. "Jones, it's okay, we'll find something. I've still got a whole pile here that we haven't considered yet," he said in a level voice that just made Emma more annoyed. After all, it was okay for him to blow hot and cold and look all gorgeous and make her wish that he liked her, but he wasn't the one who had just discovered that his mom was keeping secrets from them. Lifesaving, elemental-banishing secrets.

"No, Curtis, it's not okay. There's nothing in any of these books."

"Well, what about a Reversal Banishment?" He studied the heavy book in front of him before looking up at her, a hopeful expression plastered on his face.

"Sure, I'll just go and get my crushed diamonds and pint of darkhel blood and we'll get started," she snapped, her annoyance at him getting the better of her.

"Okay." The skin tightened slightly around Curtis's jawline as he turned a page. "Well, there's always the Lindal Banishment. Professor Vanderbilt swears by that one. In fact, I don't know why we didn't think of it first."

"Maybe because it's another three weeks until it's a crescent moon," Emma pointed out. "So what next, Curtis, the Death Curse?"

"Hey, I'm trying to help here, remember?" Curtis flinched as if she had just hit him. Not that she could really blame him since the Death Curse wasn't normally something that was even mentioned. It had been discovered by one of Sir Francis's students, way back when, as a way to banish creatures back beyond the Gate of Linaria. Unfortunately, it had a nasty side effect. The person who did the curse would die, which was why it wasn't exactly popular.

In fact, a few years ago there was some talk that all the Academies would remove the Death Curse from the main curriculum, but they had worried that by outlawing it, they might somehow glamorize it. *Because really, killing yourself to get rid of an elemental was so glamorous.* For whatever reason, it was still listed as a legitimate way to banish elementals, just not a frequently used one.

Emma let out a groan. "Curtis, I'm sorry. I shouldn't have said that. Just ignore me. I'm tired and stressed."

"Tired?" He suddenly looked concerned as he studied her face. "Actually, now that you mention it, you don't look like you've slept in days. Please tell me that you didn't go back out last night looking for that thing last night. Alone."

"Of course I didn't," she said, mainly because if she had found it, she doubted she would've been able to do much against it.

"So why are you so tired, then?"

"It's nothing," she started to say, but somehow, under Curtis's unrelenting gaze, she found the words tumbling out. "Okay, so I haven't been sleeping that well... I've been having dreams. About my mom. I keep asking her for help to fight the darkhel, and she keeps ignoring me." Emma paused and studied the table before she finally looked back up at him. *"Curtis, they felt so real."*

"Yeah, but the thing with dreams is they're not always literal. Sometimes they mean the exact opposite of what you think they do. Maybe your mom is trying to tell you something and you're just getting the message muddled. And the reason it seems like a nightmare is because your subconscious is trying to tell you it's important."

"You think so?" Emma chewed her lip as she considered it. Then, almost despite herself, she looked at him. "Do you ever dream of your mom?"

For a moment he was silent, then he nodded. "I used to dream she would come back and my dad would be so happy that he'd get a brain transplant. She never did, though, which just proves my theory about opposites happening. Maybe if I dreamed that she would stay away or had turned into a twenty-foot monster with razor blades for teeth, things might've worked out better."

Emma ignored his weak smile. "Was it horrible that she never came back?"

"I guess. I mean it's hard to say since I don't have anything to compare it to." Curtis started to draw invisible shapes on the tabletop with his finger. "To be honest, I'm not sure it would've really changed anything."

"I'm sorry to hear that. You deserve better," Emma said in a soft voice before the situation overcame her again. "But what if this isn't okay? What if we can't stop it?"

"We will," he said in a firm voice.

"But how do you know?" she persisted.

"I know because you deserve better as well," he said, his gaze unflinching. "You're doing a good job, you know."

She gave him a faint smile. "Really... because I sort of thought that doing a good job might feel a little better." As she spoke she lowered her chin onto the table. The wood veneer felt cool against her skin as despair washed over her like an old friend. "All I feel is sore and confused and completely unable to figure out what to do next. And I really am sorry about throwing the Death Curse in your face. You didn't deserve that."

"You're frustrated. And trust me, that's something I get all too well. So anyway, you never told me what you found in your mom's book." Curtis leaned his own head down on the table so their noses were only inches away from each other. Somewhere under the table she felt his outstretched broken leg touch hers. For a moment, Emma just stared at him, then realized he was waiting for an answer.

"Nothing of use." She sighed as she told him what her mom had written. "I mean, we know she managed to banish it, so why didn't she tell us how?"

"I don't know." He shook his head while his chin was still perched on the table, his dark eyes drilling into hers. "But we'll figure it out. Think of how much more we found out yesterday compared to the day before."

"Yes, and think of how much more we had our butts kicked yesterday than we did the day before," Emma countered, but he didn't seem to notice. Instead he reached out and lifted her hand off the table, entwining his fingers in hers, his gaze never leaving her face. A flutter of emotions went racing through her as the two of them sat there, chin to chin, eye to eye, hand to hand. For a second she longed to bottle the moment as she took in every inch of his face. His dark eyes, his strong jaw and jutting cheekbones, but then a guilty expression once again morphed across his face, which Emma felt like a slap on the cheek.

"Curtis," she forced herself to say. "What's going on?"

"Well, there's this giant fairy that only you can see," he said as he tightened his grip on her hand. "And right now we're trying to—"

"No." Emma gave a faint shake of her head, never taking her eyes off him. "I mean about this. About us? You can't be like this and then act like…well…like you did last night."

For a moment Curtis shut his eyes but his fingers tightened possessively around hers. Finally, he opened his eyes, which were now full of sincerity. "I'm sorry. I was a jerk last night. I shouldn't have kissed you, but trust me, it wasn't because I didn't want to." His beautiful mouth twitched before he leaned farther across the table so that his nose was almost touching hers. He was so close she could feel his breath on her cheek. "It's just there's something I really need to tell you. And the thing is that you're probably not going to—"

"There you guys are." Brenda Vance suddenly appeared at the door of the study room, and Emma felt Curtis's hand quickly untangle from hers as he lifted his head from the table and the moment dissolved around them.

"Um, can we help you?" Emma blinked as she tried to readjust to the world outside the space between her and Curtis. But even when the normal world came into focus, it wasn't one where Brenda belonged.

"You'd better be able to. I'm looking for Loni. We were supposed to meet half an hour ago to go over some more details on this assignment. I mean, I told her quite clearly that we should meet at eleven thirty. You know I have a good mind to go and speak to Principal Kessler about this. Why should my grades suffer just because Loni's a total slacker?"

Emma narrowed her eyes and felt her back stiffen. "Loni's not a slacker. And besides, Principal Kessler has better things to do than listen to you."

"But it's okay when you go and waste his time with invisible dragons?" Brenda retorted as she caught sight of the books stacked up on the table and wandered toward them, her curiosity obviously getting the better of her. "I didn't know the library had a copy of Chelmer's Alchemy of Demons. In fact, I distinctly remember Gretchen telling me that it's completely impossible to get. I can't believe she was holding out on me."

Emma grabbed the book out of Brenda's hand. "Yeah, well, it's from my mom's private collection, and before you ask, no, you can't borrow it." But Brenda didn't seem to hear as she put her bag down and settled herself at the table.

"Oh my God, your mom also has this?" Brenda picked up a second book and looked impressed. "I mean, I knew she was a great dragon slayer but she must've been some kind of scholar too. This stuff is hard-core."

"If you say so." Emma shrugged while still never taking her gaze off Curtis's haunted-looking face. He had been about to tell her something. Something important, and call

her crazy, but she would much rather be talking to him than
to Brenda right now. "But look, Brenda, this really isn't a
good time, so if you don't mind, we really need to—"

"Wow, and a key to a soul box. I've never seen one of these
in real life." Brenda suddenly picked up the crystal pendant
that was sitting on the table where Curtis had left it. She held
it up to the light so she could inspect it. Emma felt her mouth
drop open.

"*What* did you just say?" Curtis demanded in a low and
compelling voice.

"That I've never seen one before?" Brenda dutifully
repeated, but Curtis shook his head.

"No, the other part. What did you call it?"

"It's a key to a soul box. Well, I assume it is. I don't
recognize the language of the engravings but I'm pretty sure
that these slits are where it's supposed to fit in. *Why are you
both looking at me like that?*"

"What's a soul box?" Emma demanded.

Brenda rolled her eyes. "Well, if you guys listened more
in Professor Yemin's class, you might know." She reached
down to her backpack and pulled out a heavy book. She
opened it up and pointed to a photo of an ornate box. "Before
the Gate of Linaria was shut, some of the elementals—
mainly demons, from what I've read—that came through
couldn't survive. They were so corrupted and vile that
their bodies literally couldn't stand the purified air of Earth.
However, they discovered that if they took out the heart of

their darkness—aka their soul—they could survive, and so they created soul boxes. The elemental would come through the gate, lock their soul in the box, and would then go and cause all sorts of mayhem on Earth. Of course, once the gate was closed, the ones that were stuck here died off, and since no more could come through, soul boxes became obsolete. They're mainly considered a collectible these days. *Now, about that book of your mom's?*"

Emma turned to Curtis and stared at him as Brenda cautiously reached out and pried the textbook from her fingers.

Of course.

The answer to the conundrum of how the darkhel could survive on Earth while the Gate of Linaria was still shut. It must have taken its soul and put it in a box while it went looking for the Pure One. Finally, they were getting somewhere.

"So what does the key do?" Emma demanded.

"It opens the box." Brenda shrugged. "The demon or whatever is using it needs to keep the box somewhere near the gate. If you have the key, you can release the soul and it will go straight back to your demon. Then presto, they will be banished back to the other side of the gate."

"Banished?" Emma looked up in disappointment. "Why wouldn't they just die?"

"Because it says so in the book." Brenda held it up to them both as proof before reading out the passage. "'Once the creature's soul is returned, it is automatically banished back to beyond the gate.' See, all there in black and white."

"But what's to stop it from sticking its soul right back in the box?" Emma wrinkled her nose.

"About five dark priests and a lunar eclipse," Brenda said as she held the book out. "Apparently it's not exactly an easy—or pain-free—ritual to perform."

"Er, so how do you know the key will work?" Curtis asked, and Brenda, who realized that she wasn't going to get a chance to study the textbooks just yet, looked up and let out a resigned sigh.

"It's like a skeleton key. You have heard of one of those, haven't you?"

"Of course," Emma assured her in a tone that let her know that her sarcasm wasn't appreciated. "So you're saying that if something has come through the gate and put its soul in a box, then all we need to do is get the soul back out and restore it and it will be banished?"

"Er, yes, like I've just told you three times." Brenda looked at them like they were idiots before narrowing her eyes. "Why are you asking, anyway?"

"It's nothing. Just something extra that Curtis and I are doing." Emma gave a casual shrug.

"For the assignment?" Brenda suddenly looked concerned. "I didn't know we could do anything extra. Man, where's Loni? I really need to discuss this with her stat." Then without another word she jumped up and hurried toward the front of the library. The minute she'd gone, Emma started to scoop the books away before turning to Curtis.

"So at least we know how my mom got rid of it. I mean, it all makes sense now. She fought it, couldn't find the kill spot, so she opened up the soul box instead and banished it."

"Yes, but you're forgetting that even if the darkhel has put its soul in a box, we don't have a clue where the box would be. It will be like looking for a needle in an evil-infested haystack."

"So, what are you saying? You think we should just forget about it altogether?" Emma demanded. "And maybe while we're at it, we should go and work on our stupid assignment instead?"

"Hey, Jones, where is this coming from? I'm on your side, remember?" Curtis protested, his dark eyes clouding over. "And of course I don't think we should go and do the assignment. In fact, I'll be happy if I never see another fairy again, because—"

"That's it." Emma turned to him in excitement. "The fairies. We can go and ask them."

"Go and ask the darkhel to tell us where his soul box is?" Curtis frowned and shook his curls. "You know, I don't think he's going to tell us."

"No, I mean the little fairies. The annoying ones with too much backtalk. And as for telling us or not, well, who said I'm going to give them a choice?"

"But if what Brenda says is true, then the soul box must be somewhere nearby the Gate of Linaria and apparently that changes location all the time. It could be in Siberia for all we know."

"All the more reason for us to get going. Now come on. Let's go and see Mrs. Barnes about a pass-out so we can go to the mall. Because the sooner we talk to the fairies, the sooner this thing is over."

CHAPTER TWENTY-THREE

No, absolutely not," Mrs. Barnes said as Emma stood with Curtis in front of her desk.

"But we haven't even asked you anything yet," Emma protested as Mrs. Barnes shook her head and continued to type, her green-framed glasses perched high on her head. "Besides, this has nothing to do with Principal Kessler and trying to find out when he'll be back. All we want is a pass-out so we can do a Saturday patrol for our assignment."

"And the answer is still no. Emma, you're on detention, and also it's Induction tomorrow, which means no one is doing any patrolling. Parents don't like it when their children look all beaten up in the photos. It's bad for yearbook sales."

Emma, who was still struggling to catch her breath, just stared at her for a moment and wondered what her chances were of diving for the drawer where the passes were kept. After all, Mrs. Barnes had to be at least fifty; she'd never be able to catch them. Next to her Curtis seemed to stiffen as if reading her mind.

"Please, Mrs. Barnes, it's really important," he said in his smoothest voice before unleashing his lopsided grin and brushing his blond curls out of his eyes. "It's just that I didn't get to finish taking all my notes on this assignment the other day and it's worth twenty percent of our final grades."

"I'm sorry, but I've already told you that Principal Kessler doesn't—"

"Principal Kessler doesn't what?" Professor Vanderbilt poked his head around the corner. Normally when Principal Kessler was away, the weapons teacher was acting principal.

"Curtis and Emma want a pass-out so they can do a Saturday-afternoon patrol at the mall," Mrs. Barnes informed him in a foreboding voice. Ironic that when Emma didn't want to go to the mall with Curtis, Principal Kessler couldn't send her there fast enough. She paused and considered what would happen if she simply repeated this behavior.

"Hey, I never said I *wanted* to go," she suddenly piped up as she winked at Curtis, hoping he would realize what she was doing. "I hate fairies. They are stupid and dumb, and if you think there is any chance I'm going to show Curtis how to slay them, you're very much mistaken," she said in a firm voice while shooting Curtis a disdainful glance. "In fact, I might call Principal Kessler right now and—"

Curtis looked at her and tried to hide a smile.

"Mrs. Barnes." Professor Vanderbilt cut her off and turned to the secretary. "Give Emma Jones and Curtis Green a pass-out and make sure that the minibus takes them. They have two hours maximum." Then he turned back to Emma and folded his arms. "And no more arguments."

"Yes, Professor Vanderbilt." Emma obediently dropped her head and studied her shoes as Mrs. Barnes slowly shook her head in disagreement and pulled two passes out of her drawer. She then called the driver to arrange for him to meet Emma and Curtis at the front gates in fifteen minutes.

"So?" Loni was waiting for them in the quad, as arranged. Emma had sent her friend a text the minute she and Curtis had left the library to let her know what Brenda had unwittingly told them about the soul box. "Did you get them? Tyler tried to bet that you wouldn't."

"Oh really. Well, I hope you got good odds on it," Emma said as she pulled out the pass-outs and grinned. "So how did you guys do? Did the computer program narrow down the list?"

"Not yet," Tyler said. "I'm pretty sure that the dinosaurs became extinct quicker than this thing is taking to download. But hey, hopefully by the time you come back here, the darkhel will be banished and we'll just be able to use the extra paper to make airplanes to throw at Brenda when she tries to make an induction speech tomorrow."

"Not that I don't have complete faith in us, but I really don't think we should be doing the chicken-counting thing just yet," Emma said before glancing at her watch. "Anyway, we only have two hours before we've got to be back, so we'd better hurry."

✳✳✳

"So where do you find fairies at two o'clock on a Saturday afternoon?" Curtis asked after the minibus dropped them off at the mall and the driver made arrangements to pick them up at four o'clock.

"They'll be at the movie theater. Let's see. What's playing?" Emma rubbed her chin as she studied the list of movies that were showing before finally settling on the new James Bond flick.

The movie had already started, so it was dark as they made their way down the aisle of the half-empty theater. A couple of heads turned around and scowled at the sound of Curtis's crutches. At that moment Emma's phone started to beep and there were a few more angry hisses. Not exactly the stealthy approach she had been hoping for.

Emma paused for a moment to check the cell-phone screen. An e-mail from Nurse Reynes wanting to know why Emma hadn't called to arrange a new appointment. *Because she wasn't a masochist.* Delete. The second was from her dad, wanting to make sure everything was okay. *Oh yeah, never been better.* Except for killer invisible fairies and soul boxes and having to talk to annoying ten-inch fairies in the middle of a movie theater. She switched off her phone and scanned the theater; it took a while but she finally saw about eight fairies right up in front, sharing a giant Diet Coke.

"Gouge out his eyes," yelled Rupert, who was wearing a tiny David Bowie T-shirt and some skinny-legged emo jeans. "That's right, James, you're a tough guy, show them who's the man...hey, these seats are...*oh, it's you.*" He folded his tiny arms and glared at Emma. "Are you here to violate my other wing?"

"Not if you tell me what I need to know," Emma whispered as she sat down next to him and held the nail file up to his little neck. The other fairies started to head for the ceiling just as Curtis appeared, also holding a nail file in his hand, the ugly white glasses sitting on the bridge of his nose in case the fairies hit him with more glamour powder.

"Not so fast." He grinned and Trevor and Gilbert muttered a string of expletives before joining their fellow fairy on the seat. Curtis put down his crutches and settled into the chair on the other side of them, nail file still at the ready.

"What do you want?" a sulky Gilbert demanded. "Because whatever it is, make it snappy. We've had a very bad week and we've been looking forward to this movie for a long time."

"*You've* had a bad week?" Emma dug the nail file into Rupert's jugular and felt her voice raise an octave. "I'm sorry, but I don't think I heard you right, because how could your week possibly have been worse than mine?"

"Keep it down," someone from behind them yelled out, but Emma ignored them.

"So here's the deal," Emma started. "I want to know everything about this darkhel and please don't leave out the important stuff. *Like where it keeps its soul box.*"

"Like we're really going to tell you that." Trevor lifted up his tiny chin in a stubborn gesture as he elevated several inches off the chair. "What do you think we are? Stupid?"

"Curtis. Get the Skittles for Stupid and his friends." While Emma was gathering the nail files, Curtis had been in charge of getting ten bags of candy. She was going to feed the little beasts so full of sugar that they would sing like hyperactive canaries.

Curtis pulled out a packet and handed it over.

"I don't believe it. *They're trying to kill us.*" Gilbert suddenly burst into noisy sobs and Emma stared at him. "It's just too much."

"I warned you that he was a worrier. *Now look what you've done.*" Trevor shot both Emma and Curtis a venomous look before returning his attention to the other fairy. "Hey, don't let the emotions of the week get to you. Especially not in front of *humans.*"

"Um, I'm sorry, but am I missing something here?" Emma demanded as she opened up the packet with her teeth and held it out to the fairies. "Because while it's great to see you three so caring and sharing, we're on a bit of a timetable, so just take your Skittles and tell me about the soul box."

The three fairies shrank away from the packet.

Emma blinked before narrowing her eyes at them. "What? You don't like Skittles now? Let me guess, after lunch you prefer Tic Tacs?"

"Hey, if you're trying to throw doubt on our Skittle-eating ability, you can forget it. We can eat those perfect little circles of candy goodness twenty-four/seven. But those... abominations... that you're trying to give us are not real Skittles."

"Huh?" Curtis lifted up the packet. "Yes, they are. They're

just sour ones." At the very mention of the word "sour" the fairies shrank even farther back.

"They hate Sour Skittles," Emma hissed in a low voice.

"You're seriously not going to eat those just because they're sour?" Curtis demanded. "It was all they had left in the store."

"We would never eat those poison things in a million years. Veronica merely sniffed one once and she was dead before she knew it. I tell you, that candy is the work of the devil," Gilbert informed them. "Besides, if you wanted help with the soul box you just had to ask, you didn't need to threaten us."

"Gilbert—" Rupert started to say, but he was cut off by Trevor, who performed an aerial somersault before hovering in front of the other fairy.

"Rupert, we talked about this, remember? We decided."

"Fine." Rupert still didn't look very happy as he settled back into the seat and pushed out his lower lip in a sulky pout. "But I'm not going to be the one to tell them."

"Tell us what?" Emma turned to Curtis to see if he was following what was going on, but he looked equally baffled.

"Tell you where the soul box is," Trevor explained while he ignored the daggers that Rupert seemed to be mentally throwing at him. "We want to help you."

"Okay, so now I'm really confused." Curtis lifted up his glasses for a second and rubbed his eyes before lowering them back down onto his nose. "I mean, don't get me wrong:

we want you to help us, but we didn't think that you would roll over quite so easily. What's going on?"

The small fairies exchanged a look, and then Gilbert fluttered up so he was right in front of their faces.

"Look, here's the deal," the fairy said. "When we first heard our dark brother was going to attempt to open the gate again, we were pretty excited. I mean, it's always nice to see family, but then he told us how much they were looking forward to destroying the whole world and turning it into another dark realm, and, well... the truth is that we like it here. To begin with, the mall is the best invention in the world except for the Internet. And I just don't think it would as much fun if we couldn't go to Starbucks or read pinkisthenewblog every day online."

Emma shook her head. "You know, you three are the worst evil fairies in the world."

"*See, I told you this would happen.*" Rupert glared at his fellow fairies before narrowing his tiny eyes and staring at Emma and Curtis. "And for the record, just because we're helping you doesn't mean we like you guys. We're still hard-core bad."

"You'd rather read gossip blogs and watch movies," Curtis pointed out, causing Rupert to sigh.

"Okay, fine. The truth is that we're just regular, extremely stylish, paranormal beings, but if you two know what's good for you, you'll keep it to yourself," Rupert conceded.

"Now," Trevor said as he nodded toward the other fairies,

who were still hovering by the ceiling, looking down on them all with interest. "If you want the three of us to help you, we need to make it look like you are forcing us against our will because if word gets out that we helped you guys . . . well, let's just say that things might not be so pleasant."

"Fine." Emma rose to her feet and held the nail file up before saying in a loud voice so that the other fairies who were looking on from up by the ceiling could hear her. "Okay, try anything funny and it's a long slow death."

"Nice." Rupert nodded in approval and pretended to shudder in fear while Curtis retrieved his crutches. "Now go to the escalators and head down to the food court."

"The food court?" Emma blinked in surprise. "That's where I followed you on Saturday and almost got blown up. *What's going on?*"

"This is the person who is going to save us from our dark brother?" Trevor didn't look impressed as he flew around in spirals. "Because I don't mean to be negative but I think we might be in trouble."

"Just answer the question," Emma retorted as she waved the nail file at him.

"I thought you would've figured it out by now," Gilbert said in a low voice as he checked to see if the other fairies were following. They weren't.

"Figured out what?" Emma asked as they crossed the faux-marble floor of the food court and tried to ignore the competing smells of burgers and fried chicken.

"That the explosion was caused by our dark brother breaking through from the Gate of Linaria. The first time he got through, it was thanks to an earthquake that managed to jolt the gate open, but this time apparently he had a hundred warlocks conjure up a spell to let him come back through. It took years—not to mention a lot of dieting, since the gate is only open for three seconds and let's just say that our dark brothers aren't always the slimmest of creatures. Comes from all the bones they insist on eating."

Emma stopped and stared at them in horror as Curtis narrowed his eyes at the fairies.

"Are you seriously trying to tell me that the Gate of Linaria is down at the food court?" he asked.

"Well, yeah. I mean it moves around a lot but right now that's where it is. Anyway, you're here now, so our job is done."

"Hang on, we still don't know what the soul box looks like," Curtis said. "Or if it's even there."

"Just wave the key in the air and it will appear. It's not usually visible to the human eye but the key will reveal it. You do have a key, don't you?"

"Yes, we have the key," Emma confirmed, still trying to get her mind around the fact that they were about to go and see the Gate of Linaria.

"Good. Oh, and there's one more thing. Once you release the darkhel's soul, it will still take another twenty-four hours before he's banished back to the other side of the gate."

"What?" Curtis didn't look impressed. "Who makes up

these ridiculous rules? Why won't it just be banished right away?"

"Okay, do you really want a lecture on elemental banishing or do you just want to accept that what I'm telling you is true?" Gilbert had lost his worried look as he fluttered his wings in an annoyed fashion and folded his tiny arms in front of him. "Because if you want a lecture, I can give you a lecture."

"We don't want the lecture." Emma quickly put up her hands to stop him from talking any more than was strictly necessary. "Besides, we've already fought this creature twice. I'm sure we can contain it for one more day," she said, but the fairy made a clicking noise with his tongue.

"Slayer-girl," Gilbert said with dead seriousness, "what you fought was a shadow. A creature that was only at half strength. When his soul returns, he'll be like nothing you've ever fought before. Besides, before he couldn't fight for very long without having to go off and restore his power, but now, let's just say that having his soul back is like giving him a turbo-powered booster to work with."

Emma felt her eyes widen. "Please tell me that you're joking."

Rupert and Trevor shook their heads. "Gilbert is a darkhel expert. If he is says our dark brother will come back stronger once it regains its soul, then that's what will happen."

"It's true," Gilbert acknowledged, puffing out his chest.

Emma tried to contain her panic. Her two meetings with the giant fairy had been the toughest fights of her life, and the thought of having to face it again, when it was supersized with soul-induced über-powers, was hardly something to look forward to. Especially since the creature couldn't be killed.

However, if the darkhel did manage to find the Pure One in the next twenty-four hours, then it would create a future that wasn't even worth thinking about, and so she bit back her fear as she and Curtis walked toward the Chinese-food counter, which, since the explosion, was covered in heavy black plastic to hide it from the rest of the food court.

Besides, the darkhel would only be at its full strength for a day. What was some lost sleep and potential fighting compared to saving the world from being overrun by elemental fairies?

"So can we go now?" Trevor wanted to know as he pretended to skateboard across the air.

"Not yet," Emma suddenly said. "We have a few more questions. Do you know who the Pure One is? Does the darkhel know? It's just that if the creature's going to be superstrong for the next twenty-four hours, knowing who the Pure One was would make our job so much easier."

"Sorry." Gilbert shook his head. "Pure Ones don't tend to come well labeled. Our dark brother has spent most of his time on the other side of the gate researching who it is and now I guess he's just working through a list. Anyway, can we go now? We're missing our movie."

"Fine, go. But seriously, once this is over, if I catch you guys trying to help any more evil elementals sneak into this world through the Gate of Linaria, then so help me, I really will slay you."

The fairies laughed. "I love how you can keep a sense of humor even when you're in the middle of a crisis," Trevor observed as he abandoned his imaginary air skateboard in favor of doing a somersault and flipping Emma the bird. Then, without another word, the three fairies disappeared back in the direction of the movie theater.

"Okay, so it's not just me, but they're weird, right?" Curtis double-checked, and Emma nodded.

"Oh yeah. They're weird. But at least they helped us find the soul box. So let's go and do this thing. The sooner we find it, the sooner it will all be over."

"You know I still can't believe the Gate of Linaria is behind a place called Hong Kong Wong," Curtis admitted. "I thought it would be somewhere more . . . upscale."

"And not smell of stale cooking oil," Emma added as Curtis pulled back a heavy sheet of builders' plastic that concealed the burned-out kitchen. Then she noticed he was still wearing his glasses. "By the way, I don't think you'll be needing those in here. It's a glamour-powder-free kitchen."

"Oh, um, right," he said uncomfortably. He flushed, hesitated for a moment, then with obvious reluctance took off the glasses and put them in his pocket. "I guess I won't."

For a moment Emma stared at him, not quite sure what his problem was, but then she remembered they had a job to do. She stepped over a huge pile of chopsticks scattered on the floor. She'd secretly worried that the place might be full of repairmen, but fortunately the damaged kitchen was empty of anything other than the charcoaled remains.

"Wow, that must've been some explosion." Curtis whistled as he leaned forward on his crutches and surveyed the damage.

"Yeah," Emma agreed as she walked over to one of the stainless-steel benches and put down her kit. "Talk about being in the wrong place at the wrong time."

"Or the right place at the right time. I wonder if the reason you can see the darkhel is because you were here when it came through the gate," Curtis wondered aloud. He almost sounded wistful as Emma pulled the pendant out of her pocket.

"I have no idea." She headed to the far end of the kitchen and systematically started to wave it in the air. "But right now, I guess that's the least of our problems. Just yell out if you can see anything."

Curtis paused before finally nodding. "Of course." He started to glance around. "So what happened here last Saturday?"

Emma, who was just in the process of waving the pendant in the burned-out microwave, pointed over to the far wall. "Well, there were about ten fairies all hovering over there, and as I reached into my kit to get my weapon there was an explosion from over by the freezer," she said as she continued to wave the pendant in the air, desperately searching for anything that might be a soul box.

Curtis headed over to the burned-out freezer and studied it. "Ah, yes. You can see that the door has been blown out, so it must be in here." He pointed.

"Very *CSI*," Emma said, smiling slightly as she stepped past him into the freezer. Despite its being out of order, it was still chillier inside the giant appliance, and she hugged herself as she stepped over a large bag of soggy bean sprouts and went in.

She held the pendant above her head and immediately sucked in a breath.

There, where the back of the freezer wall should've been, was now a great black swirling vortex of nothingness. For a moment Emma just stood transfixed, unable to look away from the hideous whirlpool of pulsing black space that silently flashed and flickered.

Her mouth felt dry and her eye throbbed as she forced herself to look away.

So it was true.

This was the Gate of Linaria.

"Are you okay?" Curtis was suddenly at her side with the stealthlike ability that she had come to associate with him, despite the crutches he was still using.

"I'm fine. Just a little freaked out. I mean, we're sophomores at Burtonwood, and you don't exactly expect to come face-to-face with the Gate of Linaria."

"I know," he agreed in a solemn voice. "Though I've started to discover that the more time I spend with you, the more I expect weird things to happen."

"Thanks...I think," Emma said as she reluctantly stepped away from him and held the pendant up again, still looking for the soul box. It didn't seem to be there and she was just about to head back out to the kitchen again when she realized that Curtis was heading in the other direction, straight toward the far wall, as if the whole swirling black void of nothingness wasn't even there.

"Curtis, what are you doing?"

"What do you mean?" He took another step forward and Emma screamed as the void suddenly burst open and hundreds of tendrils of smoke began to slowly reach out and snake and coil their way around his plaster cast like ivy up a wall. Emma rushed toward him and grabbed his arm.

Whatever the smoky vines were, they were strong, and as she tried to pull him away, they continued to writhe and wind their way up his leg. Emma felt herself straining with the effort of fighting the void. But finally, the resistance disappeared and they went tumbling back onto the freezer's floor. Emma groaned on impact and rolled to the side to see if Curtis was okay. His face was leached of color, his brown eyes filled with confusion.

"Jeez, are you okay? What just happened?" she demanded.

"I'm not sure." He rubbed his eyes and pulled himself into a sitting position. "One minute I was just walking, and the next minute, I felt...I felt like I had just stepped into hell."

"That's because you did step into hell." Emma stared at him, still not quite sure what was going on. "You didn't see it?"

"See what?" His gorgeous face was etched with alarm. "Jones, what are you talking about?"

"The Gate of Linaria. The evil fingers of death that were trying to grab you and pull you in. How could you not see it?" For a moment Emma just stared at him before she felt a stab of panic go racing through her.

Curtis didn't answer. Instead he pulled the ugly white sunglasses back onto the bridge of his nose and peered over to the far wall. Then, as if he were seeing the gate for the very first time, his face paled and his jaw clenched.

"Seriously, you're acting very weird." Emma tried to study his face. "Why did you put your glasses back on? I don't understand."

For a moment Curtis was silent; then he pushed the glasses back onto his head and let out a sigh. "You're so smart. I'm surprised you didn't figure it out already," he said, his voice dull and laced with bitterness.

"Figure what out?" she asked, confused.

"That I'm sight-blind."

CHAPTER TWENTY-FOUR

hat?" Emma stared at him blankly, waiting for the
punch line, but when it didn't come she folded her
arms. "Come on, Curtis, stop messing with me and tell me
what's really going on."

He didn't look at her as he stated matter-of-factly, "I'm
serious. I'm sight-blind. Plain and simple. Without these
glasses I can't see a thing."

Emma shook her head in confusion. "No," she insisted
as she scrambled to her feet and watched him awkwardly
get up and retrieve his crutches. "Those glasses were only
to help you see Unseen dragons. And fairies. You told me
yourself."

He shrugged. "I lied to you. Yes, with them I can see
dragons—and fairies. But without them, I can't see anything."

"I don't understand. You go to Burtonwood Academy.
It's sort of required to be able to know when there are
paranormal creatures around."

"Oh, I know when they're around. I can hear them. Smell them. Feel when they're in the room. I can even fight them. Only problem is, I can't see them." As he spoke, his face was a mask that Emma found impossible to read. There was no easy smile, no chocolate eyes. Just planes and angles and grimness.

"So how did you even get into Burtonwood in the first place?"

Curtis sighed. "I told you that my dad isn't really a fan. Well, this one time I could feel that there was something at the beach. I mean, something really bad, so I tried to tell him not to let my younger brother go surfing. I begged and begged but my dad thought I was just being obnoxious. So he grounded me and let my brother go with his friends to the beach."

Emma gasped. "An aquafile?" she asked, since that was the most common kraken that hunted surfers.

"Yeah, I later figured out it must've been." His voice was almost devoid of emotion.

"So what happened?" She felt the color drain from her face while hardly daring to listen to the answer.

"I climbed out my bedroom window and rode my bike there, but by the time I arrived it was too late and my brother and two other kids were being dragged under the waves having the life sucked out of them. I couldn't see it but I just knew the aquafile was there and so I grabbed the scissors that I'd brought with me and jumped into the water. The thing was so bloated from what it had just done that I guess I got lucky and managed to strike a killing blow because suddenly the sense of evil I could feel was gone. I dragged the bodies onto the beach but it was too late."

"Curtis," Emma whispered as she instinctively reached out and gently touched his hand. "I had no idea. So is that when you decided to come to Burtonwood?"

He shook his head. "I'd never even heard of Burtonwood but the local newspaper ran a story about how I'd valiantly tried to save three kids from drowning and I guess it blipped on Kessler's radar as a possible aquafile attack. Anyway, next thing I knew, he came to visit, and after testing me, he offered me a scholarship. I was ten, so at the time he was confident that my sight would come through, but of course I didn't really care, I just wanted to get away from my old man."

"But your sight never did come through." All Emma could do was shake her head in disbelief as she realized just how different their childhoods had been.

"Nope, and with Induction looming, Kessler was in a bind. He said in every other respect I was the perfect slayer and he didn't want to lose me. Which is where the glasses came in. We tested them on everything but they only seemed to work on dragons—"

"And fairies," Emma pointed out.

"Yeah, though we didn't know it at the time. Anyway, it was because of the glasses that Kessler gave me your dragon designation," Curtis finished off in a soft voice as the truth started to really sink into Emma's brain. "I should've just said no. I mean, everyone at Burtonwood knew what it meant to you, but I couldn't bear the idea of going home. Of being helpless to fight elementals. I'm sorry, Jones. I should've told you sooner. I've been trying to; it's just . . . well . . . not easy to admit that you're a freak."

She stared at Curtis as he looked down and kicked the ground in embarrassment. She had been right all along.

He did have a secret.

It just wasn't exactly what she had envisioned.

She had been thinking it was because he was embarrassed to be seen with a fairy slayer or that he didn't like her, but in fact it was about as far from what she had thought as possible.

"If you hate me, I understand. I mean, it's my fault you lost your dragon spot. Not to mention the lying and the general ruining-your-life thing." Curtis still didn't look at her. For a moment Emma closed her eyes and thought of her mom and how she had longed to follow in her footsteps before finally she looked up at him and forced him to return her gaze.

"Okay, so we can just clear a few things up. The whole almost-kissing-me-and-then-fixing-my-tie thing?"

"Not one of my finest moments." Curtis flushed. "Of course I wanted to kiss you but then it occurred to me that I would be doing so under false pretenses."

"And that's why you didn't want to come down to the practice range with me?" She knew the answer but had to double-check.

"Actually, that was because I didn't want you to find out

that I couldn't see elementals. It's all been a lie." He clenched his jaw and made a hissing noise under his breath. "I screwed everything up. I wish I could fix it but it's probably too late. I'm sorry."

Emma stared at him as she let the truth wash over her.

Curtis Green was sight-blind and the guilt had been eating away at him. Well, she had not seen this one coming. Finally, he coughed.

"Okay, so you're not talking, which usually means bad things, so I'm just going to leave—"

"Wait." She blinked as she stretched out her hand to him and he looked at it, as if not quite sure if she was going to touch him or hit him. "As much as it hurts to admit, you're not the reason I lost my spot. I've seen you fight and you have everything it takes to make an amazing dragon slayer. Plus, as Loni has been trying to remind me for the last six weeks, I was the one who tested positive for fairies."

For the first time since he had accidently almost walked through the Gate of Linaria, Curtis lost the haunted expression and was just looking confused. "Er, I'm not sure you understand what I've just told you."

"I understand," she assured him.

He continued to study her face before blinking. "The thing is I hadn't really expected our conversation to go quite this way. I had pictured a lot more yelling and maybe a few I-wouldn't-go-near-you-if-you-were-the-last-guy-on-earth kind of stuff."

"You must be mistaking me with some other hotheaded

Aries who wanted to be a dragon slayer and might've mentioned her eternal hatred for the guy who got her spot," Emma mumbled as she thought of some of her previous behavior.

"Trust me, I could never mistake you for anyone else." A small smile hovered on his lips. Then, before she could even begin to allow his words sink in, Curtis let his crutches fall with a clatter to the ground and closed the distance between them. "And now there's something I've wanted to do for a while... *Emma*."

"There is?" she croaked as she realized he had just called her by her first name. She watched in mute fascination as he tilted his head and his perfectly formed lips came crashing down on hers in a way that she had never dreamed possible. The sensation was instant as she felt herself being engulfed by his broad shoulders while her senses were filled with the smell of vanilla cookies.

His arms snaked around her back and his mouth explored hers. Emma pressed into him and felt her whole body start to tingle with the rightness of it all. It was perfect. Curtis was perfect. He was... *wait, why was he pulling away... and why wasn't he kissing her anymore?*

"Is everything okay?" she asked in a cautious voice. "You're not going to have another freak-out, are you?"

"There's something I think you should see." He gently steered her around so that she was facing the same way he was, his arms still protectively wrapped around her shoulders, as if he was afraid that she would disappear on him.

"What are you—"

But the rest of her words were lost as there, hovering in the air, just behind where she was standing, was an elaborately decorated container about the size of a backpack. The wood was so dark it looked almost black, while deep red gems were studded in the lid and glistened around it like some sort of blood-soaked halo. For an inanimate object it seemed to radiate a lot of evil. Like darkhel, like soul box, she supposed, while not finding the thought remotely comforting.

"You found it," she croaked. "You really found it."

"We found it," he corrected as he stepped back and watched Emma fish the pendant out of the pocket of her shirt. The large circle in the middle of the box was a mirror image of the crystal. "So go on," he encouraged, and Emma felt her hands start to shake.

Is this what her mom had done when she had banished the darkhel?

The idea of Curtis and her repeating history gave her a small thrill. Of course it wasn't the same as being a dragon slayer, but at least she was following in her mother's footsteps in some small way. Even if it had taken Emma four days and a bunch of friends to inadvertently figure out.

She took a deep breath and slipped the pendant into the front of the box. It was a perfect fit and she watched as the top opened up like a flower and a dark wisp of smoke curled out. For a moment it hovered over her head before it formed into a small, tight ball and then it went speeding out of the freezer and off into the food court.

A second later the box itself disappeared and the crystal pendant fell to the floor with a clatter. She bent and picked it up before turning back to Curtis, slipping her hand into his and shooting him a shy smile. He squeezed her hand and gave her a dazzling smile that made her feel short of breath.

There. It was done. The darkhel's soul had been returned, and in twenty-four hours the vile creature would be banished back to the other side of the gate, where it belonged.

Emma just hoped that things didn't get worse before they got better.

CHAPTER TWENTY-FIVE

I still can't believe you did it," Loni said as they sat in Emma's dorm room carefully activating the dozens of tiny wards that Loni had attached to the silver knives and carefully coated in salt, while they waited for Tyler and Curtis to come back with some food and the list of potential Pure Ones.

"I know, it's crazy, isn't it?" Emma agreed as she used her screwdriver to flip the switch in the ward before adding it to the growing pile. "I mean we actually banished the darkhel. Well, almost banished it," she corrected while desperately trying to ignore the irony of finding herself in the position of longing for rather than dreading tomorrow's induction ceremony. Even though she wouldn't be made a dragon slayer, she would at least know that the darkhel was gone.

"Yeah, that's great too but I'm actually talking about you and Curtis," Loni said in a mild voice before she put down the ward she had been working on and grinned. "So seriously, I want all the details."

"What?" Emma felt her cheeks start to heat up. "I don't

know what you're talking about. I mean, we're in the middle of a crisis here and I'm not sure that talking about boys is really appropriate."

"Well, that's where you're wrong," Loni retorted. "Not only is the crisis nearly averted but more importantly you two came back from the mall glowing like you'd been dipped in neon paint and then plugged into a power station. So I want details and I want them now. Was there kissing?"

Emma felt a tingle go through her as she nodded and smiled. "Yes, there was kissing. And even some talking. So do you really want to know what happened?"

"Do ogres like eating the eyeballs of their victims? Of course I do." Loni eagerly leaned forward. It didn't take Emma too long to fill her friend in on everything, though she didn't feel it was her place to mention Curtis's secret.

"Well, if I've said it once to Tyler, I've said it a hundred times. You and Curtis are perfect for each other." Loni let out a dreamy sigh when Emma had finished. "And not just because of the star-sign thing, but just because it makes so much sense. *Oh, and it also means that Tyler owes me a hundred bucks.*"

"You put a bet on me?" Emma demanded.

"No," Loni quickly said, then relented. "*Well, yes.* But only because I'm a hopeless romantic. Plus Tyler, cynic that he is, gave me really great odds. Are you mad?"

"No, I'm not mad," Emma assured her. "Especially since I know how much you wanted to get those jeans you saw at the mall the other day, so I guess your ill-gotten gains will help pay for them. But, Lon, if you don't mind, don't say anything about it just yet. It's just that until we know for sure that the darkhel is banished, I can't help but feel uneasy. Like my stomach is all twisted in knots, you know?"

"I know." Loni nodded just as there was a knock on the door and Tyler and Curtis appeared with a tray of burgers and a piece of paper.

"Well, ladies, I hope those wards are done because we come bearing food," Tyler announced with a flourish.

"Great." Loni reached for a burger. "But of course you know that if you ever call us ladies again, you will have to be disposed of in a most despicable manner."

"I did figure it was a long shot," Tyler admitted as he sat down on the corner of Emma's bed and waved a piece of paper in the air. "Anyway, I also have a list. There are thirty-five males who are in the system as having B-negative blood."

"Thirty-five?" Emma wasn't a math genius but even she knew that she and Curtis would be stretched trying to keep an eye on them all until tomorrow when the darkhel was banished for good.

She ignored the food and immediately grabbed the paper and started to study the names of the people who were unlucky enough to have the wrong blood. Curtis leaned his crutches against the wall and limped over to join her. Being so close to him made her skin tingle and she shot him a shy smile.

"Hey," she said.

"Hey," he replied in a murmur as he leaned over her

shoulder and studied the list she was holding, his breath tickling her neck. "So who do we have here?"

"Too many people," Emma retorted while only just resisting the urge to lean back into his chest. "Oh, but we can take Professor Luton off the list because he died the Christmas before last," she said as she started to look through the names. "And didn't James Anderson move to England six months ago to work in the London office of the Department? The darkhel definitely said that the Pure One was close by."

"Well, that's two less people to worry about," Curtis said as he drew two neat lines through the names and Loni and Tyler joined them to examine the list. "And that means we need to go through this list and take off anyone who isn't at Burtonwood anymore or who wasn't here at least five years ago."

"I see Chris Tripper," Tyler said as he joined them. "And I'm sure he's salamander slaying in Australia right. Seriously, you should see the size of them. I think it's the heat but they're twice as large as the North American salamanders."

"Okay, he's gone too," Curtis said as they went through the list one by one. Then he frowned and turned to Emma. "William Jones? Emma, what's your dad's name doing on the list?"

"Is it?" Tyler looked alarmed, but Emma just shook her head.

"He used to do some contract work for the IT department but he gave up the contract when my mom died. I guess that's why he got included." She shrugged. Tyler obviously hadn't been joking about how thorough Burtonwood was with physicals.

"Aren't you worried?" Loni looked at her.

"Of course not. Besides, he's in New York. The darkhel could never get him. You can take him and Ryan Gibson, his business partner, off the list. Now, who is...*oh my God. I can't believe this*." Emma suddenly yelped as she caught sight of two names farther down the page. Then she let out a groan as she realized how obvious it was. How could she have not figured it out sooner?

"Emma? What's wrong?" Loni demanded as she started to glance around the room. "The darkhel isn't here, is it?"

"What?" Emma looked at Loni blankly for a moment before suddenly shaking her head. "Oh, no, I'm sorry, I didn't mean to scare you, it's just I've figured out who the Pure One is."

"Who?" Loni, Tyler, and Curtis all asked at once.

"Well," she amended. "I should say that I've narrowed it down to two people. It's either Garry or Glen Lewis. It's just so obvious."

"It is?" Tyler looked at her blankly. "What makes them more likely than anyone else on this list?"

"The fact that when I saw the darkhel on Friday afternoon on the playing fields, it was heading directly to where Glen and Garry were playing Frisbee. Anyway, the darkhel was really pissed at me for getting in the way. It even said that I couldn't protect 'him' forever. Don't you see? It could tell the

Pure One was close by, but I stopped it from getting to him."

"Who stopped it?" Tyler coughed.

"Okay, fine, it was Tyler and his completely brilliant bet that saved either Garry or Glen from having their throat slit and their blood dripped over the Gate of Linaria in a grizzly ritual. Happy?" Emma corrected.

Tyler grinned and nodded. "Very, and can I just say that you have a very nice way with words. And you know, it does make sense. The Lewis twins have been at Burtonwood for seven years, so that fits in with when Emma's mom was still alive."

"But what if you're wrong?" Curtis didn't look convinced. "If we do a twenty-four-hour bodyguard on Garry and Glen, then we're leaving a lot of other people unprotected."

"Actually, not that many," Loni said as she looked up from Emma's laptop, where she had been Googling. "I've got four more deaths, five relocations, and three other people who I've never heard of, which leaves us with eighteen possibilities besides the Lewis twins. Ten students, seven teachers, and one support staff."

"So we protect them all but we keep an extra eye on Garry and Glen as well," Tyler reasoned.

"Yes, but how?" Curtis tightened his jaw.

"Don't forget that we've got wards up," Loni reminded them. "So there's a good chance that we won't even be seeing Mr. Ultimate Elemental Evil again. But as an extra precaution, I do happen to have these as well. Ta-da."

"Er, what are they?" Tyler was the first to speak as he

stared at the small round metal balls that were in the bag Loni was holding out. "Because they look like marbles."

"Actually, they are. Well, they're ball bearings rubbed in salt. They're not as powerful as the wards, but I figured that if we could slip them into people's bags and pockets, it might give them a bit of extra protection. It was actually after Emma suggested I use the cutlery for the wards that I realized that ball bearings might be good for personal protection."

"Please, if you ever decide to become a world-famous inventor, don't mention my contribution to anyone," Emma begged.

"Okay, the weird thing is that after everything that's been happening lately, that plan sort of makes sense," Tyler admitted as he got to his feet. "So how about Curtis and I start trailing the Lewis twins and Emma and Loni can start putting up the wards and slipping these bad boys onto some unsuspecting potential Pure Ones."

"Shouldn't I go with Curtis to help check on the twins?" Emma asked, but Curtis and Tyler instantly shook their heads.

"Trust me." Tyler spoke first. "You don't want to witness some of the things that those guys say or do. Plus, if you're both trailing them, then there are a lot of other potential Pure Ones who are vulnerable."

"I know." Emma frowned. "But I'm sure that it's one of the twins, and if the darkhel is going to be stronger than ever, then isn't it better for us to both be there?"

"Yes, but you're forgetting that the chances of it turning

up are slim to none," Loni reminded her as she held up her wards. "And by this time tomorrow we won't even need to worry about it. So really all we're doing is taking precautions."

Precautions with cutlery and ball bearings. Somehow Emma couldn't imagine that her mom had gone through all of this. However, she reluctantly realized her friends were right. As much as she longed to stick close to the Lewis twins (now, there was a phrase she didn't think she would ever be saying), she knew that it made more sense if she and Curtis split up. She shot him a final parting glance, and she and Loni got to work.

After they had set the wards around the Burtonwood perimeter, one by one they searched out everyone on the list. To distract them from her real purpose, Loni asked them if they'd had a safety check on their lasers lately. And while she bandied around a lot of technical terms, Emma managed to slip salt-covered ball bearings into bags, jackets—and, in Trevor Mitchell's case, the side pockets of his cargo trousers (that was a little awkward). It was slightly harder to pull off the stunt with the adults who were on the list, but Emma came to the rescue by asking them what their thoughts were about the Department of Paranormal Containment's new human resources policy, with particular reference to scheduled breaks while on a covert slaying mission—who knew that having a detention and having to write out the policy brochure five times would come in so handy?

By ten o'clock that night, it was all done and it proved easier to do than Emma had thought. Of course, they would probably have to do it all over again tomorrow morning when everyone changed their clothes and bags, which was a bit depressing, but Emma tried not to think about it as she and Loni hurried back to the sophomore lounge, where they had arranged to meet the guys. She shivered in the cool night air as they hurried to the meeting.

At the other end of the lounge Garry and Glen were having a noisy conversation about just how many demons they had killed on the code-blue mission the other day. Emma immediately shot Curtis a look of sympathy for being stuck with the job of keeping them in his sight until tomorrow afternoon.

"So?" Tyler immediately asked. "Did you get everyone?"

"Almost," Loni said as she held up the neat list she had been using to keep track of it all. "There was no sign of Professor Yemin, though apparently even though he stays on campus, he has a house in town as well, so he might be there. And there are also two students, one other professor, and the support staff who aren't here, but we're hoping that means we can just cross them off the list. Even better, so far Emma hasn't had any sightings of the darkhel. Unless she's just not letting on."

"Trust me, you'd know if I'd seen it," Emma said in a dry voice as she dropped down into the chair farthest away and tried to ignore the bad feeling she had in the pit of her stomach.

"So maybe it means my wards have worked?" Loni said in a hopeful voice.

"Maybe, though the little fairies had said that the darkhel found it hard to maintain its strength while the gate was shut, so maybe's just taking a breather." As Emma spoke, she restlessly got to her feet. "Actually, I might go and do a patrol, just to make sure it's not lurking anywhere."

"Emma, relax. We were just out there two seconds ago," Loni reminded her. "And there was no sign of it anywhere."

"I know, but I don't want to take any chances. Until three o'clock tomorrow no one on that list is safe."

"Do you want me to come with you?" Curtis started to get to his feet, but before Emma could say yes, Tyler started to cough.

"Actually, buddy, I think our guys are leaving, which means it's probably our cue to go as well," Tyler said, and for a moment Curtis paused as if racked by indecision, but Emma gave a slight nod.

"I'll be okay. You go, but make sure you call me if there is *anything* unusual."

"Ditto." Curtis caught her hand for a second and lowered his mouth to hers. It was just a fleeting kiss, which no one but Loni seemed to notice, but it was enough to help calm Emma's rising anxiety. "And please, be careful."

"I will," she promised as she watched him make his way out of the lounge, his crutches swinging back and forth in a soft rhythm.

"Oh my God," Loni squealed the minute the guys were out of earshot. "That was the most adorable thing I've ever seen in my life. And weird. I still can't get over the fact that you two—"

"I know." Emma allowed herself one short smile before a more somber mood overtook her. "But I really can't think about it. Not yet. Not until this is over. And speaking of which, I'd better get back out there."

"Well, I'm coming with you," Loni said in a firm voice that Emma didn't dare argue with.

✳✳✳

By midnight there was still no sign of the darkhel and Emma felt exhausted, so when Loni finally insisted that she call it a night, she reluctantly agreed.

But it wasn't until her friend left and she was in her room alone that she let out a sigh. She had a bad feeling that tomorrow was going to be even worse than today. And not just because of the induction ceremony (which had actually been pushed so far down on her "suck list" that it wasn't funny) but because until they knew the darkhel had been banished, they were going to need to be on full alert.

As her mind continued to churn, she spread her slaying kit out on her bed and methodically started to clean and check everything, just like her mom had taught her. But just as she was putting away her sword there was a loud banging on her door and she jumped in surprise.

"Emma, are you there?"

"Curtis?" Emma put down her sword and hurried over to see Curtis cautiously peering up and down the hallway to check that no warden was around. "What are you doing here?"

"Hoping I don't get caught. Can I come in?"

"Of course." She quickly ushered him in and shut the door. Then she frowned as a surge of panic went racing through her. "Has something happened? Are Garry and Glen okay?"

"Well, I wouldn't say they were okay, since I'm fairly sure they're demented. Thankfully they're currently snoring like fifty-year-old men—it's the only thing they don't seem to do in tandem. Anyway, Tyler's camped outside their room and so far the wards all seem to have held. That or the darkhel has decided Earth sucks and has gone back to the other side of the gate of its own accord."

"I wish," Emma said quietly as he reached and wove his fingers through hers. "So what are you doing here?"

"I came to see how you were holding up," he said as his grip tightened, and for a moment Emma felt the stress of the day fade away. Then he glanced over to the small leather book that was lying open on her bed. "Are you still freaked out about your mom being mixed up in all of this?"

"No," Emma said before letting out a reluctant sigh. "Maybe. I just wish that it didn't seem so much like a big secret part of her life that I didn't know about. I want to find out how it all fits together and then I want it to all be over. Plus, I can't help it, I feel so inadequate. I mean, it probably took my mom two seconds to figure out about the soul box, and if we'd been faster, it would all be over now and we wouldn't be trying to protect people with cutlery and salt."

"You can't know that, so don't beat yourself up over it. If anyone can figure this out, you can, Emma."

"I wish I had your faith." She gulped, but instead of

answering, he leaned forward on his crutches and gently kissed her, his mouth soft against hers. Emma felt some of the tension that had been mounting ease as the kiss deepened and his crutches fell to the floor. Finally, he pulled away and blinked as if he'd forgotten where he was for a moment.

"Wow, okay. Well, I guess I'd better go, because if I don't let you get some sleep soon, Loni will kill me."

"You're scared of Loni?" She arched her brow.

"Hell yeah." He gave an emphatic nod of his head, causing his curls to splay out across his brow. Emma couldn't help but reach up and push them out of his eyes. He let out a little moan and kissed her again. This time it was Emma who eventually pulled away.

"Actually," she confessed, "I'm a little scared of her too. Sometimes I think she likes to channel her inner Mrs. Barnes. But, Curtis—" She suddenly felt shy as she wove her fingers through his and peered up into his eyes. "I'm glad you came around."

"Me too." He shot her a lopsided grin before he awkwardly bent down to retrieve his crutches and headed for the door. "Good night... Emma."

Emma waited until she could no longer hear his crutches swinging back down the corridor to hop into bed and turn off the light.

She touched her lips, which were still tingling from where Curtis's mouth had been. After everything that had happened in the last six weeks, she didn't really think that too many things could surprise her anymore, but she had obviously been wro—

She sat up abruptly as she glanced around the room. A low, scraping noise was coming from over by the window and for one crazy minute the grin on her face increased as she wondered if it was Curtis climbing up to her window. Then she realized that he had a broken leg and she was on the third floor. Suddenly, as a familiar static sound hummed in her ear, all the happiness that she had been feeling disappeared in an instant.

She jumped to her feet and instantly reached for her sword. The room was dark except for the faint glow of her digital alarm clock and she cautiously made her way over to the window, clutching the sword as she went. The drapes were closed, and she used the point of her weapon to push one back slightly.

The minute she did, she caught sight of the darkhel's face pressed up against her window and her heart started to hammer in her chest as she realized that she had never bothered to put up any wards in her own room. Could she be any more stupid? She shuddered as she realized that not only did the darkhel look bigger as the faint moonlight outlined its giant shoulders and wings, but it seemed to have an extra glow around it that sent ice-cold stabs of panic racing around her body. The creature's red eyes were like two pinpoints in the dark, and then it opened its barbaric, misshapen mouth and bared its teeth.

It focused in on her as she quickly closed the drapes. "What? Did you think your puny wards could stop me from coming in?" it said in a low, guttural voice as its giant wings batted the air and kept it hovering up by her window. "Well, actually, they would have if I hadn't destroyed them all."

Emma opened the curtain again and saw that the creature was holding out one of Loni's modified knives so that she could see that the circuit board was completely crushed. Its hand itself was a hideous mound of weeping, blistered skin. "Of course I'm not going to pretend it didn't hurt. But I was really missing this place. There's something about it that I just like."

"I don't know why you're acting so smug," she forced herself to reply. Her mom had taught her long ago that it was one thing to feel afraid; it was another thing to show that fear to your enemy. Suddenly, the advice didn't seem as easy as it sounded as she gripped the hilt of her sword and returned the beast's glare. "Since by this time tomorrow you will be long banished."

"I have enough time."

"No you don't. If you knew who the Pure One was, you would've already opened the gate by now. Face it, you're clueless. And you failed. In fact, it must piss you off that first my mom banished you and now I've done it as well."

"Can it be?" For a moment the darkhel paused before a hideous smile spread out across its misshapen mouth. "Oh, how precious. Mommy didn't tell you."

Emma instantly felt the blood drain from her face. "Tell me what? Stop talking about my mother as if you know her. *You don't know her.* You don't know anything."

"Really?" the creature snapped, and she watched in horror as the window started to push open, and too late she realized that the darkhel's giant talons had been creeping under the aluminum frame and slowly edging it open the whole time they'd been talking. Emma's heart started to pound.

"Shut up," she yelled as she thrust her sword and used all of her strength to send it plunging into the creature's talon. "Just shut up and go away."

The creature didn't even flinch and Emma realized that Gilbert had been right when he'd said that the darkhel with a soul was even harder to fight. She was just about to stab it again when she caught sight of Loni's silver hooped earrings that were lying on the desk. Her friend had taken them off earlier and had obviously forgotten to take them with her.

Silver.

She dove for one just as the darkhel finished lifting the window open so that the glass was no longer separating them. For a moment it looked like it was going to speak again, but before it could open its hideous mouth, Emma stabbed the pointed silver end of an earring into the darkhel's neck and then watched in relief as the creature instantly fell back into the night sky, its whole body seeming to shake with pain. Then it stared at her for a moment, its red eyes full of hate and agony, and without another word it disappeared into the night. Emma slumped back in relief as the sharp static buzz in her ear abruptly stopped, letting her know the darkhel had left Burtonwood. All she could guess was that despite all of its boasting, the combined efforts of the wards and being stabbed by a silver earring had taken its toll.

So the campus was still safe for now, but she had plenty of other things to worry about.

Like what did it mean about her mom?

What else hadn't her mom told her? Were there more secrets she needed to know? Emma paced the room, longing for this all to be over so that her life could go back to normal. Even the thought of being stuck hunting tiny fairies for the rest of her life was more appealing than trying to untangle what the darkhel's words had meant.

She picked up the small leather-bound book again and frantically flipped through the pages looking for something. *Anything.*

But no matter how many times she read through it, there were no hidden clues buried in its chapters. Just her mom's loopy writing saying "I know how to banish it" and then, on the final page, "It is done."

Emma wanted to scream in frustration, but instead she pushed the book away as the curling tension she had been feeling all day threatened to explode in her stomach. Why hadn't her mom been scared as she waited for the countdown until the darkhel was banished? Did she go around putting pieces of silver cutlery around Burtonwood and slip ball bearings in people's bags and clothing?

But even as she thought it Emma knew it was a stupid question. Of course her mom hadn't done any of those things. Louisa Jones had been a dragon slayer, so dealing with this darkhel was all in a day's work for her. She probably figured out a way to banish it instantly so that she could go home, cook dinner, and no doubt get up the next day and go back to her real job of killing dragons.

Unlike Emma, who was barely managing to hold it together.

No wonder Principal Kessler hadn't assigned her dragons. Even though Curtis was sight-blind, he was still a thousand times better than she was. He could kill things that he couldn't even see. Whereas Emma had seen the darkhel three times and hadn't even come close to killing it. Hurting it maybe, but not killing it.

As she closed her eyes she willed herself to dream about her mom and then look for the hidden message or meaning that might be buried deep within the book.

But this time there were no dreams, and when Emma woke up two hours later to the sound of the alarm, she didn't feel relieved at all. She just felt abandoned and not looking forward to what the new day was going to bring.

CHAPTER TWENTY-SIX

I t did what?" Loni screeched in a high-pitched voice the
next morning as she and Emma hurried across the quad
to the cafeteria. "Why didn't you come and get me?"

"Because then we both would be exhausted today," Emma
replied as she glanced around. The whole place was buzzing
with the excitement that only an induction ceremony could
bring. If only Emma could share the feeling. "And again,
I'm really sorry about using one of your favorite earrings as
a weapon."

"I don't care about the earring. I care about the fact that
you stayed up all night and didn't think to come and talk to
me." Loni was looking seriously annoyed now and Emma
winced.

"Sorry, and if it's any consolation I did get a couple hours
of sleep and the good news is that it looks like your ward
idea would've worked if the darkhel hadn't destroyed them.
Yay you," she added, but Loni remained unimpressed.

"I still don't like it and next time an invisible fairy comes
and knocks on your window in the middle of the night—

and tells you that it's destroyed all the wards—I want you to promise to come and get me."

"Except there won't be a next time," Emma reminded her, but since Loni still looked mutinous, she raised her hands in surrender. "Fine, next time an invisible fairy comes to visit me at night I will definitely tell you. Happy?"

"Hardly," Loni assured her before taking a grudging gulp of her coffee. "Anyway, what did it want?"

"What do you mean?" Emma wrinkled her nose. "It's evil. It wanted to freak me out in a devious and cunning way."

"Yes, but why? Why would it tell you that it had broken the wards?"

"To show that I hadn't beaten it? You know what alpha males are like. They can't bear to lose." Emma shrugged. "Actually, if you ask me, it was because it was pissed off. It didn't like when I taunted it about not having the Pure One yet. Maybe it was trying to find out what I knew about it."

Loni didn't look convinced, but before she could press the matter further, Curtis appeared and Emma felt herself giving him a shy smile.

"Hey," she said as he leaned his crutches against the table and lowered himself down onto the chair next to her. "So how did it go last night with the twins?"

"Okay. Tyler's just waiting for them to come out of the bathroom. But there was no sign of trouble all night. What about you guys?"

"I think I'll let Emma tell you about her night." Loni glared.

Emma let out a reluctant sigh. "Fine. Okay, so the thing is that the darkhel turned up at my window last night at about one in the morning. I guess it likes making house calls."

"What?" Curtis instantly lost his easy smile as his jaw tightened and his eyes narrowed. "I can't believe you didn't come and get us."

"Thank you." Loni nodded in appreciation at his agreement.

"Look, guys, I'm sorry I didn't tell you, but let's not forget that I'm the one who can see it, plus I've already fought it twice. I'm not exactly helpless when it comes to this thing."

"Why didn't you call me?" Curtis's face was pale. "That thing opened up your window and destroyed Loni's wards. It could've come back at any time and—"

"I'm okay," she said in a soft voice as she suddenly felt his fingers grip hers under the table and he shot her a look that was so intense she was pretty sure that the temperature in the cafeteria went up by about ten degrees. "Besides, even though Loni's wards were destroyed, I still get a static buzz in my ear everytime it's near. That's how I knew it hadn't returned.

"I still don't like it. Until this thing is banished, we can't take any chances," Curtis said as he increased the pressure on her fingers. Emma returned it.

"Okay, so here's the new plan," Loni suddenly announced as she got to her feet. "There are still six hours until we know for sure that that giant fairy guy has been banished, so I figure that Tyler can keep following Garry and Glen. I'll go and rebuild the wards, this time setting the subsonic blast so high that the freaking fairy won't be able to get anywhere near them much less smash them. I should've done this in the first place, but I was worried that the pitch might set off some of the other wards. I'm such an idiot. Anyway, while I do that, Emma and Curtis can split up and hunt down everyone on the list and make sure that they're all still in one piece. Does that work for everyone?"

Emma felt Curtis squeeze her hand one more time as she got to her feet. She certainly hoped it was going to work.

* * *

"Okay. I've remade twenty-two wards complete with an ultrasonic and a subsonic pulse, not to mention double the salt, and set them to pump out three hundred volts of positive electrons. I don't even think Superman could get through them now," Loni announced from the other end of Emma's cell phone, two hours later. "So how is it going?"

"Well, it's been a little crazy trying to hunt everyone down on the list. It was a lot easier yesterday when campus wasn't so crowded," Emma said. "I've only found two so far, but hopefully Curtis is having better luck. The thing is that…I—" Before she could finish there was a familiar static noise that started to hum in her ears and she looked up to where Rupert, Gilbert, and Trevor were hovering just above her. "Lon, I've got to go. The little fairies are here."

"What? They got through my wards?" Loni sounded dismayed.

"Hey, who are you calling little?" Trevor demanded. "I'll have you know that I'm actually considered tall."

"Ask them if they could even feel the effects of the wards," Loni commanded. "I mean, I've just checked them and they're working."

Emma, who quite frankly had much better things to ask the fairies about than the wards, knew that Loni wouldn't be satisfied until she got an answer.

"Okay, so did you guys notice any wards as you flew in here?"

"Oh, is that what that weird feeling was. I thought it was just my new shoes pinching. Why? Don't tell me you thought those things would actually work?" Trevor wanted to know.

"That's it?" Loni wailed. "Some foot tingling? I can't believe they didn't work."

"But they *did* work," Emma insisted. "The darkhel showed me his burned hand where he had crushed them. It was blistered and hideous."

"Our dark brother is blistered and hideous. That's probably just a paper cut or something because I can assure you those wards wouldn't have even made him blink."

Loni made a strangled groaning noise but Emma ignored it as she started to get an uncomfortable feeling in her stomach.

"Look, Lon, let me deal with this and I'll call you back."

"Sure," Loni muttered before hanging up. Emma put her cell phone away. As she did, she noticed there was a text message from her dad, but since she didn't want to miss any calls if Curtis or the others needed to reach her, she ignored it. Once this was all over she would call him.

She caught sight of Rupert hovering over by a group of sophomores who were eating donuts. He was just above their heads and was holding a small silver bag in his hand. Then he casually flew down and plucked a donut out of the nearby box, the oblivious sophomores not even blinking.

"Did you just use glamour powder on them?" Emma raised an eyebrow at him.

"What? They had jelly donuts and I'm hungry, what else was I supposed to do? Besides, we're in enemy territory. Someone might want to kill us." Rupert gave an unrepentant shrug as he took another bite of the donut.

"Can't think why," Emma muttered. "So, what are you doing here? I'm sure it's not to see me get inducted."

"As thrilling as the idea of seeing you officially turned into a fairy murderer is, we're actually here about our dark brother."

"So far he's been a no-show, and if you were right about how long it would take before he's banished, there's only two hours left. I think we might be safe."

"Well, that's what happens when you think, slayer-girl, because it gets you into all kinds of trouble." Rupert finished his donut and did three aerial somersaults before ending up hovering just inches from her nose, his tiny face a mosaic of sugar and jelly.

"What do you mean?" Emma suddenly felt a familiar nervousness bunch up in her stomach. "Is he here? Have you seen him?"

"We don't need to see him to know he's here." Trevor looked like he was riding an invisible skateboard as he too suddenly flew down in front of her. "Every air elemental in a twenty-mile radius can feel his presence."

"And we can also tell that he's almost found the Pure One." Gilbert joined the other two just as they all suddenly clutched at their stomachs.

"What? How? Are you sure?" Emma said in alarm as her stomach muscles tightened. She winced in pain.

"Oh, we're sure all right. Though I don't know why you're asking us when it's obvious that you can feel his presence too. And that you understand how close he is to succeeding."

"What?" Emma stared at them all like they were certifiably crazy. "What are you talking about?"

"The sore stomach?" Gilbert hinted.

"The anxiety?" Rupert added.

"The unbearable pain and general feeling of unease that you can't quite put your finger on?" Trevor finished off. "It's been building for the last twenty-four hours. How could you not have noticed?"

"I—I've had a lot on my mind." Emma frowned as she thought back to the growing anxiety she'd been feeling. And she did have an upset stomach as well; she just hadn't paid enough attention to it. "So are you telling me that it's all some sort of darkhel radar?"

"Were you not just listening?" Trevor growled.

"But normally it's just a static sound in my ear," Emma protested as she rubbed her ears, as if to check they were working. "And it's been static-free all night and this morning until you guys turned up."

"Hello, static doesn't mean anything. It's just a little electric-charged buzz we put out into the air—you know, like a jazzy little theme song. It hardly means danger. Not like the danger that's coming. You know you really are very ill-informed."

"Enough," Gilbert growled at them all. "Because while you might not be worried about what could happen if our dark brother finds the Pure One before he is banished, that's okay because I'm worried enough for all us. Especially since it's almost time."

"How do you know?" Emma started to ask just as a violent spasm went shooting through her stomach and left her doubled over in pain. Okay, scrap that question. As she watched the three fairies also clutch their torsos, she reached into her pocket and fumbled for her cell phone. Then she took a deep breath and tried to compose herself as she called Curtis. There was no answer and so she quickly dialed Tyler. But before she could even hit send, Tyler came racing toward her, his face the color of snow.

"Em, it's not good," he panted, wringing his hands in an agitated manner. "It's Garry and Glen. They're gone."

"Gone?" Emma felt the noise around her suddenly fade away as she stared at him. "But how?"

"I don't know." Tyler shook his head. "I mean one minute they were in the bathroom trying to make a baking-soda-and-white-vinegar bomb—please don't ask—and the next thing they just weren't there. *And hey, are those fairies?*"

"Yeah, and what about it, pal?" Trevor demanded as he started to open up the small bag that held his glamour powder.

"No." Emma quickly shook her head. "Don't do it. He's with me."

"Well, tell Mr. He's-with-Me that right now we don't have time for his petty worries because we've got bigger fish to fry. And by 'fish,' I mean our dark brother, and by 'fry,' I mean that you need to figure out a way to stop him," Gilbert informed her as his wings fluttered in a blurry motion.

"Yes, well, the two guys that Tyler just said are missing are two of the potential Pure Ones. We've been following them since yesterday. It's just that I thought...I hoped that between the lack of static in my ears and the fact that I stabbed it last night, they were—"

"Safe?" Rupert swooped down in front of her and raised a mocking eyebrow. "Well, slayer-girl, I think we can assume that you were wrong."

Emma tried to regulate her breathing as she lifted a hand to her head and pushed back her bangs as if the gesture would somehow help everything make sense. It didn't. She turned back to Tyler.

"We need to call Curtis and see how it went finding everyone on the list."

"Speak and he will appear." Tyler pointed to where Curtis was speeding toward them, faster than Emma would've thought possible on a pair of crutches.

"Okay, I can't find anyone on the list," he said as he came to a halt, his ugly white glasses perched on his nose. Then he looked up and frowned. "Why are the little fairies here?"

"If one more person calls me little, I'm out of here." Trevor folded his arms and pushed out his bottom lip in a sullen pout.

"They're here because the darkhel's getting close to finding the Pure One," Emma quickly explained.

"Yes, because apparently she couldn't figure out the signs on her own," Trevor muttered before Gilbert nudged him in the ribs. Emma ignored them both as she turned to Curtis and she felt his fingers weave into his. Immediately, her panic lessened.

"So how many on the list did you look for?"

"I looked for all of them, Emma. When I couldn't find the first person, I went to the next, asking anyone I could think of, but the answer was all the same."

"But"—Emma pointed to the list—"I saw Ian Wishart and Scott Atkinson."

"You might've seen them this morning, but they're not here now."

"You think he's taken all of the potential Pure Ones?" The words choked in her throat as she looked up to where the three fairies were all fluttering impatiently in the air. "So what's he going to do to them? Has he...*has he killed them*?"

"Normally I would've said yes since our dark brother isn't really one for houseguests, but since the blood he spills on the Gate of Linaria needs to be fresh, I would say that until he starts the ritual, they will still be alive."

"But why take all of them? Why not just take the right one?"

"Because he's probably too stupid to figure out which one is the right one," Rupert informed her while pretending to do some air-surfing. "Well, stupid or lazy. Knowing him, he'll just go through them one by one until the Gate of Linaria opens. *Which, slayer-girl, is why we need to get moving.*"

Emma hitched her slaying kit higher up her shoulder. "We need to get to the food court right now and pray that we're not too late."

"Okay, so this is not good," Tyler suddenly announced in a hoarse voice. "I mean, I'm a betting guy but I really, really don't like these odds. For a start we don't even have passouts. And how are we going to get there?"

"We'll figure it out," Curtis said in a tight voice, his jaw clenched. But before they could move, Loni suddenly came hurtling toward them, her heart-shaped face unnaturally pale.

"Emma, we've got trouble—big, big trouble. Oh, hey, the fairies are still here. Don't tell me that they're going to glamour me again."

"They'd better not." Emma shot Rupert a stern look and he sulkily put away his bag. Then she turned back to Loni. "They're actually here to help. And we know all about the darkhel. He's managed to get everyone on the list. He probably took half of them last night after I thought I had injured him. It was a ruse. You were right when you said there was a reason that he came to tell me about the wards he'd destroyed. It was to distract me. He totally played me and I fell for it."

"What?" Loni's voice was barely above a whisper.

"You didn't know?" Emma said in alarm. "I thought that's why you were here looking so freaked out?"

"No." Loni shook her short spiked hair. "I was actually here to tell you that your dad and Olivia are here."

"What! My dad? But that's not possible. He's at a wedding in New York."

"He changed his plans," Loni informed her, her voice still shaking. "But, Emma, here's the thing: I've just been talking to Olivia and she's starting to freak out. One minute your dad was standing next to her and then he just suddenly disappeared. Right into thin air...and we can't find him anywhere."

The world went quiet and a tingly sensation went racing up and down Emma's leg until soon the only thing she could hear was her heart pounding as she realized that there was one question she had never bothered to ask herself.

Why had her mom been caught up in this whole thing in the first place?

After all, she was a dragon slayer, so fighting darkhels wasn't part of her job, unless...

She felt the color drain away from her face.

"Emma, are you okay?" Curtis asked from beside her, but she hardly heard.

Unless she had a very good reason.

Like protecting her husband from being killed.

CHAPTER TWENTY-SEVEN

Emma felt sick. How had she been so stupid? In the distance, Loni, Tyler, and Curtis were arguing over the best and fastest way to get to the mall, but Emma hardly heard them as the truth hit her like a sledgehammer. The darkhel was going to kill her father. The thought was unbearable. She had already lost her mom, and now she was going to lose her dad too?

"Emma." It was Curtis's voice that finally snapped her out of her daze, and she looked up to see that Loni was escorting a sobbing Olivia toward them. No points for guessing that Loni had given Olivia the Cliff's Notes version of what was happening. "We decided that the quickest way to get to the mall was to get Olivia to drive. Do you think you can talk her into it?"

For a moment Emma just stared at him blankly, but before she could answer, Olivia finally caught sight of her and flew into her arms.

"Is it true?" she sobbed. "Is something really going to hurt Bill?"

"Absolutely not." Emma shook her head as she tried to hug Olivia around her pregnant belly.

"Because it's all my fault. When Bill told me it was Induction, I refused to go to the wedding. I'm so sorry. And then when that thing took him....*I couldn't even see it*." Olivia was becoming hysterical now.

"Olivia," Emma pleaded. "I know you're freaked out, but if we have any chance of helping him, we need to get to the mall. Can you take us there? Please, Olivia, we need your help."

"D-did you say we need to go to the mall?" Olivia stopped crying and ran a hand across one of her watery blue eyes.

"That's right. The dar—the thing that's got him has gone there," Tyler explained. "So we need to get there pronto. By the way, what are your thoughts on busting through the boom gate? Because I have a feeling that's the only way we're going to get past security."

"What?" Olivia looked at them, a horrified expression on her face as she started to sob again. Emma quickly shook her head at Tyler, who immediately mouthed a silent *sorry*.

"It's okay. He didn't mean that; it's just that technically we're not supposed to leave campus, but let's just go to the car and we'll figure something out," Emma explained as they led Olivia as quickly as possible toward the parking lot. They finally reached the Volvo and everyone piled in.

At that moment the three fairies came flying into the car window.

"Boy, that was fun. Did you see his face when we picked up his coffee cup and he thought it had disappeared." Trevor chortled before his face fell. "You know that's the kind of stuff I will really miss if our dark brother opens the gate."

"Which is why we're not going to let him," Curtis informed them in a tight voice.

"Is Curtis talking to someone?" Olivia put on her seat belt over her swollen belly and looked confused.

"Yes," Emma said. "It's just the fairies. And I know it's weird that you can't see them, but if it's any consolation, they've put so much glamour powder around Burtonwood today that practically none of the sight-gifted can see them either. Not to mention—" Emma suddenly sat up bolt upright. *"Of course—that's it."*

"What's it?" Loni looked at her in alarm.

"I think I've figured out a way for us to get out of Burtonwood." She turned to Olivia. "Okay, this is going to sound very weird, but when you drive up to the barrier, we're not going to be in the car. Well, we *will* be in the car but you—and more importantly the security guard—won't be able to see us."

"What?" Olivia puckered her normally sunny face into a contorted mask. "I don't understand."

"Okay, here's a crash course in fairies. When they sprinkle that powder, it makes them invisible even to most of the sight-gifted. But it also makes anything that they touch invisible as well. That's why they can eat so much food at the mall. I mean, they wouldn't get very far if they were invisible but their Starbucks and their Skittle packets weren't."

"Trevor, Rupert. I don't like where she's going with this." Gilbert looked like he was going to fly out the window as worry lines puckered up on his tiny face, but Curtis quickly hit the switch and the windows went up.

"Look," Emma snapped in a curt voice. "If you really want to help, you're going to need to touch all of us except Olivia so that the guards can't see us when she goes out of the parking lot. Unless of course you're looking forward to seeing your dark brothers coming through the Gate of Linaria and ruining all your fun."

Gilbert swallowed hard. "Slayer-girl's right. We need to touch the humans and put them under the glamour. *And afterward we need to wash our hands. Really, really well.*"

* ** *

Half an hour later Olivia pulled the Volvo up to the entrance of the mall. The glamour had worked perfectly, and the moment the fairies touched Emma, Curtis, Tyler, and Loni as they sat in the car, they had become invisible to the outside world. However, despite Olivia's assurance that she couldn't see any of them, Emma still held her breath as they passed the guard station. Thankfully, the guard had taken one look at Olivia's pregnant belly and waved her on.

As soon as they were clear, the fairies had insisted on being let out of the car, and the minute they were gone, Emma and her friends became visible again. Olivia didn't say anything, but it was obvious by the way she gripped the steering wheel that the whole experience had unnerved her, and they had made the rest of the trip in silence.

As soon as the car stopped, Emma went to jump out before she suddenly turned back around and lightly touched Olivia on the arm.

"It's going to be okay, you know," she said in much the same way everyone had been saying to her all week, and as inane as she knew it was, she suddenly understood why they had been saying it. Not because it was true, but because it let people know that you wanted it to be true. Then she pushed her emotions down. If she thought too much about what the darkhel might do to her dad, there was a good chance she would collapse in a heap and never get up again. And at this particular moment that wasn't something she could afford to do.

"How do you know it'll be okay? I mean, if I was your mom, I could've stopped it, but I didn't do anything. One minute he was there and then he was gone." Olivia looked like she was going to cry again but instead took a deep breath and clamped down on her lower lip.

"Yeah, well, between you and me, my mom wouldn't have had the patience to sweet-talk the guard while he checked the car. She totally would've floored it and taken down the boom gate. Anyway, we're here now, but, Olivia, it would be better if you waited outside."

Olivia nodded. "Emma, please get him back. You and the baby need your dad."

"I know. I will." Emma paused for a moment and hugged

her stepmother before turning to the backseat, where Loni, Tyler, and Curtis were all crammed in. "Will you guys stay here with Olivia? Make sure she's okay?"

"Sorry, but you're not going in there alone," Loni said in a firm voice as she got out of the car and Curtis followed. "We're in this together."

"Touching, really, but maybe we could lose the Three Musketeer stuff and get a move on?" Rupert suddenly dived toward them. After their release from the car, the fairies had chosen to fly on ahead, and judging by the amount of sugar around their mouths, they had been waiting for some time.

"Yes, where have you been?" Gilbert tapped at the tiny watch on his wrist as a worried expression morphed across his face. "Our dark brother has arrived, and if you were any later he would've had time to tap all the arteries and drain all the blood that he needs—"

"Okay, enough with the details." It was actually Tyler who cut them off. "Go and do your thing and I'll make sure that Olivia is okay."

"Thanks." Emma reached out and squeezed his hand.

"Yeah, it's so touching that I might possibly throw up," Trevor muttered. "Now come on already. Follow us; we know a shortcut."

Without another word, the three fairies darted off to the main entrance and into the thick Sunday lunchtime crowd. Thankfully Emma had been chasing fairies through the mall for six weeks now and she had no problem following them as they swooped and swerved their way through like three tiny but very erratic bullets. They turned left into a fire exit, and after going down a flight of stairs, Emma suddenly found herself right outside the burned-out shell that was once Hong Kong Wong. A few seconds later Curtis and Loni joined her, panting as they tried to catch their breath.

The black plastic was still hanging over the entire counter, cutting it off from the rest of the food court, but instead of going straight inside, Gilbert came to a halt and nervously started to wring his tiny hands.

"So what's the plan?" he demanded, his wings making a whirring sound.

"I kill it. Do you have any tips?" Emma's voice was flat. The small fairies all gulped at the same time.

"Sorry, I wish we did. We might be family but there are still trust issues, and no darkhel has ever revealed where their point of weakness is. Pity. Isn't there some sort of Sir Francis hotline you can call?" Gilbert asked.

Emma shook her head. "There's no hotline."

"That's a flaw." Rupert fluttered his wings. "Definitely. If I were you, I'd be wanting a hotline."

Emma didn't bother to respond. Instead she glanced around the half-full food court and made sure no one was looking in their direction. Then she nodded to Curtis and Loni and pushed back the black plastic so that they could slip undetected into the fire-damaged kitchen.

The moment the black plastic fell shut behind them, she

dropped her slaying kit and pulled out her sword. Curtis was right beside her, wearing his glasses, unbelievably silent despite his crutches, and then Loni, clutching at her laser like it was a light saber. There was no sign of the darkhel, but over in the far corner Emma caught sight of a group of bodies, all lying limply like rag dolls at a toy hospital, their arms bloodied and bruised. The smell of blood cloyed in her nose until Emma felt like she was choking on it.

Curtis and Loni seemed to be struggling as well as they all hurried over. Among the bodies Emma was able to discern the Lewis twins and Professor Yemin as well as several other people on the list.

"They're alive." Loni's voice was a little above a whisper as she dropped to her knees and started checking everyone out. "They're all alive."

Emma let out her breath, but then froze as she caught sight of her father, lying on a countertop in the middle of the room. She only just managed to stifle a scream as she raced over to his limp body. His face was waxen and pale and his arms were covered with deep angry-looking bruises, just like the others, and for one dreadful minute Emma thought she was too late. Then she saw the shallow rise and fall of his chest and she felt a tremendous surge of hope.

"Dad, it's okay. I'm here," she said as she tried to drag him up into a sitting position. There was no answer but she didn't let it put her off. "And everything's going to be fine. I just need to get you out of here and—"

"I don't think so . . ." The darkhel suddenly emerged from the burned-out freezer. It had a large bowl gripped tightly in one talon and a heavy book in the other. Instantly, Emma's stomach cramped up and she doubled over in pain.

Next to her Curtis stiffened in shock, and as Emma managed to straighten up, she realized why.

Last night at her window, the darkhel had definitely looked larger than before, but nothing could have prepared her for the full reality of what it had become since its soul had been restored.

It was now at least ten feet tall, and its whole body was broader and thicker, with sinewy muscles bulging out from its arms and thighs. The room seemed too small to accommodate its enormity. At the sight of the creature Emma was filled with a sense of dread like she'd never felt before.

Only the red eyes seemed the same, and they were now fastened in on her.

She glanced at her watch and realized there was still another hour before it would be banished. She felt sick at the impossibility of the task that loomed before her.

"We can do this, Emma," Curtis whispered from next to her as if reading her mind. "Just don't let it scratch you."

"That's the plan," she said before turning to Loni, her voice urgent. "While I distract it can you try and get as many of them out of here as possible?"

"Of course." Loni's face was deathly pale, but Emma

hardly noticed as the darkhel raced headlong toward them. Without pausing to think, she pulled a silver knife out of her pocket, and as she ran toward the beast, she took aim and threw the knife. It twinkled as it spun across the destroyed kitchen before hitting the darkhel in the shoulder and bouncing harmlessly onto the ground. For a moment the beast paused and looked irritated as it rolled its giant shoulder as if trying to shake off the pain.

It was fair to say it didn't look happy and so Emma quickly followed up on her attack by throwing a nail file. This time it didn't even stop when the weapon bounced off its thick skin, just continuing to charge at her. Out of the corner of her eye she could see that Loni was dragging out the limp, injured bodies one by one.

Emma held up her sword and waited until the darkhel was almost on top of her before she used all her strength to thrust it upward into its chest. The sword plunged deep into the darkhel's body and she felt herself grunt with satisfaction in knowing that this time she had actually damaged it.

But her elation didn't last for long as the creature once again reached out with its talons. She ducked just in time, but her sudden movement threw her off balance and she went crashing to the ground. Every part of her hurt as she realized that the creature really was stronger than it had been before. Now it was looming over her, bearing down on her, its red eyes full of loathing.

However, before it could strike at her, Curtis suddenly appeared and tried to drive his sword through the creature's ribs. The ploy didn't work and she could see him wince in pain at the exertion of the movement. However, it gave her time to get back to her feet, though as she did so, she realized that the darkhel was no longer trying to attack her. Now its deadly gaze was fixed firmly on Curtis.

"No," she screamed. Then, in what seemed to be Matrix-like slow motion, the beast lunged at him, its deadly poisonous talons aimed directly at Curtis's throat. One scratch and Curtis would be dead. Instinctively, she pushed him out of the way and they both went crashing down to the ground.

She groaned in pain and she tried to wriggle into a sitting position as the darkhel raced at them again. Next to her Curtis was groggily rubbing his temple as the darkhel pivoted around and once again tried to slash at them.

"Curtis, move," she yelled, too late, realizing that his white sunglasses were lying in a broken pile on the floor. Emma felt the blood pound in her temples as she caught sight of Curtis's grim expression. *Oh God, what had she done?*

"Your glasses. I'm so sorry. If I hadn't pushed you—"

"Then I would be darkhel shish kebab by now," Curtis managed to say as he scrambled to his feet, ignoring the damaged glasses. "So stop looking at me and concentrate on what it's doing."

Emma spun around just in time to see the darkhel once more coming at her. This time she didn't raise her sword. Instead she just held it in her hand until the creature was almost upon her. At the very last instant she lifted it up and thrust it deep between the creature's ribs.

For a moment the darkhel paused, then reached out and swiped her with a deadly talon, but before she could parry the blow, Curtis stepped in and blocked it with his crutch, then ducked and struck the creature just above the knee.

Emma gasped as she realized that Curtis, without his glasses, was working purely from intuition. The creature, meanwhile, just stared at the crutch for a moment before reaching out with a giant arm and sending Curtis flying back into some tables. Emma instantly leaped forward, but the moment she did, the darkhel flicked her away like she was an irritating mosquito then picked her up and threw her back into the tables. She felt the wood splinter as she landed awkwardly on her ankle. She groaned in pain as the darkhel's foot came crashing down on her chest, slamming the air out.

"Enough." Its voice was low and throbbing with malice. "It's over. And although I know I should kill you, I think it would be more fun to let you live. So you can reflect every day for the rest of your miserable life on how you failed to stop me. Just like your mother."

"My mother didn't fail." Emma gasped for air as the creature pressed its heel harder into her chest. "She banished you. That's called winning in my book."

"Oh, foolish human. You are truly pathetic." The creature loomed over her. It was so powerful now that she felt the strength draining from her just by looking at it. "Not to mention stupid. Do you really not know the price your mother paid?"

"What are you talking about? My mother released your soul from the soul box, just like I did. She was the one who left me the key," Emma said as she thought of the crystal necklace.

"Well, I'll grant you that she did manage to find the key. It's just a pity she could never find anything to open with it," the creature hissed, its vile breath hot against Emma's skin as it reached down and effortlessly plucked her up by the neck. "Your mother used what I believe she called the Death Curse."

Emma's breath caught in her throat as the creature tightened its grip. She gasped for air as she tried to make sense of what it was saying. "You're lying."

Her mother had been one of the strongest slayers who had ever lived.

She died from an infection in the hospital.

It took four days. Emma was there. She'd seen it...

"Oh...don't tell me you didn't realize that your mother never found my soul box? That she had to use another method to banish me back beyond that stinking gate? That she gave her life to stop me from finding what I was seeking?" The darkhel's voice was full of mockery.

Emma felt sick.

The darkhel's grip continued to tighten around her throat, but it was the creature's words that were doing the real damage. The darkhel had killed her mother.

The beast had killed her mom.

But before the world went black she caught sight of

Curtis hobbling forward and thrusting his sword deep into the creature's side. Emma instantly fell to the ground, her ankle flaring with pain. The darkhel didn't even wince as it sent a giant fist pummeling into Curtis's face, and Emma whimpered as the skin around his eye split open and started to bleed profusely down his golden cheek.

"Now. The two of you can watch." The darkhel grinned as it stalked over to where the bowl it had been carrying was lying on the floor. It scooped it up and carried it over to the countertop where Emma's dad was lying unconscious. "Now…let's begin." Emma watched in horror as the creature flipped open the heavy book and started to chant some words in Latin.

CHAPTER TWENTY-EIGHT

Emma screamed as she tried to crawl forward on her injured ankle over to where her father was lying prostrate on the counter, but the darkhel ignored her as it continued to chant.

"What's happening?" Curtis demanded. Fright had turned his face an ominous greenish color. "How much longer before it's banished? Can you hold it?"

Emma stared at him for a moment as the full impact of the situation washed over her. The darkhel had won. Which meant that she had lost.

"What's going on?" Curtis repeated. "Talk to me. Tell me what it's doing. You've got to be my eyes."

"I can't do it, Curtis." She shook her head and let the pain have its way with her. "It's too strong. I don't know how to fight it. No one does. Not Sir Francis. Not my mom—she used the Death Curse." Emma started to sob. "It killed her and now it's going to kill my dad. I've failed them. I've failed you. Your glasses are broken, which means—"

"No!" he screamed, his voice laced with steel. "You haven't

failed anyone. Now go fight this thing. You're a fairy slayer and it's a fairy."

"Curtis, please, you know as well as I do that I just made up all that fairy-slaying stuff. I mean, who tries to kill things with hairspray?" Emma let defeat crawl through her like an old friend. It was just too hard. "I'm so sorry I dragged you into this. It's all been for nothing."

"Stop it. Just because it's not in Sir Francis's book doesn't mean the darkhel can't be killed. After all, it's not in the book to touch a stupid statue on the face every time we pass it, but we all do it. You can't give up." Curtis's face was racked with pain as he pulled himself up into a sitting position and blindly threw a single nail file at the darkhel.

Despite Curtis's inability to see his target, the file embedded itself in the darkhel's sinewy arm and the bowl fell to the ground with a clatter. From up by the ceiling Trevor, Rupert, and Gilbert let out a roar of approval.

However, Emma couldn't share their excitement. All Curtis's attack had bought them was an extra minute.

The darkhel glared at the three small fairies as it reached down and scooped up the bowl. "Laugh now, but the gate will be open soon and my true brothers will able to teach you some lessons in what it really means to be a fairy."

"Well, if you're so different than us, why does metal feel like a hot lance running through your bones?" Trevor retorted in a loud voice.

"Of course we use these nifty antimagnetic wrist straps,"

Gilbert added, sounding more like infomercial than anything else. "They really help draw away the pain. Amazing, and cheap too. I guess we forgot to tell you about them."

"Enough." The darkhel howled as it took another step closer to the table where Emma's father was lying. "I'm nothing like you."

"Keep telling yourself that if it makes you feel better, but I can see the burn mark the nail file left on your arm," Rupert retorted. "You're exactly like us. Just without the good taste in clothes. I mean, what's with all the leather? And I swear that belt of yours has a skull and crossbones on it. Please, could you try any harder to be a cliché?"

"What did you just say?" Emma felt something tugging at the back of her mind and she looked up to the ceiling, where Rupert was still hovering in small rapid circles.

"Skull and crossbones? Cliché?" the fairy asked.

"No. Before that. You said the darkhel's just like you."

"No, I'm not," the darkhel howled as it opened up its giant wings and spread them out. The room suddenly seemed tiny as they angrily beat the air until all the loose plastic that had been covering the benches lifted up as if in protest. Then, without another word, the creature held the bowl under Emma's father's neck and Emma screamed as she realized it was planning to slit her dad's throat and drain the blood.

Finally, the lethargy and despair she had been feeling disappeared as an idea suddenly came to her.

"Curtis." Emma ignored the pain in her ankle as she

forced herself to stand up. Then she reached out and grasped his hand. It felt solid and warm in hers. "I know what to do but I need your help. The darkhel's standing by the table. It's just about to get to my dad. Can you please buy me some time? I know you can't see it, but—"

"Emma, I've spent my life fighting things I can't see. I've got your back," Curtis assured her as he rose to his feet, grabbed one of his crutches, and limped his way over to near where the darkhel was standing, still beating its wings in a furious rhythm as it held a deadly talon up to Emma's father's neck. "What are you going to do?"

"I think I know why we have to touch Sir Francis's head every time we pass the statue. It's not for luck—it's to remind us to think for ourselves. So I think I'm going to be a fairy slayer and break every rule there is." The adrenaline started to surge through her.

He nodded, then, without preamble, he lifted one of his crutches high in the air and sent it smashing into the creature's face, his aim true despite his lack of sight. The darkhel fell back away from the table and went tumbling to the ground, while high above them, Rupert and Trevor let out another gutsy cheer of appreciation.

Emma ignored them as she forced her injured foot to cover the distance between herself and her slaying kit. She emptied the entire bag onto the ground until she found the unused packets of Sour Skittles. Then, without wasting a second, she crushed them one by one with her fist before ripping them open. Skittle dust blew up in her face and clogged her nose, but she ignored it as she grabbed her mom's favorite dagger. As she worked she noticed that Loni had managed to drag everyone else out of the room and was now making her way to the table where Emma's dad still lay.

Emma sent her friend a silent prayer of gratitude as she watched Loni pull him off the table and drag him outside the burned kitchen.

"Can you possibly be serious?" the darkhel snapped as it got to its feet, its face a mask of fury and anger. "How many times do I have to tell you that you can't win? You can't kill me, and by the time I'm banished, it will be too late because—"

"Who says I can't kill you?" Emma hurried back toward her enemy, waving the packet of Skittles in her hand. "Curtis, stand back, I know exactly what to do."

"So there is a Sir Francis hotline." Rupert flew down. "I knew it."

"Don't be a moron." The darkhel knocked the small fairy out of the way. "It's not some great idea she's borrowing from a dead slayer with delusions of grandeur. It's just a trick."

"Well, trick *this*," Emma shouted as she lunged and then jumped up off her good ankle. As she became airborne, she used her mom's dagger and slashed it across the darkhel's throat. The minute the foul creature fell to the ground, she leaned over and started to pour the crushed Sour Skittles into the open wound. The darkhel reached up and pushed its

talons deep into her calf muscle, ripping away at the tendon
as it tried to use her leg to help it stand up. Emma ignored
the pain that lanced through her.

"It won't work, you know. You can't kill me," the darkhel
said, its voice full of rage and venom.

"I can kill you." She poured more Sour Skittle powder
into the angry gash across its neck. The powder instantly
started to bubble and blister, and Emma used the butt of her
dagger to smash it deeper into the wound. "And by the way,
this is for my mom."

"You're wasting your time." It gurgled in a weakened
voice as it dug its talons farther into her flesh. But instead
of standing up and throwing her against the wall, as she
had half expected, the darkhel continued to lie on the floor.
Emma tried to stay focused as she poured another Skittles
packet onto the wound and watched as vile yellow fluid
started flowing out like lava down the side of a volcano.

"This is for my dad." She gritted her teeth as she reached
for another packet.

"And this one's for Curtis." Still the creature didn't loosen
its grip, but Emma forced herself to ignore the pain as she
poured the final packet of smashed-up Sour Skittles into the
gaping, hideous wound and ground the powder in.

"And this? This one's for me," she said as she stood back
and watched in anticipation as the wound continued to hiss
and fizz, eating into the darkhel's thick dark skin until a
deathly stench of burning flesh and evil started to sting her
nostrils. But before Emma could quite figure out what had

happened, the darkhel suddenly lifted a gigantic arm and sent her flying back across the room. She landed in a heap next to Curtis.

"Emma—" he started to say, but she hardly heard as she watched the darkhel once again stand up to its full height, again spreading its giant wings the entire breadth of the room.

"I told you that you couldn't kill me," it snarled as it started to stalk toward her, its dark red eyes narrow and glowing. "And the sooner you—"

But whatever it had been going to say was lost as it suddenly widened its eyes and clutched at its chest. Next its gigantic wings wilted like a flower on a hot summer's day and its lethal talons fell limply to its side as the darkhel dropped to its knees, its face a picture of stunned disbelief. Then it fell to the floor, its mouth grimacing in an almost comical way. Somewhere in the background Emma could hear Loni screaming.

"What's going on? Emma, what's happening?"

"I think she's killed it," Gilbert announced as he tentatively flew down from his spot on the ceiling and inspected what was left of the darkhel. Emma watched the creature's giant chest cavity slowly sink away as if something was sucking it down from underneath until all that was left was a large pool of foul black liquid.

"Is he right? Did you kill it? It doesn't feel like it's still here." Curtis turned to her, his left eye swollen.

"I don't know." For a moment Emma just stared at him

as the reality sank in. "I—I mean, yes, I'm pretty sure he's dead."

"Oh yeah," Trevor confirmed. "He's definitely dead. Nothing alive could possibly smell that bad."

Emma took a deep breath and sighed with tentative relief as Loni raced over, her face pale.

"But how did you do it?" her friend demanded.

"Don't laugh." Emma gingerly let Loni and Curtis help her to her feet. "But I used Sour Skittles. I figured if they were lethal to Trevor and Company, then maybe a whole bunch of them ground up might do the trick on this fellow."

Loni widened her eyes for a moment, then said, her voice filled with concern, "So how do you feel?"

"Like I've done five rounds with an invisible fairy," Emma replied as she started to scan the room. "But what about my dad? Is he...I mean, did the darkhel—"

"Scratch him?" Loni interjected before quickly shaking her head. "Thankfully no. And none of the others are scratched either. Though they have been thrown around quite a lot and are in shock, not to mention suffering a few broken bones, but it could've worse, so much—"

But whatever Loni was about to say was lost as Emma's dad suddenly limped into into the kitchen, followed by what looked like a Department of Paranormal Containment medic, but all Emma was aware of was that her father had now enveloped her in his arms and her face crumpled and she started to sob.

"It killed her. Mom. That's how she died. She figured out that you were the Pure One and that it might try and get to you, and the only way she could stop it was to give her life."

For a moment her dad was silent, then he tightened his grip, his voice hollow and hoarse. "She never even mentioned anything about sacrificing her life. Not once. I would've tried to make her change her mind."

Emma shook her head and pushed away her tears. "It wouldn't have worked. Mom wasn't just protecting you; she was protecting us all. That's just how she was."

"I know." Her dad's face was racked with pain. "I wish it could've been different but trying to stop her from doing what she thought was right was like trying to stop a hurricane. That's one of the things I love most about her."

Emma stiffened. "You said you love her. In the present tense."

"Of course." Her dad looked surprised. "Always. I could never stop loving your mother. Did you really think I could?"

Olivia suddenly appeared in the doorway, Tyler at her side, looking around the burned-out kitchen in confusion. The minute she caught sight of Emma and her dad, she let out a strangled sob and hurried over.

"You're both safe." She grasped both their hands and squeezed them tightly. "Are—are you okay?"

"We're fine." Emma pushed away her tears as her dad put a protective arm around Olivia's thickened waist, and for the first time in...well...ever, she didn't feel sick at the sight of it. "We're both fine," she started to add, but before she could get all the words out, the world began to buckle and spin beneath her.

"Emma, your leg." A pair of strong hands caught her just before she fell and she twisted around in time to see Curtis behind her, holding her up. She knew something was wrong and she followed his gaze down to her leg.

There was a long angry slash running all the way down from her thigh to her ankle and the wound was bleeding profusely over the floor. Emma bit down on her lip as she realized just how much damage the darkhel had done. And now that she looked at her leg she could feel burning hot tendrils of poison go racing up and down her entire body like it was on fire. She turned back to Curtis and winced. "I think I might've screwed up. It really hurts."

"Of course you didn't screw up. It's just a scratch. You'll be fine, Emma."

But whatever he was about to say next was lost as Emma's head started to spin and the world went black.

CHAPTER TWENTY-NINE

Emma was floating somewhere on a white cloud. It was nice. She felt weightless, and when she looked down at her leg, it was exactly like it had always been. A tiny scar under the knee from where Tyler had once bet that she couldn't climb over the hedge at the far end of the practice field, but otherwise intact. No sign that a darkhel had ever dug its poison talons into her exposed flesh.

She flexed her toes. They definitely felt normal. Then she realized that someone else was standing beside her. *Mom?* She widened her eyes. *You're here.*

Of course I'm here. Her mom smiled at her and Emma felt a surge of happiness go racing through her.

This is so great. Emma settled deeper into the cloud. *There's so much I want to talk to you about. The darkhel. The Pure One. Why didn't you leave more notes? It was so hard to find. I was really scared.*

But you did it, my darling. I knew you could. You have no

idea how proud I am of you. Who would've thought that my daughter would be a fairy slayer? The only person in history to have ever killed one.

Thanks. Emma started to beam but the smile quickly fell from her face as her mom stood up and pressed a kiss into her dark straight hair. *Mom, what are you doing? Please don't go. Not again. You need to stay here with me.*

Her mom turned back with a sad smile. *Emma, my love, it's not me who is going, it's you. This is not where you're meant to be, but don't worry, I'll always be here waiting, watching, loving. Now just close your eyes, sweetie, and everything will be fine....*

"Emma, don't freak out, but you're in the infirmary," a voice said from somewhere nearby, and Emma forced her eyes open. She noticed that a familiar hand was entwined with hers and that the room smelled of vanilla cookies.

"Curtis?" She turned her head and saw that he was lying in the bed next to her, an angry bruise making its mark under his left eye. However, whatever pain it was causing him didn't stop him from shooting her a lopsided grin. She immediately felt better.

"I'm right here. You're okay."

"But how? The darkhel scratched me. I felt it. And why don't I feel woozy? I always feel woozy when I'm in a hospital."

"It's probably because you've just spent the last eighteen hours sleeping," Curtis said as she wriggled into a sitting position. "It tends to stop all wooziness."

"Where's my dad and Olivia? Are they okay?"

"They're fine, just very tired. In fact, it took the doctor about fourteen hours to convince them you were okay and that they should go get some sleep. Even then they didn't go willingly. I think they'll be back soon," he assured her, and for one perfect moment Emma let herself bask in the warmth of his golden smile before the vision of his ruined glasses, lying crushed and useless on the ground, forced its way back into her mind. Of Curtis's devastated face as he looked at them. His future destroyed. Destroyed by her.

"I didn't save you, though, did I?" she asked in a desolate voice just as a dull sound of static rang in her ears. She glanced up to see Rupert, Gilbert, and Trevor darting into the ward with what looked liked bunches of plastic flowers in their tiny hands. She hated to think what LEGO set or Barbie doll they'd stolen them from.

She ignored them as the guilt continued to well up in her like a fountain.

"Emma—"

"No, Curtis." She folded her arms to let him know that he couldn't dismiss her so easily. "You might not want to talk about it, but I do. I just want you to know that I'll do whatever it takes to convince Principal Kessler not to send you home." As she spoke the fairies continued to hover around the ceiling, shooting her impatient glares.

"Emma—"

"I'm serious. Maybe I could go out with you and be your eyes or something? We worked pretty well together, so he might go for it. Or—"

Rupert let out a small cough, and Emma turned her attention toward the ceiling.

"Yes?" she said in a testy voice. It wasn't that she didn't appreciate their help, but their timing right now wasn't the best.

"We just wanted to check that you were okay." Trevor flew toward her, holding out the bright pink plastic flowers. "And to say thank you for everything you did for us."

"Speak for yourself." Rupert poked his chin into the air and didn't move from his spot by the ceiling. He looked very rock-and-roll. "I'm not saying thank you. Did you see how liberal she was with those Sour Skittles? Powder was flying everywhere. I could've been killed!"

"And you would've been if our dark brother had had his way." Gilbert flew back up to his friend, his wings flapping in an angry whirl around his neat plaid shirt. "We've discussed this. The slayer-girl actually saved your life, remember? And if Trevor and I can forgive her for the Sour Skittle incident, you can as well."

"Okay, so I guess technically you're right," Rupert reluctantly acknowledged before darting down and hovering just in front of Emma's face. "Well done, slayer. Though next time just be a little more careful with where you spray the candy. That stuff's dangerous."

"She'll try and keep it in mind." Curtis cut them both off in an impatient voice. "And now, if you want to leave the flowers and get going, that would be great because we're sort of in the middle of something."

"Ooh, touchy," Trevor retorted before he swooped down and deposited the flowers in Emma's lap and winked. "Anyway, we've got a new bookstore to try out. Apparently they put real chocolate flakes in their cappuccinos," he said, and without saying another word, the three of them disappeared out the door.

"Okay, so that was weird. Since when do fairies make house calls?" Emma said as she absentmindedly picked up a tiny plastic bouquet of flowers. She was just about to push it behind her ear when she suddenly frowned and turned back to Curtis. "How did you know they had flowers with them?"

"What?"

"How did you know?" she repeated. "You're sight-blind, remember, and while you told me you could still hear and sense their presence, it doesn't explain how you knew about the flowers. They were holding them when you said it, which means you couldn't see them, right?"

Curtis grinned as he reached over to the small cabinet that was between their two beds and handed her a small flat canister. Her dad used something similar for his contact lenses and Emma studied it for a moment before glancing back up at him.

"Oh my God—" She turned toward him, her cheeks flushed with hope. "Don't tell me that you've got special contact lenses to let you see dragons?"

"Not just dragons." He unleashed his trademark smile and Emma felt her toes curl. "Pretty much everything. Apparently Principal Kessler's been in touch with the guy who invented those glasses that I was wearing. Anyway, it turned out he'd moved onto smaller and more specific lenses. They still can't work on regular sight-blind people, but apparently because I can hear and feel the presence of elementals, they can work on me."

"Curtis, that's so wonderful. I can hardly believe it."

"Yeah, it's pretty co—" he started to say, but was cut off as Principal Kessler and Nurse Reynes walked into the room.

"I thought I told you to let her sleep," the nurse chided.

"I'm starting to think I should've woken her up ten minutes earlier," Curtis mumbled as a frustrated expression crossed his face, which only made Emma grin even more. However, she tried her hardest to bite back her smile as Principal Kessler took a seat next to her bed.

"So, Emma Jones, it appears you've had a busy week, what with finding an unknown fairy elemental. The oldest and most dangerous one to boot. Not to mention the fact that you've turned into an über-slayer."

"I'd hardly call it über-slaying. I used candy to kill an invisible fairy," she protested as she wondered how long Principal Kessler planned to stay in the room. While it was nice to know she wasn't going to get another detention, she would really much prefer to talk to Curtis.

Unfortunately, Principal Kessler didn't seem to be in any hurry to leave. He turned to Curtis and shot him a surprised look.

"I gather you didn't get a chance to tell her about it?"

Curtis shook his head. "Besides, I still don't really understand it myself."

"Understand what?" Emma stared at them both as Nurse Reynes pulled a large black folder out of her purse.

"Understand the reason behind why you could see the darkhel," the nurse explained as she flipped open the folder and proceeded to show Emma a series of figures that made no sense at all. "And why in your simulation fights Professor Meyers reported a marked increase in your strength and agility. Not to mention why you didn't die from the scratch the darkhel gave you, and why you've healed so quickly from your injuries."

Emma automatically wriggled her twisted ankle and realized it didn't hurt. She pulled back the sheets, but instead of lacerated wounds, she saw only a faint line of pink running down her calf. She looked back up at Principal Kessler and the nurse and frowned.

"I don't understand. What's this all about?"

"We have reason to believe it's because of the accident you had the previous Saturday."

"You mean when I hurt my eye at the food court?" Emma stared at them both in an effort to figure out what they are talking about.

"That's right. We think it's because a small piece of the Gate of Linaria landed in your eye."

"You're joking, right?" she asked, but neither of them laughed.

"I don't think they're joking," Curtis unnecessarily added. "Hence the reason why they dubbed you an über-slayer."

"All because I got something in my eye?" Emma looked to Principal Kessles for confirmation, and he nodded. "So what does it mean exactly?"

"Truth is that we don't have a clue, but if we want to understand it better, we'll just have to monitor you." Nurse Reynes shifted uncomfortably in her chair. "Assuming, of course, you turn up for your appointments."

Emma let it all sink in. From fairy slayer to über-slayer all in a week?

"And, Emma..." Principal Kessler coughed, a guilty flush staining his normally tanned face. "I just wanted to say how sorry I am that I didn't listen to you. I normally pride myself on having an open mind and an open door to all our students. I guess I failed you."

"I probably didn't help matters," Emma conceded in what she hoped was an appropriately über-slayer manner, "since I was pretty focused on trying to get you to change your mind about Induction. There's probably a lesson in there somewhere."

"Yes, no doubt, and speaking of Induction, I want to offer you a dragon-slaying spot. We've never had two dragon slayers in one year, but I think you've shown that this is an exceptional case. I know how much it means to you to follow in your mom's footsteps."

"Thank you. But—" Emma paused. "That won't be necessary."

"What?" Curtis spluttered.

"What?" Principal Kessler wasn't far behind.

"I said it won't be necessary. Curtis is the best dragon slayer. I mean, he was slaying them when he couldn't even see them. Besides, I think it's important for me to continue to be a fairy slayer. After all, what if my dad passes his Pure One genes on to my half brother when he's born? That's a pretty sucky inheritance—to find out that you have some wonky gate-opening blood flowing through your tiny innocent veins. How can I protect him if I'm not a fairy slayer? And you know what? I think my mom would understand if I'm not a dragon slayer, because she was all about looking after our family."

"But there's nothing to suggest that the darkhel will ever be able to break through the Gate of Linaria again." Principal Kessler ran his hand through his gray hair. "You killed it."

"Yes, but there might be more darkhels. And by the way, I think there should be a lot more disclosure about how to kill them, so if you don't mind, I'll be staying a fairy slayer. Not to hunt the likes of Rupert, Trevor, and Gilbert—who between you and me aren't exactly as bad as they like to pretend—but so that I can keep an eye on things. Especially that gate. It seems like Sir Francis knew what he was talking about after all, and if his tests think I should be a fairy slayer, then who am I to argue?"

"But—" Principal Kessler started to say, but Nurse Reynes coughed and held up her hand.

"There's nothing about this conversation that can't wait

until later," she said as she nodded for Principal Kessler to follow her. Then she turned to Curtis and glared at him. "And I don't want you talking to Emma for too long. Do you understand me?"

"Yes, ma'am." He nodded and then waited until the two adults were gone before he pushed back the sheets of his bed, awkwardly swung his plastered leg to the floor, and lowered himself into the chair next to Emma. He then used his good hand to pick up hers. The sensation of his touching her made her stomach go gloopy.

"So, are we okay?" she asked in a tentative voice.

"What do you mean?" He wrinkled his nose as he weaved his fingers through hers.

"About me breaking your glasses. I was so worried about you. I kept thinking that you'd have to leave Burtonwood and go back to your dad's house and it all would've been my fault."

"But if you'd been stuck with fairies, it would've been my fault," he countered, and Emma felt a small smile tug at her lips.

"How about we just call it even?" she suggested.

"You know, for a hot-tempered fairy slayer, you're pretty cool." He twisted slightly so he was facing her and suddenly Emma felt her heart start to pound in a way that had nothing to do with her worries over what they'd been through together and everything to do with the fact that Curtis Green was amazing.

"Yeah, well, for a sight-blind dragon slayer with a broken

leg, a burned hand, and a massive bruise around your eye, you're not so bad yourself."

"You just wait until I'm fully recovered. There's no way you'll be able to resist me," he assured her, and Emma raised her eyebrows.

"I'm actually having problems resisting you right now," she teased, but the rest of her words were lost as Curtis leaned up and let his mouth search out hers.

Emma found herself sighing in happiness. The feel of his lips on hers was hot and tender all at once, and as the kiss deepened, she edged her way closer to him, her fingers unconsciously threading through his curls.

"There's no way I'm paying up on that bet," a voice said, and Curtis made a growling noise under his breath as Emma reluctantly pulled away to see Loni and Tyler standing at the end of the bed.

"Of course you're paying up," Loni informed him. "Just because my wards didn't keep the darkhel out doesn't mean they didn't work. You heard the guys from ops: they said that the theory is sound and that the idea of using a subsonic blaster was—"

"Inspired. Yeah, so you keep telling me, but I'm still not paying up."

"Yes, you are. And at least the money will be going to a good cause since I've seen the most gorgeous bag at the mall and my horoscope said that today I will experience a reversal of fortune. You can't argue with the stars."

"I can when they cost me twenty bucks," Tyler protested

as Loni pulled up the chair Nurse Reynes had so recently discarded and settled into it. Next to her Tyler picked up some leftover Jell-O and, after giving it a tentative sniff, started to pile it into his mouth. "What do you guys think about honoring Loni's inconclusive bet?"

However, instead of answering them, Curtis let out a small cough and pressed his forehead against Emma's as he lowered his voice.

"Um, do you think they're going to stay here long?" he asked as his dark eyes caught hers. Emma felt her stomach churn in longing as she returned his gaze, while the rest of the world started to slip away again.

"Probably," she said softly. "But to be honest, right now I really don't care."

Curtis smiled as he once again pulled her toward him and searched out her mouth.

Perfect.

Turn the page for a sneak peek at Amanda Ashby's

ZOMBIE QUEEN
of Newbury High

one

$\mathcal{M}$ia Everett was doomed. It was a fact she had known ever since Rob Ziggerman walked into biology class half an hour earlier. Instead of sitting next to her, as had been his habit for the last month, he'd made a beeline for Samantha Griffin. All of which meant the rumors must be true.

"How can this be happening?" she demanded in a low voice as she turned to Candice, who was carefully inspecting the skin of her elbow by poking it with a pencil.

"I have no idea." Her friend shook her shoulder-length red hair in disgust as she offered up her arm for inspection. "I'm only seventeen. It hardly seems fair, but it's definitely leprosy. No doubt about it. See the way the skin is falling away like that? Textbook case."

"Candice, I'm not talking about you, I'm talking about how my life is about to be ruined." Mia sunk farther down into her seat as their teacher, Mr. Haves, continued to talk in an animated voice about something bug-related. Normally Mia liked biology, but then again, she normally had Rob Ziggerman in all his blond, beautiful glory sitting next to her, so what was there not to like? "It's important."

"And leprosy isn't?"

Mia gritted her teeth, once again wishing Candice wasn't such a hypochondriac. This week it was leprosy, the week before it was some weird tapeworm that you could only get from a certain part of the Amazonian rain forest. Which, considering Candice hadn't even left the state of California, was highly unlikely.

"*What?*" Candice raised an eyebrow. "Why are you looking at me like that? I'm serious. My arm could fall off by tomorrow."

"Yes, it could. *If in fact you had leprosy.* All you've got is a bad case of dry skin." Mia forced herself to keep her voice low. "Now, can we please start focusing on my crisis? Did you find out anything?"

"Fine." Candice let out an exaggerated sigh and reluctantly pulled her sleeve down. "So this is what I heard. When Samantha broke up with Trent three weeks ago, she assumed that the guys would be lining up to ask her out. Unfortunately, she forgot to take into account that while she might have a hot body from doing all that cheerleading, she still has a major personality flaw—aka, she's a total witch. Anyway, with the senior prom only four days away and still no invitation, she's decided to focus on Rob."

"She doesn't have a prom date and so now she wants

mine?" Mia wailed as she felt her stomach churn in a way it hadn't done since she had first heard that *Buffy* was going to be canceled.

"Looks like it," Candice agreed in a whisper as Mr. Haves turned off the lights and started to fiddle with his laptop until a picture of a cockroach flashed up on the whiteboard.

"But that's so unfair. Why would he take me out on six perfect dates"—*well, okay, five actually, because going to watch him practice football probably didn't count as a date in the technical sense of the word*—"and then ask me to the prom, if he was going to run off with Samantha Griffin the minute she looked his way and tossed her hair? I mean, he said I was cute and that he liked the fact I wasn't high-maintenance. He said it was refreshing."

"He also said that Indiana was the capital of India in geography the other day," Candice pointed out.

"Okay, so he's not exactly a brainiac," Mia conceded. "But unlike most of the other jocks around here, he doesn't think he's God's gift to the world, either. He's just a regular guy who is sweet and kind—"

"And has abs that would make David Beckham weep," Candice added, and Mia found herself nodding. Yup. There was no denying that Rob Ziggerman was gorgeous. With a capital GORGEOUS. None of which was helping with the problem at hand.

"So where does this leave me?" Mia stared unhappily at the back of Rob's head. His blond hair was styled in a sculptured mess that she longed to run her fingers through (not that she would, of course, because despite being sweet and kind, he did have a thing about his hair). Sitting as close as she could get, Samantha was leaning all over him, leaving no doubt about what her intentions were.

"With a spare prom dress?" Candice guessed before shooting her an apologetic grimace. "Look, you've lived across the street from Samantha for the last ten years, so you know as well as I do that what Samantha wants, Samantha gets. Just accept it and be happy you dated a football player for a few weeks."

"Well, she's not going to get her own way this time. No way." Mia gave a firm shake of her head. "We just need to think of a plan. Ooh, maybe if I start using makeup and do my nails, I can beat Samantha at her own game."

"That's your plan?" Candice peered at her from under her mascara-free eyelashes as if to remind Mia that their makeup kits didn't consist of much more than Clearasil and lip gloss. Then Mia glanced back to where Samantha was now laughing at something Rob had said, and she felt her resolve strengthen.

"It's not such a dumb idea," Mia defended. "I mean, it's a slight problem that I don't have a PhD in eyeliner application, but how hard can it be? Besides, I could always ask Grace to help."

"You hate your sister," Candice reminded her. "And more to the point, Grace hates you. Plus, she's friends with Samantha.

It's that whole cheerleading-club thing. She would never go along with it."

"True," Mia reluctantly agreed as she realized no good could come from telling her fifteen-year-old, pom-pom-wielding, vacuous-Barbie-doll sister about this. "But I've got to do something or I'll be the laughingstock of the school. I mean, how can I go to the prom if Rob dumps me?"

"Oh yes, how embarrassing to not have a prom date. We wouldn't want that," Candice bristled, and Mia found herself wincing in guilt. They'd made a pact to go to the senior prom together to prove they didn't need guys to have fun. Though in all fairness, they'd made this decision based purely on the fact that with Candice's ongoing medical obsession and Mia's encyclopedic knowledge of anything *Buffy-* and *Angel*-related, neither of them had any expectations of being asked in the first place. Let alone by a guy like Rob Ziggerman.

"Candice, I didn't mean that." Mia shot her friend an apologetic look. "It's just, if he hadn't asked me, then no one would've cared less if I did or didn't have a date. But now . . ."

"But now, instead of everyone just thinking you're that weird girl who once tried to get the school to have a Joss Whedon day, they'll think you're the girl Rob dumped," Candice finished, and Mia let out a groan.

"I've really screwed up, haven't I?"

"No, you haven't," Candice finally relented. "Your only sin was being so refreshingly adorable that Rob couldn't resist you."

"Thanks." Mia shot her friend an appreciative glance and sighed. "Now if only I could figure out how to make it happen all over again."

"Got it," Candice suddenly whispered. "Since Rob seems incapable of taking his eyes off Samantha's disgustingly low-cut top, we have to assume that boobs are his fatal flaw. So what about getting a push-up bra to help distract him? We could cut the next few classes and go to the mall."

"But the senior assembly is this afternoon." Mia looked at her friend in surprise. "That's when the football team will be getting their awards. Rob will be there."

"Yes, and if you don't act soon, you'll get to see Samantha and her thirty-six-Ds bouncing up to congratulate him afterward," Candice said in a matter-of-fact way.

"You're right." Mia glanced down at her own less-than-impressive chest. "A push-up bra it is, and maybe we could also—"

"Maybe you could both pay attention?" someone suggested in a mild voice, and Mia looked up to where Mr. Haves had suddenly appeared by her side. "So, Mia, would you like to tell us what happens next?"

Mia hoped no one had heard her push-up-bra plan as she looked up at his encouraging smile. Normally, when teachers did that it was because they were evil passive-aggressive maniacs who liked to see students squirm, but Mr. Haves just genuinely seemed to like helping kids learn. Which as a rule was a good thing, just not today. She peered over to the whiteboard, where there was an amplified photo of a cockroach. Gross.

"Well?" Mr. Haves continued. "What do you think is going to happen to our friend, *Periplaneta americana* next?"

"Um. . . it's going to fly away?" she guessed, and then wished she hadn't as the sound of Samantha Griffin's unmistakable snicker sounded out. Which was more than a little annoying since Samantha wasn't exactly an A-plus sort of student.

"Not quite. Can anyone else tell me?" Mr. Haves looked hopefully around the class, but when no one raised a hand, he glanced in the direction of his favorite student, Chase Miller—aka the new boy. Well, he'd been at Newbury High for about six months now, but for some reason Mia had never really talked to him. Apparently he was from Boston or somewhere like that. He was tall with short light brown hair and green eyes that were set above a pair of razor-sharp cheekbones. He also tended to keep to himself.

"The jewel wasp is going to put venom into the cockroach's brain so it can control its mind and body, making it a brainless minion."

Okay, and now she remembered why she never talked to him, because he was weird. After all, who in their right mind would know stuff like that?

"Excellent. Well done, Chase." Mr. Haves clapped as he walked back to the front of the room and brought up the next photograph. "The jewel wasp will lay its eggs on the cockroach. After the eggs hatch, the larvae will feed on the roach. Then the larvae use the roach's abdomen as the perfect living-dead incubator until the newly hatched wasps can feed on—"

Much to Mia's relief, the rest of his words were drowned out as the bell rang, quickly followed by the sound of scraping chairs that echoed around the room.

"Can you wait for me? I won't be long." Mia turned to where Candice was busy studying something on her cell phone.

"Sure." Her friend gave a vague wave of her hand without looking up and so Mia piled her books into her bag and took a moment to pat her shoulder-length brown hair into place before hurrying toward Rob. However, just before she got there, Mr. Haves appeared in front of her.

"Mia, could I have a quick word, please?"

"Oh." She gulped as she watched Rob stride out, engrossed in something Samantha was saying, the faint smell of his cologne catching in her nose as he went. Mia realized this probably wasn't the time or the place. "Uh, I guess so."

"Actually, I'll meet you outside." Candice waved her phone in the air. "I've got to make an important call. When it comes to leprosy, you've got to move quickly."

"Did she just say 'leprosy'?" Mr. Haves lifted a surprised eyebrow as he beckoned Mia to follow him to the front of the classroom.

Thanks, Candice.